IN MINOR KEYS

IRISH STUDIES

IN MINOR KEYS

The Uncollected Short Stories of

GEORGE MOORE

Edited with an introduction by David B. Eakin and Helmut E. Gerber

Syracuse University Press 1985

98332

ISBN 0–8156–2338–0

Irish Studies

Irish Studies presents a wide range of books interpreting important aspects of Irish life and culture to scholarly and general audiences. The richness and complexity of the Irish experience, past and present, deserves broad understanding and careful analysis. For this reason an important purpose of the series is to offer a forum to scholars interested in Ireland, its history, and culture. Irish literature is a special concern in the series, but works from the perspectives of the fine arts, history, and the social sciences are also welcome, as are studies which take interdisciplinary approaches.

Irish Studies is a continuing project of Syracuse University Press and is under the general editorship of Richard Fallis, associate professor of English at Syracuse University.

Irish Studies, edited by Richard Fallis

Children's Lore in Finnegan's Wake, Grace Eckley
The Drama of J.M. Synge, Mary C. King
Great Hatred, Little Room: The Irish Historical Novel, James M. Cahalan
In Minor Keys: The Uncollected Short Stories of George Moore, edited by David B. Eakin and Helmut E. Gerber
The Irish Renaissance, Richard Fallis
The Literary Vision of Liam O'Flaherty, John Zneimer
Northern Ireland: The Background to the Conflict, edited by John Darby
Peig: The Autobiography of Peig Sayers of the Great Blasket Island, translated by Bryan MacMahon
Selected Short Stories of Padraic Colum, edited by Sanford Sternlicht
Shadowy Heroes: Irish Literature of the 1890s, Wayne E. Hall
Ulster's Uncertain Defenders: Protestant, Political, Paramilitary and Community Groups and the Northern Ireland Conflict, Sarah Nelson
Yeats, Douglas Archibald

Contents

ACKNOWLEDGEMENTS

For permission to quote passages from unpublished letters by George Moore to Curtice H. Hitchcock, Richard I. Best, Groff Conklin, A.J.A. Symons and Seumas O'Sullivan we are grateful to J.C. Medley and to the appropriate authorities of the libraries at Arizona State University, Humanities Research Center (University of Texas), University of Kansas, National Library in Dublin, and the Henry E. Huntington Library and Art Gallery. Citations from these letters are from the forthcoming *George Moore on Parnassus*, compiled and edited, with critical and biographical commentary, by Helmut E. Gerber. We appreciate Mr J.C. Medley's interest and generosity, without which the short stories in this volume could not have been printed.

Like all researchers on George Moore, we are indebted to Edwin Gilcher for his generously given advice on bibliographical matters and his constant interest in our project. To all those who helped search out copies of the periodicals and newspapers in which these stories first appeared we are grateful: Professor J.O. Bailey, Mr Richard Buhr, Professor Pierre Coustillas, Professor Ian Fletcher, Ms Jane Conrow and Ms Jewel Hayden of the ASU Interlibrary Loan Services and her staff, Ms Jan Madden, the Superintendent of the Newspaper Library at Colindale (London), Mrs Marilyn Wurzburger of the ASU Special Collections Department, and many friends who have permitted us to plague them with countless queries about various kinds of minutiae.

Finally, we thank Carol Rawls, our patient and always good-humoured typist, who frequently called our attention to our errors and oversights and who prepared the final typescript.

H.E. GERBER and DAVID B. EAKIN

TEXTUAL NOTE

We have reprinted the stories that follow from the first published version in English. We have tampered with the original texts only to the extent of silently correcting obvious printers' errors. We have not altered peculiarities of punctuation, rhetoric, or diction, for these may well be Moore's.

We do not reprint 'Le Sinistre de Tonbridge' although this French version of 'Two men, a Railway Story' appeared one month before the English version, for it is very nearly identical and was in any event likely prepared after the story had been written out in English. We also omit 'An Art Student', first published in *To-day*, Spring 1895, because it became sections XIV–XVII of 'Mildred Lawson' in *Celibates*, with only one passage markedly rewritten. It is very likely that Moore wrote out the whole of 'Mildred Lawson', lifted out three sections, slightly altered, retitled the three sections 'An Art Student', and sent this portion to *To-day*. This seems to be the same practice Moore had used in serializing ten chapters detached from *Esther Waters* before the whole novel appeared in book form. We also do not reprint 'Euphorion in Texas', first published in *English Review* for July 1914, because Moore collected this title himself in the 1915 Heinemann edition of *Memoirs of My Dead Life* and in subsequent editions. We omit 'The Hermit's Love Story', first published in *Cosmopolitan* for June 1927, and *Nash's Magazine* for August 1927, because it became Chapter LVIII ('Dinoll and Crede') in the third American edition (1928), revised and expanded, of *A Story-Teller's Holiday* and in all later editions.

We recognize that other as yet unlocated and unidentified stories by Moore may come to light, most likely short pieces which he published early in his career. During the 1880s Moore occasionally published unsigned and even pseudonymous work. We suspect, however, that relatively few stories of this kind will be found. Moore's artistic ego was such that it is unlikely he would have kept silent for long about his authorship. It is much more likely that the unsigned and pseudonymous material will turn out to be reviews, letters to editors, polemic essays, and the like.

'Under the Fan' is reprinted from *Tinsley's Magazine*, XXX (February 1882), pp. 135–54.

'A Russian Husband' is reprinted from *Walnuts and Wine: A Christmas Annual*, edited by Augustus M. Moore (London: The Strand Publishing Co. [1883]), pp. 18–21.

'Dried Fruit' is reprinted from *Court and Society Review*, II [Christmas Number] (7 December 1885), pp. 41–5.

'Two Men, A Railway Story' is reprinted from *Court and Society Review*, IV (20 April 1887), pp. 375–7. The story, with few substantial changes, was first published in French as 'Le Sinistre de Tonbridge' in *La Revue Indépendante* (March, 1887), pp. 409–24.

'A Strange Death' is reprinted from *The Hawk*, IV (22 October 1889), pp. 431, 433, 435; and IV (29 October 1889), pp. 463–4.

'A Faithful Heart' is reprinted from *The Speaker*, V (16 April 1892), pp. 469–71; and V (23 April 1892), pp. 501–2.

'Parted' is reprinted from *The Daily Chronicle* (London), 22 May 1893, p. 3.

'An Episode in Bachelor Life' is reprinted from *The Sketch*, IV (24 January 1894), pp. 691–3.

'An Episode in Married Life' is reprinted from *The Sketch*, V (21 February 1894), pp. 179–81.

'Emma Bovary' is reprinted from *Lippincott's Magazine*, LXIX (May 1902), pp. 589–95. With minor, general mechanical changes, the story was translated into German by Max Meyerfeld and published in *Die Nation* (Berlin), No. 9 (29 November 1902), pp. 142–4. The English version was rewritten as 'Priscilla and Emily Lofft' in *In Single Strictness* (London: Heinemann, 1922), pp. 28–46, reissued as *Celibate Lives* (London: Heinemann, 1927), pp. 26–43.

'The Voice of the Mountain' is reprinted from *The Gael* (New York), No. 7, vol. XXIII (July 1904), pp. 247–9.

'A Flood' is reprinted from its first publication in the *Irish Review*, I (March 1911), pp. 7–19. This version was reprinted in the *Living Age*, CCLXIX (27 May 1911), pp. 548–55, and, with very minor changes in punctuation, in the *Smart Set*, XLI (November 1913), pp. 57–62. The story was revised and published separately as *A Flood* (New York: G[roff] C[onklin] at the Harbor Press, 1930) and included in *The Smart Set Anthology*, edited by Burton Rascoe and Groff Conklin (New York: Reynal, 1934), pp. 291–300.

'At the Turn of the Road: An Irish Girl's Love Story' is reprinted from *Cosmopolitan*, LXXXIII (July 1927), pp. 54–8, 184–6. It also appeared, with minor changes in style and a different subtitle ('A Tragedy of the New Forest'), in *Nash's Magazine*, LXXIX (February 1928), pp. 28–32, 106–9.

'The Strange Story of the Three Golden Fishes: A Comedy of a Man Who Always Was Lucky – Especially in Marriage' is reprinted from *Cosmopolitan*, LXXXIII (September 1927), pp. 78–81, 138–40. It also appeared, with some changes in *Nash's Magazine*, LXXIX (November 1927), pp. 54–7, 132–5.

Introduction

Although George Augustus Moore (1852–1933) wrote many short stories that fit one or another of the modern definitions of the genre, a survey of the wide range of his output might profitably include works that strain the conventional definitions. That his work in short fiction is extraordinarily diverse should be no surprise. Moore was an experimenter in all the literary forms he attempted: poetry, drama, essay, polemic, novel, and autobiography. He was constantly testing new subject matter, new attitudes, new styles, and new techniques. Perhaps for this reason he resists being securely fixed by some durable label.

He published five collections of short stories of various kinds. Because he constantly revised, rewrote, amalgamated, and rearranged these stories, it is difficult to say how many distinctly separate stories he actually wrote for inclusion in these volumes. 'John Norton', for example, is a rewriting and condensation of his first novel, *A Modern Lover* (1883); 'Mildred Lawson' is a long story into which he absorbed 'An Art Student', an earlier uncollected story; and 'Some Parishioners', in the first English edition of *The Untilled Field* (1903), is divided into four stories in the revised Continental edition, published in the same year. Some stories are mainly revised for style while others are so fundamentally rewritten that they should probably be counted as separate works. The five collections of stories are *Celibates* (1895), *The Untilled Field*, *A Story-Teller's Holiday* (1918), *In Single Strictness* (1922), and *Celibate Lives* (1927). Their complex publication data for variant versions have been authoritatively noted in

11

Edwin Gilcher's primary bibliography.[1]

The stories in these five volumes evidence great variety in length, style and manner, and content. The literary influences on the content and on the manner of these stories are equally diversified: Zola and other French writers, Turgenev, Irish myths, and contemporary journalism. In *Celibates, Celibate Lives,* and *In Single Strictness,* Moore provides penetrating psychological studies in celibacy, loneliness, and the religious temperament; in *The Untilled Field* and *A Story-Teller's Holiday,* he provides stories of character and circumstance most noteworthy for their style, a rhythmic prose which Moore called his 'melodic line', enriched by symbolism, myth, and folklore. Even if Moore had written nothing else in the short prose form, one would have to conclude that his collected stories provide both considerable variety and excellence.

Moore, however, wrote far more short imaginative prose pieces than the five collections suggest: character sketches, scenes, anecdotes, scenarios, 'moods and memories', 'imaginative conversations', and so on. Many of these he absorbed into his autobiographical writings and collections of essays: *Parnell and His Island* (1887), *Confessions of a Young Man* (1888), *Impressions and Opinions* (1891), *Memoirs of My Dead Life* (1906), *Hail and Farewell* (1911, 1912, 1914), *Avowals* (1919), and *Conversations in Ebury Street* (1924). Many of the 'pseudo-fictions' in these collections are readily detachable from the context in which they appear. A few characteristic titles will suffice to illustrate Moore's diversity and range.

Parnell and His Island, for example, contains such didactic yet imaginative sketches as 'An Irish Country House', 'The Landlord', and 'A Hunting Breakfast'. These 'essays', based on reality but dressed up in the language of fiction, indeed often become the bases of further fictional reworkings; they are, in many respects, not unlike Dickens's *Sketches by Boz.* *Confessions* contains the portrait of the woman of thirty (Ch. V), who recurs frequently in Moore's work; the self-portrait of the mysterious woman whose letter is printed in part (Ch. VIII); and the portrait of 'dirty Emma' (Ch. IX), whom

Moore remembered when he was writing *Esther Waters*. Even in *Impressions and Opinions*, most of which consists of reviews and more or less straightforward, if highly personal, essays on painting, literature, acting, and drama, Moore cannot resist making a fiction out of a collection of historical letters. Under the pretext of reviewing *The Letters of the Duke of Wellington to Miss J.*, Moore writes a scenario for a novel about Miss J. and the Duke. Having presented his fictional conversion of history, he then concludes by briefly suggesting how Henry James, Zola, Daudet, Maupassant, and Balzac might have transposed the historical material into fiction. So, too, in *Memoirs of My Dead Life* and other similar collections, Moore allows an 'echo-augury', a name, a title, a phrase, or an idea, to impel his imagination into conceiving a descriptive prose poem, an imaginary portrait, or an imaginary conversation. In addition to interpolating such short pseudo-fictions into collections of diverse kinds, he also published a number of stories and prose poems separately: *Euphorion in Texas, Peronnik the Fool, A Flood,* and *The Talking Pine*. In addition, he wrote two short novels, *The Lake* (1905) and *Ulick and Soracha* (1926). The first was intended for inclusion in *The Untilled Field* but outgrew conventional length; it was in the later collected editions of Moore's works included in *The Untilled Field*. The second short novel was in fact absorbed as Chapters XLIV–LVII in the 1928 and subsequent editions of *A Story-Teller's Holiday*.

Rather than five volumes of collected short fictions, it would be more accurate, if short fiction may be defined broadly, to speak of the equivalent of at least eight or nine volumes. Finally, there is the equivalent of one more volume of stories published in periodicals and newspapers but never collected in book form. Such stories make up the present volume, under a title proposed by Moore : *In Minor Keys*.

(ii)

The several ideas embedded in the phrase 'in minor keys' were plainly on Moore's mind when, upon his return from France in 1880, he began to write prose fiction of various

13

kinds. The phrase itself, however, does not appear to have occurred to him in a literary connection until early in 1894, when he used it in the preface to Lena Milman's translation of Dostoevsky's *Poor Folk*. The phrase acted upon his imagination like the echo-auguries principle which he half-seriously set forth in *Confessions*. The idea of minor keys became pervasive; it lodged itself in his mind for his entire career. Under various guises he explored the idea, modified it, applied it, and expanded it. Only in 1927, however, did he finally propose to compile a collection of recently written and projected short stories under the title *In Minor Keys*. We have given the present volume this title not merely to fulfil Moore's wishes, but because the title seems in several ways particularly relevant to the diverse stories Moore wrote over a period of nearly fifty years and left uncollected.

Although Moore used the phrase 'in a minor key' at least once before 1894, he used it then literally as a musical reference. Thus, in *A Drama in Muslin* (1886, p. 162), he wrote of dresses that are as 'white silk clear as the notes of violins playing in a minor key'. The passage at best is an experiment in the theory of correspondence of which Moore had gained some superficial understanding from his readings of the French symbolist poets. More to the point, because the musical vocabulary is applied metaphorically to a device in literature, is the following passage from Moore's preface to *Poor Folk*:

> And to maintain a sensation in vibration to the last page is surely genius. The mere act of concluding often serves to break the spell; the least violence, the faintest exaggeration is enough; we must drop into a minor key if we would increase the effect, only by a skilful use of anti-climax may we attain those perfect climaxes – sensation of inextinguishable grief, the calm of resignation, the mute yearning for what life has not for giving. In such pauses all great stories end.[2]

One significance of 'in minor keys' therefore seems to be the use of an anticlimactic, a subdued, ending. A second significance is suggested in two earlier passages of the preface. First, Moore writes that Maupassant 'saw the modern struggle for

14

existence as numberless little dramas' (p. viii). A few pages later, with particular reference to Kipling, Maupassant, and Dostoevsky, Moore defends anecdotes, 'little dramas', or 'little literature':

> ... the anecdote related, however blithely, however vividly, however picturesquely, remains little literature, just as little men remain little men however smartly they dress, however gracefully they deport themselves. But that we should prefer little literature when it is good ... to the pseudo great goes without saying. (p. x)

'In minor keys' seems to be Moore's way of designating a story in which a slight event may have a large consequence or in which he implies a significant moral idea marked by a subdued or underwritten ending.

Moore had also alluded to the idea of the slight event implying significant consequences in his essay on Turgenev. Here he wrote that 'the slightest events are fashioned into marvellous stories'.[3] The same idea is hinted at even earlier in 'Dried Fruit' (1885), in which Moore writes that the street is 'absorbed by its own little affairs and troubles' and that the old couple, at the end, is amused by 'the thousand and one little incidents of suburban existence'. This couple's is a 'calm of resignation'. Similarly, in 'Le Revers d'un Grand Homme', first published in the *Hawk* on 28 January 1890 and reprinted in *Impressions and Opinions*, Moore wrote, 'A paragraph in a newspaper, a word dropped in conversation, the sight of a special landscape in a special light, a moment of *ennui* or of joy, it is such things as these that dictate the first idea of a book.'[4] As such things 'dictate the first idea of a book', such things often are taken as the meaningful substance of Moore's stories in minor keys.

It took Moore twelve years, from about 1882 to about 1894, to become fully conscious of the literary use of 'minor keys' and to theorize about the concept. In stories, novels, essays, and plays after 1894 Moore went on to explore the literary techniques implicit in the musical phrase in many ways, with greater subtlety, and with increased artistic awareness. Perhaps the best, certainly the best-known, illustration of Moore's use of the device occurs in *Esther Waters* (1894). The novel opens quietly as Esther arrives at Woodfield and it closes many years later with almost the identical passage as Esther returns to Woodfield. In the course of the novel Esther's fortunes rise and fall, rise again and fall again, and she finally ends as she had begun, but older, worn, and residing in a house that is also old and worn, but with a son who is ready to set forth in life along a chancy road towards an unpredictable future. As in many of the short stories, the 'little circle of life' ends in the 'calm of resignation'.

Finally, long after the exploratory early stories had probably been forgotten and after nearly forty-five years of using the concept of 'minor keys' in stories which he himself collected as well as in novels, Moore, in 1927, proposed to formalize the concept in the title of a collection of new stories. Actually, the idea of such a collection had occurred to him as early as 17 August 1925, when he wrote on the subject to Lady Cunard. At that time, however, he was too tired and often too ill to undertake the work. In spring, 1927, Moore again referred to his project in an interview with G. Laurence Groom:

> 'Et votre nouveau livre?'
> 'Un recueil de nouvelles si uniformes de tons qu'elles feront un véritable roman. Pour cela, j'évite de prendre des récits publiés dans diverse revues, et qui différeraient trop de manière et de ton, mais je compose mes contes à la suite, et dans le même esprit. J'intitulerai le volume: *In Minor Keys*.'[5]

Apparently he had in mind a collection of stories grouped on a unifying principle, perhaps along the lines of *Celibates, The Untilled Field,* and *A Story-Teller's Holiday*. Despite illness and exhaustion, he published three new stories in periodicals and he began three or four others but either abandoned them or left them unfinished. Of the latter, unfortunately, little is known other than the slight traces Moore left of them in his letters. That he was serious about the projected volume is evident from the fact that Moore contracted with Crosby Gaige in May, 1928, for a book of five stories.[6]

Before surveying chronologically the stories we have

collected under a title Moore proposed late in life for a book of five stories, it is instructive to speculate on the contents of the volume Moore had in mind.

(iii)

Three stories originally intended for inclusion in *In Minor Keys* can be identified readily enough. Moore's letters to various recipients between 1925 and 1927 frequently refer to these stories which he published in periodicals. Three others that may have been candidates for inclusion were not published and are not extant in manuscript. His letters of the time, however, clearly suggest that one had been partly written and two perhaps completed. A less certain seventh candidate may have been a story he had already published three times but was revising late in 1929. An equally uncertain eighth story is a prose poem or a 'dream' of twenty-five lines.

The eight stories from among which Moore may have considered five to make up *In Minor Keys* are the following (starred titles seem to us the most likely candidates for inclusion):

*1. 'At the Turn of the Road: An Irish Girl's Love Story'. This is probably the same story as 'The Unexpected Guest', to which Moore refers frequently in letters dated late in 1925.

*2. 'The Strange Story of the three Golden Fishes: A Comedy of a Man Who Always Was Lucky – Especially in Marriage'.

3. 'The Hermit's Love Story'.

4. 'A Flood'.

5. 'The Talking Pine'.

*6. 'Christina Harford and Her Divorce'.

*7. [The Sarky (Sarkey?) Story.] The story is untitled in the letters which refer to it.

*8. 'A Lost Masterpiece'. This is the same story as 'The Houseparty', a title referred to in some of Moore's correspondence.

The first two stories were without doubt candidates for the proposed collection, for in the letter dated 19 June 1926,[7]

Moore indicated his intention to include in a volume two stories which had been sold to *Cosmopolitan*. These two stories we have included in the present collection. The third story may at one time also have been intended for inclusion, but it was apparently dropped from consideration. In a letter dated 14 October [1926],[8] Moore wrote that he was adding a story to a new edition of *A Story-Teller's Holiday*. 'The Hermit's Love Story', after having appeared in *Cosmopolitan* and *Nash's Magazine* in 1927, in fact became Chapter LVIII, called 'Dinoll and Crede' in the preface, of the third American edition (1928), revised and expanded, of *A Story-Teller's Holiday*. This story we have not included in the present collection because Moore himself collected it.

The fourth story, 'A Flood', Edwin Gilcher, Moore's bibliographer, has suggested, may also have been a candidate for inclusion. This story had been published twice in 1911 and again in 1913. It is associated with the proposed new volume of stories because in 1929 Moore was revising the earlier version. In a letter dated 30 October 1929, Moore wrote that 'the text published by *The Smart Set* [November 1913] was inferior, or shall I say inadequate. I have rewritten the story, and hope to publish it myself in a volume sometime next year; but if you care to pay for it, you can have the new text.'[9] The new text was published separately in an edition of 185 copies by Groff Conklin's Harbor Press in 1930. The story can hardly be said to have been 'rewritten'; the first five pages or so were indeed revised from the 1913 and earlier versions; the remaining pages show little more than minor editorial tinkering. Despite Moore's proposal 'to publish it myself in a volume sometime next year', there is some doubt that the volume he had in mind was *In Minor Keys*. Nevertheless, we print the story in the present collection because it was not collected by Moore and because the small separate edition is very scarce.

The last three stories were not published and no manuscripts have been discovered, although Moore had begun writing all three and may even have finished two. Evidence of their probable content appears sporadically in the letters of Moore's last five or six years. Since they do not seem extant in a form that would warrant reprinting, it is useful to present here briefly such information about them as we have been able to glean.

Of these three stories, 'Christina Harford and Her Divorce' would probably have been the most interesting. Almost all the information we have on this story appears in Moore's tantalizing redaction in a letter, dated [? May 1929], to Lady Cunard (Hart-Davis, p. 175). Here Moore proposes to offer the story to the *Evening Standard*, but it definitely did not appear in this newspaper, nor has it turned up elsewhere. All we have is Moore's brief description of a long story he appears to have completed:

> *Christina Harford and her Divorce* runs to nearly 20,000 words. There is no scene in court, no evidence is given, merely a statement that after the case Christina finds herself a castaway. Christina does not become a nun but the story pursues its way through a convent and out of it without a break. As in all of my stories, everything I have to say is included in the story. It contains no attack on anybody's religion nor are moral questions discussed. The recommendation of the story is its humanity.

Sir Rupert in his editorial note refers to the story as 'a complete mystery', a description which, we think, more aptly applies to the whereabouts of a manuscript or typescript. The probable content and its major source is less mysterious.

Moore twice made use of material dealing with sensational divorce cases as reported in newspapers, once in a poem, 'A Farewell to 1886', and once in an article 'The Legal Laundry'.[10] Most relevant to the story of Christina Harford is the poem of 1887 which was prompted by the much-publicized divorce case of Virginia and Donald Crawford. Married in 1880 at age eighteen, Virginia Crawford (*née* Smith) was six years later named as co-respondent in a sensational divorce suit filed by her husband and involving Sir Charles Dilke, the Duke of Marlborough, and Captain Shaw of the London Fire Brigade. The details of the domestic melodrama were copiously reported in the London *Times* from 5 February to about 7 August 1886; Donald Crawford published a verbatim report in the same year and followed this almost immediately with a second edition of his *The Crawford Divorce Case* and with his supplementary *Crawford v. Crawford*, also in 1886. The domestic issue soon became a political one, as W.T. Stead used his newspapers and magazines in an effort to ruin Sir Charles Dilke's political career. In the aftermath, Mrs Crawford was unquestionably hounded; Henry Yates Thompson, the owner of the *Pall Mall Gazette*, for which Mrs Crawford, with Stead's editorial support, was writing pseudonymously, had her dismissed, and Harold Frederic as late as 1892 published allegedly slanderous remarks against her. Stead, partly for humane and partly for political reasons, kept Mrs Crawford secretly in his employ. Through Stead's influence with Cardinal Newman, she was received into the Roman Catholic Church and spent some time as a laywoman in a convent. She became very active in Catholic-supported humanitarian causes, worked on behalf of greater political rights for women, translated from French and Italian, and published literary criticism.

In 1895 Moore was seeking authoritative information on convent life in preparation for writing *Evelyn Innes* (1898) and *Sister Teresa* (1901). W.T. Stead at this point recommended Virginia Crawford and introduced her to Moore. As the 'Nia' of a massive correspondence, she was for nearly forty years Moore's paid research assistant. She not only helped him with the research on his double novel but also with *The Lake, The Brook Kerith* (1916), *Héloise and Abélard* (1921), *Ulick and Soracha, Madeleine de Lille,* the novel he was working on when he died, and other matters, including overseeing his servants and his dealings with publishers, agents, and printers when he was ill or travelling. Clearly, theirs was a friendly and warm working relationship.

What is most interesting about 'Christina Harford and Her Divorce', a title which suggests Virginia Crawford's name, is his insistence on avoiding all the tawdry sensationalism of the newspaper accounts and concentrating on the stoical endurance of a very remarkable lady.

Although evidence of the 20,000-word story seems to have vanished, it may finally have been dismembered and absorbed in the uncompleted *Madeleine de Lille*. This work, too, has left only traces in Moore's correspondence with Virginia Crawford. In any event, the subjects of the story (the religious temperament, convent life, and the conflict between the profane and the divine) interested Moore all his life. Cast in a minor key, the story would have been a most appropriate inclusion in Moore's proposed collection of five stories.

Much less is known about the mysterious story of Sarky. In the extant letters we have seen, we have found only two specific references and an unconfirmed one. The origin of the idea for this story about a little cat is suggested in Clara Warville's report[11] that Sarky was the name of a Persian cat belonging to Noel Coward's father, who lived at 111 Ebury Street near Moore. Nothing is known of the content. One can only speculate from Moore's report of how he narrated the story to Lady Cunard's guests that it was a light piece, that the death of a small cat was probably to be one of the little events around which a story might be developed.

Information about 'A Lost Masterpiece' is limited to what Moore provides in a few letters to A.J.A. Symons.[12] From the letters to Symons, dated 30 July, 4, 5, 11, and 28 August, and 2 September 1930, some of the content of the story can be reconstructed. The setting was to be a house party in the home of Mr Ogleby, a book collector. At the outset the host is guiding his guests around his library while they await Johnson Creswell, whose name later seems to have been changed to Eric Cran (there was a real John Edwards Cresswell, but not confirmed as a book collector). The expected guest arrives and has a story to tell, though it is not clear precisely what Eric Cran is in quest of. We are told that he is searching for rare French books for his collection; he is also in search of an Edgar Somerville, but we know nothing about this elusive character, except that he may be on the trail of a lost masterpiece, perhaps a rare or lost title by Walter Savage Landor. Cran's search begins in the spring of 1906, he lingers 'among the nuns and the pigeons and the old mansions of Dieppe', and he journeys to Rouen and Paris.

Because Moore was himself no book collector and was

generally impatient with bibliographical research, he called on Symons to supply the names and titles that a collector might want in his library. Symons was also to supply appropriate comments that a collector might make on various rarities. The story was apparently to be cast in the form of oral narration and have something like a Chinese box effect: Somerville's story told within the story of Cran's search and both stories within the framing situation of a house party of diverse characters in a book collector's home.

Moore was clearly making use of his own travels in France, his frequently used knowledge of convents and old houses, and of authors he had read and admired, such as Amyot, Balzac, Shelley, Keats, Landor, Montaigne, Rabelais, and Ronsard. As further preparation for the story, Moore read Sir Edmund Gosse's 'Boythorne in the Flesh',[13] an essay on some of Landor's lost and obscure works. In Gosse's volume, he probably also read 'The Science of Manuscripts' and the essay on Frederick Locker-Lampson, the collector who assembled the Rowfant Library. The general idea of the story may also have had its beginnings in the two early stories, 'Dried Fruit' and 'A Strange Death', in both of which the contents of a character's library are used to suggest aspects of his life and personality.

Interestingly, the germ of the story may have been advanced by Moore's reading of a story by Seumas O'Sullivan in 1926. On 3 August 1926, Moore wrote to Seumas O'Sullivan [pseudonym for James Starkey], the Irish poet and short-story writer: 'I admire the lovely stories you publish under the title of *Common Adventures* . . . On the thither side of life you wander and . . . dream, and never more beautifully than in the story of the book collector.'[14] The scene of O'Sullivan's 'The Bookman', unlike Moore's, is set in Dublin; the bookman is impoverished and in reality knows nothing about rare books, though he is obsessed with collecting 'rarities' which the narrator knows to be valueless. The story is told with a delicate blend of pathos and irony. There is no resemblance between O'Sullivan's central character and any of the characters we glimpse in Moore's letters to A.J.A. Symons. The point of similarity is in the central idea of a collector feverishly searching, as O'Sullivan says, for 'a particular golden nugget', a lost masterpiece. Moore's characters were clearly intended to be sophisticated, well-to-do persons and his collectors were intended to be genuinely knowledgeable about rarities.

The story for which Symons was to 'scribble in the names' and 'fill in the gaps' turned out to be very troublesome. At one point Moore threw 'a week's work into the wastepaper basket' and started over. By September, 1930, the story was not progressing well, as he wrote Symons, 'not from lack of invention, but from heat, medicine bottles and general lassitude!' Perhaps because of several operations and long periods in a nursing home, Moore never completed the story.

On the basis of the preceding discussion, we include in our collection three stories of the eight Moore may have considered for inclusion in his proposed collection of five stories. In addition to these three, we include eleven others which Moore did not collect. In fact, most of the early stories he had probably forgotten by the time he began planning a new collection. The title Moore proposed late in life seems to us appropriate to the eighteen uncollected stories he had written between 1882 and 1931.

(iv)

In *Confessions of a Young Man* Moore provides a few hints on the basis of which one can speculate about the importance to him, apart from their quality, of many of the early stories. In Chapter IX, for example, he wrote that when he returned to England in about 1880–1, 'my English terribly corrupt with French ideas and forms of thought, I could write acceptable English verse, but even ordinary newspaper prose was beyond my reach, and an attempt I made to write a novel drifted into a miserable failure . . . '[15] The attempted novel may have been *The Aristocracy of Vice*, of which there is no trace. One might speculate on the basis of their titles that this aborted novel, perhaps begun about 1879 or 1880, made use of material from *Worldliness*, a comedy said to have been

23

printed about 1874 but of which no copies have been found. In *Confessions*, Moore describes his assault on the London literary world for which he candidly admits his unfitness:

> French wit was in my brain, French sentiment was in my heart; of the English soul I knew nothing, and I could not remember old sympathies, it was like seeking forgotten words, and if I were writing a short story, I had to return to Montmartre or the Champs Elysées for my characters . . .
>
> Handicapped as I was with dangerous ideas, and an impossible style, defeat was inevitable. My English was rotten with French idiom; it was an ill-built wall overpowered by huge masses of ivy; the weak foundations had given way beneath the weight of the parasite; and the ideas I sought to give expression to were green, sour, and immature as apples in August. (Dick, X, 150)

He began to read much contemporaneous fiction, including some of Henry James's novels and short stories. In reference to James, Moore comments, 'But Mr James and I are agreed on essentials, we prefer character-drawing to adventures' (Dick, X, 152). Having wearied of writing and trying to publish some journalism, he tells us, 'I turned my attention to short stories. I wrote a dozen with a view to preparing myself for a long novel' (Dick, XII, 181).

Such recollections of Moore's return to England from France are revealing, depite some exaggeration. It is at least likely that the early journalism and the early short stories were efforts to train himself in the writing of English prose and to recapture a sense of 'the English soul'. Even this early Moore knew he would have a long struggle to develop a personal and finely honed style. Even this early he knew that the chief emphasis in his fiction would be on character-drawing.

Before Moore published his first known short story, he had written besides *Worldliness* (1874?) two small, imitative collections of verse, *Flowers of Passion* (1878) and *Pagan Poems* (1881); *Martin Luther* (1879), a play with Bernard Lopez; a few poems published in periodicals; and perhaps some half-dozen book reviews and articles. Most of this early work, especially the two collections of poems, had been severely reviewed as the work of a 'bestial bard', but its sensationalism had attracted attention. In addition, Moore had won favour with hostesses as a clever conversationalist and as an interesting personality likely to shock people. Through family connections, especially his brother Augustus's, he had access to some editors and publishers. As a Frenchified Irishman and an ambitious young man just returned from France, he was bound to be noticed.

In 1880 and 1881 he had attracted the attention of Richard Hold Hutton, the editor of the *Spectator*, which published a handful of Moore's reviews and poems. Still, it was a short-lived association, for Moore published nothing else in the *Spectator* after 1881. Perhaps more important, Moore ingratiated himself with William Tinsley and his friend Byron Webber, who may have been responsible for the appearance of Moore's first short story, 'Under the Fan', in *Tinsley's Magazine*, edited by Edmund Downey.[16] Webber, according to Downey's account, was responsible for Tinsley's publication of Moore's first novel, *A Modern Lover*. Moore himself humorously reports an early encounter with Downey and Tinsley in Chapter XII of *Confessions*, confidently depicting the latter as a mere 'literary stepping-stone'. The publisher–author relationship was again short-lived, but it effectively launched Moore's career as a novelist and short-story writer.

'Under the Fan' (February 1882), Moore's first known published story, may well have had its origins in some of the aborted works begun before Moore left Paris and work he began in the Strand lodging-house upon his return to London. One early source for the story could have been *The Aristocracy of Vice*, the aborted novel he had started in Paris and mentions enthusiastically in an undated letter to his mother: 'I have a novel on hand the title is *Aristocracy of Vice* it treats not of the demi monde but of the three quarter world' (Hone, p. 75). According to Hone, 'It got completely out of hand and was abandoned in despair' (p. 88). Moore's habit of reusing materials, as well as his penchant for continual rewriting, suggests that 'Under the Fan' may have derived something from the discarded novel. The theatrical world of the short story might well have been the 'three quarter world' of the novel. Certainly Moore's other activities at this time suggest his interest in the theatre. He had already co-authored *Martin Luther* and written the three-act comedy *Worldliness*. It is likely that 'Under the Fan' may have derived certain materials or at least something of the structure from the latter play. The three chapters of the short story clearly resemble a scenario for a three-act comedy; similarly, some of the scenes, particularly the dinner scene, are handled as if once intended for the stage.

'Under the Fan' is the longest story in the present volume and one of the most interesting on several counts. The theatre attracted Moore throughout his career, but in the early eighties he was particularly interested in the lives of the travelling actors, even at one point travelling around the countryside with a theatrical group for first-hand information. Dick Lendsell, the manager in 'Under the Fan', like Dick Lennox, the actor-manager in *A Mummer's Wife*, is probably based on Dick Maitland, who introduced Moore to theatre life (Dick, p. 235, n. 9). At about this time, possibly earlier, he and his brother Augustus had also translated the lyrics for Robert Planquette's comic opera, *Les Cloches de Corneville*. It is of course the *opéra bouffe* of this general type that the young actress of 'Under the Fan' is striving to put behind her in pursuit of more legitimate theatre.

Besides reflecting this general interest in theatrical life, 'Under the Fan' also evinces Moore's continued fascination for 'the woman of thirty', a subject he garnered from Balzac. In *Confessions* she becomes the ideal woman for the refined and cultured bachelor, markedly in contrast with the young wife who 'evoke[s] no ideal but that of home; and home is in his eyes the antithesis of freedom, desire, aspiration' (Dick, V, 89). Mrs Wallington White, widow, is Moore's early version of the woman of thirty, rich, self-consciously cultured, and painstakingly social. She is not exactly the ideal for the worldly narrator of *Confessions*, but she is the ideal wife for the drab, unresourceful Lord Wedmore.

In technique, 'Under the Fan' shows both Moore's skill in dramatizing a scene and his early interest in the possibilities of minor incidents having large-scale significance. Particularly revealing of Moore's skill as a dramatist is the dinner scene in the second chapter. The participants are finely delineated by key characteristics in spite of the genre's obvious space limitations. The overall effect is a gormandizing milieu of unconventional social behaviour, bawdy jokes, paired-off couples (or threesomes), parenthetical stage directions, and strained wit. The scene, as Milton Chaiken has pointed out,[17] is reminiscent of the scene in *A Mummer's Wife* when Dick Lennox furtively arranges for his travelling theatre group to usurp the sumptuous luncheon prepared for an unwitting local businessman (Ch. XII). Both scenes suggest a fluidity of action in which diverse characters all come alive in the comparatively short narrative passages.

Two other scenes in 'Under the Fan' reveal a significant use of 'minor keys'. As the story opens, Mrs White is sitting with Lord Wedmore in her box at the theatre, avidly eyeing the performance of Miss St Vincent in the comic opera. When the show is over, Mrs White gracefully yet with a touch of superciliousness throws a bouquet of flowers squarely at the actress's feet. The exchanged looks reveal an unequalled hatred: 'It was one of those thousand duels which take place in our midst, whose collective force, although unnoticed by the historian, is certainly equal to the battles which decide the fate of empires.' Clearly Moore sees the scene as a vignette, delicately drawn to capture the rivalry and bitterness of the two women. 'Throwing the bouquet,' the narrator points out, 'was the finishing touch to a picture designed by a master.'

The proposal scene also warrants a closer scrutiny. After the dinner Wedmore and Miss St Vincent take a cab to her lodgings, but the coldness of the night dampens the would-be romantic ambiance. When Wedmore stammers out his proposal, Miss St Vincent can only think that she must dispassionately decide between a life of wealth with Wedmore or a life of love and shared interests with fellow-actor Mr Shirley. The inclement weather nearly causes Miss St Vincent to accept the proposal, if only to get in out of the cold. A sudden thought, however, rescues her as she conceives of a compromise she can work out with Mrs White the next day. 'How often,' the narrator comments, 'are our gravest steps in life decided by some trifling incident!' It is directly from the actress's hastily formed scheme and the resultant conclave between the two women that the unsuspecting Lord Wedmore's life is determined.

Because Moore usually concentrated in his fictions on the psychological study of his characters and because he rarely depicted scenes of brutality, 'A Russian Husband' (1883) seems at first glance uncharacteristic of his general, lifelong manner. In addition, the use of Russian materials does not coincide with Moore's predominant interests at this time. His most evident interest in Russian literature did not come until the late 1880s and 1890s when, with Lena Milman's urging, he reread Turgenev, Dostoevsky, and probably Tolstoy. Around 1887 or 1888 he wrote an interesting and self-revealing essay entitled 'Turgueneff';[18] he also wrote the preface to Milman's translation of Dostoevsky's *Poor Folk* in the spring of 1894. From *Confessions* we know that Moore had been impressed by Russian writers, at least by Turgenev (Ch. X), during his stay in France, but no external evidence exists that he was reading any Russian works during the early 1880s. He could have drawn the basic story from a newspaper article or perhaps from conversations he had had in Paris at the homes of fashionable hostesses.

There are, at any rate, three aspects of 'A Russian Husband' which clearly make the story characteristic of Moore. First, the content of this story, like 'Under the Fan', owes something to the author's French affiliation. Madame Ardloff, the heroine, is a Parisian whose Russian husband had spent five years in Paris before they were married. It was at this time common for the Russian aristocracy to frequent the French capital and to marry French women, often with a mind to take back a smattering of culture to their native land. Secondly, the early eighties was the one time when Moore was unabashedly experimenting with the scientific, detached naturalism he had discovered in Zola during his stay in France. Moore's naturalism of course culminated in *A Mummer's Wife* in 1884, but in that novel the emphasis is on the dispassionate reporting of Kate Ede's psychological disintegration. In 'A Russian Husband' Moore used the naturalist technique of scientific objectivity, most successfully in the flogging scene where the young Pole Vanca is fatally flagellated by the jealous Count Ardloff while his wife is forced to watch the painful proceedings. Moore used the naturalist method not only for detailed analysis and description but also for suggesting the trapped lives of these Siberian inhabitants. The uninviting snow-covered steppes of the Russian landscape both externalize the dreary inner lives and mercilessly crush any rebellious attempts to escape. The end of the story poignantly focuses on the forced resignation of Madame Ardloff; not only must she witness the slow death of the one person in whom she had found a kindred spirit, but she must, for fear of arousing further jealousy in her husband, endure the agony beneath a façade of detachment implying that his death is of no importance to her. She must afterwards ride back to her snow-capped villa knowing that all hope of escape is irrevocably quelled.

Thirdly, this story characteristically explores the technique of 'minor keys', most notably in the way in which Vanca's death is precipitated. The troubles begin at the dinner party given by the Count when the jealous husband observes what he rashly considers too much intimacy between his wife and the young Polish officer. Bored with her life in the Siberian desert and emotionally estranged from her uncultured husband, Madame Ardloff has naturally developed an easy rapport with one whose interests also look beyond the surrounding barren expanses. That the two are conversing so freely is bad enough in the Count's eyes; but Vanca's crucial mistake comes when he innocently picks up the small white glove Madame Ardloff has taken off and nonchalantly twirls it in his hand. The impudence is too much for the now irate Count; Vanca is at once arrested, degraded of his rank, and executed at dawn the next day.

Like 'A Russian Husband' and *A Mummer's Wife*, 'Dried Fruit' (7 December 1885) continues the interest Moore had shown in the interrelationship of character and environment. Moore had prefixed his naturalistic novel with an epigraph from Victor Duruy in *L'Introduction Générale à l'Histoire de*

29

France which clearly heralds his faith in the Zola doctrine:

> Change the surroundings in which man lives, and, in two or three generations, you will have changed his physical constitution, his habits of life, and a goodly number of his ideas.

The principal character of 'Dried Fruit', the studious, lonely John Barnwell, blends so well with his respectable boarding-house community that it is suggested his departure would harbinger a decline in property values. The environmental importance is particuarly well handled by opening the story with a telescopic overview of the community, zooming in first on the neighbourhood gossips and then directly on Barnwell's rooms at Mrs Lewis's boarding-house, and, after the all-important recognition scene between Barnwell and his long-lost love, panning out again for another view of the unchanged neighbourhood. The technique again focuses on the significance of minor incidents, which from a detached Olympian vantage point seem inconsequential but which have, if not profound, at least enduring consequences for the participants.

Another technical aspect of the story that is of some interest at this early stage of Moore's career is his attempt to make use of the interior monologue. The use of the device anticipates its use by Moore's friend Edouard Dujardin in *Les Hantises* (1886) and *Les Lauriers sont coupés* (1887). Moore was to use the technique frequently and more tellingly in *Confessions, Mike Fletcher* (1889) and the opening pages of 'Mildred Lawson' in *Celibates* (Dick, p. 253, n. 1).

Much of the material in 'Dried Fruit' is reminiscent of themes and subjects Moore had already used or would use again in his literary output, as well as certain materials drawn from his personal life. The travel books in Barnwell's library on Egypt, Greece, Spain, France, etc., relate to Moore's father and also suggest his studious grandfather. Moore himself had reviewed Alexander A. Knox's *The New Playground; or, Wanderings in Algeria* in the *Spectator*, 7 May 1881. In 'The Clerk's Quest' (*The Untilled Field*) he would write again about a man who loves a woman from afar and preserves her in his dreams. The 'dirty-faced' servant of

'Dried Fruit', Emma, is clearly reminiscent of the servant of the same name in *Confessions* whom Moore met when he was living in the Strand lodging-house. These sketches of the servant are the bases for the full-length portrait of a servant in the heroine of *Esther Waters* (1894). When Julia, Barnwell's lost love, wonders, 'where were last year's roses', we are reminded of Moore's early poem in the *Spectator* (11 December 1880), 'The Love of the Past,' later included in *Confessions* as 'The Sweetness of the Past':

> The rose of the past is better
> Than the rose we ravish to-day
> 'Tis holier, purer, and fitter
> To place on the shrine where we pray
> For the secret thoughts we obey.

As late as 1906, in *Memoirs of My Dead Life*, Moore was again using his metaphor of 'dried fruit' in the chapter entitled 'Spent Love'. Specifically referring to religion that over a prolonged period becomes a 'pleasant, familiar habit', he says, 'Some fruits are better dried than fresh.' 'Our habits,' he continues, 'are our stories, and tell whence we have come and how we came to be what we are.' The scene in 'Dried Fruit' when Julia is coincidentally asked to wait for the boarding-house's landlady in John Barnwell's study is particularly revealing of this general sentiment. While she waits, Julia inspects the books and miscellany of the room's absent tenant, all the while speculating on what kind of man he is. The device of 'reading' a character from the books he owns was apparently to be more central to 'A Lost Masterpiece', the incomplete story Moore was writing a few years before he died.

A little later, when Julia discovers a picture of herself taken some thirty years earlier, the story begins to shift to another theme Moore deals with in 'Spent Love', that of idealized love. 'We humans,' Moore avows, 'are more complicated than animals, and we love through the imagination, at least the imagination stimulates the senses, acting as a sort of adjuvant.' The thirty-year-old unaccepted proposal is forgotten by Julia in the interim but cherished by Barnwell as a

31

means of preserving a love which could never be consummated. Even when the two rediscover each other in their twilight years, the love has dried into a comfortable Platonic relationship but at the same time has been stimulated by the saccharine remembrances of love past.

Having published 'Dried Fruit' in *Court and Society Review*, Moore went on to publish letters to the editor in the magazine, most significantly the serialized version of *A Drama in Muslin* (14 January through 1 July 1886), articles (5 and 19 January 1886), and poems (20 May and 9 December 1886). He also attracted the attention of readers who contributed letters and notes about him. In addition, he published two translations from Mallarmé (19 January 1887) which he included in *Confessions* the following year. Because he had useful friends in France and was beginning to win the interest of an English audience, between 1885 and 1888 he began to explore and expand both the English and the French market for his work.

Moore's French, as he himself candidly admitted, was never grammatically or idiomatically as correct as he would have wished. However, he could write competent poetry in French, he could translate from the French, and he could write lively letters in French, such as those to Zola and Dujardin, for example. With the help of Paul Alexis and other French friends, work by Moore appeared in *Le Voltaire* and in *Le Figaro* during 1886 and the first half of 1887: 'Le Poète Anglais Shelley', a review of a London production of *The Cenci*, in *Le Figaro*, 22 May 1886; 'La Femme du Cabotin', Mme Judith Bernard's translation of *A Mummer's Wife*, in *Le Voltaire*, 9 July through 18 October 1886; 'Lettres sur l'Irlande', M.F. Rabbe's translation of the articles later published in book form as *Terre d'Irlande* (1887) and as *Parnell and His Island*, in *Le Figaro*, 31 July through 4 September 1886.

Moore's personal involvement in French translations of his work was variable. Sometimes he had no control over the French version; sometimes he prepared revised versions of an English edition as the basis for a French translation and even advised the translator; occasionally he may have worked quite closely with the French translator, especially those he knew well like Dujardin, H.D. Davray, and G. Jean-Aubry. Although it is not certain to what extent he did this, he may have written some small works or parts of larger works in French himself and then asked friends to correct and polish his French.

In any event 'Two Men, A Railway Story' (20 April 1887) appeared first in French as 'Le Sinistre de Tonbridge' in *La Revue Indépendante* (March 1887), founded and edited by Edouard Dujardin. No translator is named. Because the English and French versions of the story are almost identical, it is possible that Moore wrote the story in English and, with Dujardin's assistance, translated it into French. The differences between the two versions seem to be little more than a matter of greater frankness of diction in the French than in the English version. Briefly, the difference may be illustrated by comparing a few lines from the last two paragraphs of each version:

Son corset dessine son ventre proéminent et ses larges seins. [Not in the English version.]

C'est l'odeur écœurante de l'abattoir.
The smell is the soft sickly smell of the shambles.

Apart from the slightly stronger language in some passages of the French translation, the two versions are too similar to warrant printing both.

More interesting is the different emphases suggested by the two titles. Clearly, the French title emphasizes the sensational wreck whereas the English title emphasizes the personalities and psychologies of the two leading male characters. The story itself suggests a division of purpose or at least an imbalance between cause and effect, between initiating circumstance and consequence.

Again, as in many of these stories, the catastrophe is initiated by a minor occurrence. The horrible train wreck results from the trifling 'signs of intimacy' that one jealous man, James Hall, observes between his co-worker, John Nixon, and the barmaid. As jealousy gnaws at him, Hall, the stoker, resolves to murder the taunting Nixon. Methodically, Hall's jealousy grows into hatred and blind rage as they are making the Tonbridge run. The fight on the train, the loss of control over the iron monster, and at last the wreck itself are depicted objectively and in great detail. In the last sentence of the story, Moore seeks to resolve the story in a minor key, as Mrs Heath laments, 'Oh, I knew those men would get a fighting over me.' Unfortunately, in this instance, the gruesome and vivid details of the wreck overpower the minor-keyed opening and ending of the story. It is finally 'le sinistre' and not the muted jealousy and suppressed frustration that is memorable.

In this story, despite persistent signs of a marked interest in the psychology of his characters, Moore is still working in the manner of the French naturalists. The description of the wreck reads like a sensational newspaper account. The descriptive details of the bar and the Thames embankment and the fleeting glimpses of the countryside as the train rushes towards its destiny read like minutely recorded personal observations. The fight, the intermittent efforts to bring the train under control, and the references to the mechanism of the train's controls all read like the results of an interview with a railway man or an engine driver. In the light of all this, the French seems more appropriate than the English title.

From 1885 to its demise in 1887, Moore published frequently in the *Bat*, with which his brother Augustus was associated. He wrote on the Théâtre Libre, Zola's *L'Œuvre*, the convent which served as a setting in the early pages of *A Drama in Muslin*, the art of the Impressionists, a poem on the Crawford divorce case, and so on. When the *Bat* was superseded by the *Hawk*, under Augustus Moore's editorship, George became a frequent contributor, mainly on drama and painting. It was in the *Hawk*, 'a smart journal for young men about town', that he published many of the essays he later collected in *Impressions and Opinions* and *Memoirs of My Dead Life*, as well as the next four short stories.

In 'A Strange Death' (22 and 29 October 1889) Moore

turned his interest to point of view. Each of the two chapters chronicles the short-lived visit of forty-five-year-old Edwin Harrington in the 'lonely and ugly village' of Charmandean, an excursion the feeble Londoner has made at the recommendation of his physician. The first chapter is told from the narrow-minded villagers' viewpoint, with the townsmen watching the mysterious unnamed stranger's arrival at the railway station, his taking lodgings at a local farmhouse, and his seemingly bizarre behaviour. Uncertainty and misguided speculation readily convince the town of the man's sinister purposes. The chapter ends with the men of the village about to break down Harrington's now barricaded bedroom door. Chapter II, beginning in Harrington's London study, at once shifts the interest to the man's docile and effete condition. His attraction for Charmandean, ironically selected for its picturesque name, is dispelled when he encounters the stares and suspicions of the inhospitable townsmen. Anxiety mounts to fear and finally to terror when the unlucky Harrington realizes his movements are being closely spied on. In the final scene, he is 'seized by blind terror' and reacts like a hurt animal as he tries to ward off his pursuers, only to fall dead of heart failure when the bedroom door is suddenly flung open.

The generally macabre flavour of the story could have been derived from Villiers de l'Isle-Adam, whom Moore had met in 1877 through Bernard Lopez. Villiers's *Contes cruels* offers a variety of tales with a sudden, ironic twist, often mingled with a touch of the bizarre. There is also, in 'A Strange Death', a suggestion of Edgar Allan Poe, whom Moore had probably read as early as 1873–80 while he was in Paris. The two early volumes of poetry, *Flowers of Passion* and *Pagan Poems*, both contain outré narrative poems à la Poe as well as shorter macabre pieces in the manner of Baudelaire, whom Moore was consciously imitating.

The five pre-1890 stories seem to be trial runs in various directions by the aspiring author. While there is internal evidence that Moore was experimenting with the minor-keys concept, little external evidence exists of designed consistency. More noticeable indeed is the diversity of subject matter, of prose style, of literary influence, of narrative technique. Two factors suggest that the diversity is more than mere floundering. First, Moore had been exposed to a variety of literary means both in France and during his first decade of serious writing in England. The trial runs suggest that he was seeking the most workable outlet for his fledgling talents. Secondly, Moore was consistently on the lookout for new publishers. He did not know what would sell and what would not; he was not, at the same time, always willing to compromise to the tastes of the prudish Victorian publishers and circulating libraries. While he was willing to curry favour with Willian Tinsley for his first story, 'Under the Fan', he risked a defiance of the circulating libraries a year later with *A Modern Lover*, still later waging an outright attack with *Literature at Nurse, Or Circulating Morals* (1885). With *A Mummer's Wife*, he contracted with Zola's staunch English supporter, Vizetelly, for an inexpensive one-volume edition to rival the circulating libraries' domination of the market with their 'triple deckers'. In fact, the 1880s show Moore concentrating on exposure as he contributed fiction, poems, reviews, letters, and polemics to an increasing number of the London literary periodicals, among them the *Spectator, St James's Gazette, Mayfair Magazine, Pall Mall Gazette, The Bat, Court and Society Review, Lady's Pictorial, Fortnightly Review, Athenaeum*, and others. By 1891 Moore had to his credit six novels, one volume of criticism, a satirical pamphlet, a volume of sketches on Ireland, and a fictional autobiography. At this time his reputation was such that he became the regular art reviewer for the *Speaker*.

Between 1891 and 1895 Moore reached the first major peak in his artistic career. He became well known for his work as art reviewer for the *Speaker*; he collected his art reviews in *Modern Painting* (1893), which became for many readers their first introduction to the French Impressionist painters and the artists of the New English Art Club; he serialized ten chapters of *Esther Waters* in the *Pall Mall Gazette* (October 1893); in 1894 he published the complete novel in book form and it was received with general acclaim as the best realistic novel in English; and one year later he published *Celibates*, his first collection of short stories and clearly a major work in this genre. By the end of 1895 his work was regularly appearing in a wide range of major magazines and newspapers. He was no longer the seeker for literary outlets but an artist who was being sought. His trial flights in autobiographical writing, literary criticism, art criticism, the short story and the novel had all led to major works in the various genres.

'A Faithful Heart' (16 April 1892) was published at about the time Moore was writing *Esther Waters*. In each work he portrays a woman from the lower social echelons patiently enduring a prolonged life of hardship but finding solace in the martyr-like devotion to her child. Both stories in some sense treat of a *mésalliance*, at the same time forgoing any Cinderella ending as the solution for social ills. Moore had dealt with socially disparate romances and marriages earlier in *A Drama in Muslin*. There, however, the setting was Ireland, the emphasis on the pursuit, and the family resistance decidedly more didactic – more Irish, as Moore would have it. In 'A Faithful Heart' the chief interest is on the constancy of the ever-oppressed Mrs Shepherd, forced to endure 'ten years of self-denial', to keep her marriage to the paranoid Major a secret, to abnegate the wealth of her husband's family, to abstain from intimate friendships, in short to acquiesce unthinkingly but wholeheartedly in the stern, excessively cautious decision of her husband. As with *Esther Waters*, the stress is on the pathos of little lives. The point of view is much better handled than in some of the earlier stories, with a clear reporting of the Major and Mrs Shepherd's thoughts, believable dialogue, and little authorial intrusion. The result, despite the heavily stacked deck against Mrs Shepherd, is that she does come alive for the reader; she is not an automaton 'puppeteered' by a naturalistic pen. By placing her hope and her own aspirations in their young daughter, she elicits a merited, even if slightly contrived, sympathy. 'She regretted nothing', we are told after she has visited the sumptuous estate of her husband's family and enjoys 'at least one noble moment', and she remains the Major's 'good little woman'.

In 'Parted' (22 May 1893) Moore shifts his setting to a

considerably lower economic stratum and focuses on the habitual drunkenness and general futility in one of London's run-down neighbourhoods. The treatment of the Lincoln Lane inhabitants illustrates both Moore's use of the circumstantial naturalism of the French school and his own modification of it by placing more emphasis on the psychology of characters, on the states of mind begot by the environment and perpetuated by a dearth of inner resources. The study of alcoholism in Liz Dale looks back to Kate Ede's gradual deterioration in *A Mummer's Wife* and ahead to Sarah in *Esther Waters*. There is, too, a gleam of the 'faithful heart' in the steadfast, essentially charitable Bill Dale as he essays to reform his alcoholic wife. The overall effect is none the less one of trapped lives, trapped both by the sordidness of London's working-class environment and by the inevitable psychological torpor such environments engender. The Dales are figuratively parted by the wife's alcoholism and Bill and the idealized Annie Temple are parted by a failure to seize the moment, yet in the end all remain firmly bound to the stifling purlieu of London's inner city. Even Dale's one decisive action, leaving his razor blades in the view of his suicidal wife, is undercut both by his own ensuing fear that he may be the cause of her death and by the guffawing of the insensitive tenants when they learn of his misdirected anxiety. That the razor blades are only pawned for more liquor is just the irony needed to dispel the husband's illusions of escape. Although at the end of the story Annie thinks that 'fate had decided too quickly', it is character in conjunction with environment that has decided.

'A Novel in a Nutshell' is the descriptive heading before each of the two stories which appeared in the *Sketch* in early 1894, and clearly neither is strongly developed. Yet each is singularly interesting as a clear-cut exemplification of one of the two basic notions which lie behind Moore's concept of minor-key literature. The first story, 'An Episode in Bachelor Life' (24 January 1894), is another study of feminine sensibility. As a study of the colourless, down-trodden servant girl, it is suggestive of the more finely developed characterization of *Esther Waters*; as a study of loneliness and frustrated, unrequited love, it anticipates the stories in *Celibates* the following year. Certainly the ending of the story is in keeping with the dictum Moore outlined the same year in his preface to *Poor Folk*, insisting on the 'sensation of inextinguishable grief' and 'the mute yearning for what life has not for giving'. Knowing that her master is having an affair with a woman of his own social rank and knowing that he is ignorant of her own love for him, the hapless Clara is left with few other options than to abandon her post. The ineffable love she feels must remain unarticulated, even while her employer bitterly accuses her of ingratitude for quitting her job. The world of Clara's dreams now becomes, in the 'pause' of the story's anticlimax, 'a squalid kitchen, where coarse girls romped to a tune played on a concertina by a shoe-boy sitting on the dresser'.

In 'An Episode in Married Life' (21 February 1894) the emphasis is on the minor, almost trifling incident that at once changes the direction of a budding love affair. It is an unexplained, spur-of-the-moment quirk of James Mason's imagination that impels him to meet his newly acquired paramour in the garb of a French Pierrot, complete with the traditional whitened face. Having anticipated a quiet, romantic evening with a sophisticated man of letters, Madame de Beausac can only react with horror and disgust. She hurries home, embraces the child she had guiltily neglected, and thankfully realizes the error she almost made. Moore leaves the reader in no doubt of his intention when he humorously concludes, 'And so did a powder-puff save a woman, when other remedies had failed, from the calamity of a great passion.'

This story may have some special interest in that it opens with a reference to a specific time ten years earlier – 15 May 1885 – in Paris. Mme de Beausac is another woman of thirty such as he had portrayed in *Confessions* (Ch. V), and the central male figure, James Mason, is an English novelist probably in his early thirties. Moore's attraction to the woman of thirty is partly derived from Balzac's story 'La Femme de Trente Ans', but it may also have a more personal source. In 1879, when he was still in Paris, Moore wrote to his mother, 'I am playing my cards now to become the lover of the Marquise d'Osmond, she is very swell if not very young . . . The first thing a young man who wants to get on in Paris must do is to get under the wings of some lady with a good name and in a high position that done with tact he can wriggle himself anywhere' (Hone, pp. 78–9). 'An Episode in Married Life' seems more like an exercise in recall than a pure fiction. It expresses the callow cynicism of the young man-about-town of the Parisian period rather than the mind of the forty-seven-year-old successful author who wrote the story.

There is a misleading eight-year gap between the two *Sketch* stories and the next story we reprint from 1902. Moore's output in the genre was by no means diminishing, but the instant success of *Esther Waters* changed the position that as professional and now proclaimed writer he would hold in the literary world. He continued to contribute short stories, as well as poems, reviews, letters, and general-interest pieces, to the London periodicals; but he also began the practice of collecting his own published material for inclusion in separate volumes of short stories, art criticism, and memoirs. It was a practice he would never abandon, learning along the way that the most profitable means to make money was through the 'correction of form' – or if at times not the correction, at least the reissue of his works in revised editions.

Between 1895 and 1901, besides producing a large output of periodical writings, Moore was writing his double novel, *Evelyn Innes* and *Sister Teresa*. These two works, although they failed to receive the critical attention which he expected, are important precursors of his later work. In these novels he absorbed techniques from music, he probed religious themes, and he began to develop the style he later referred to as his 'melodic line'. These two novels signalled his recognition that he had taken the earlier naturalist-realist mode as far as his imagination allowed.

In 1901, although he began preparing for the move in 1898, Moore started his ten-year pilgrimage in Ireland. The move was triggered by requests from William Butler Yeats and other Irish literati in an effort to capitalize on both

Moore's working knowledge of the theatre and his now
well-known name. Yet Moore himself was also prompted by
a faltering faith in the cultural climate of England, a displeas-
ure with the state of the English theatre, and a strong reaction
against the British involvement in the Boer War. In addition,
in the Irish cultural revival he believed he had found a cause.
He readily embraced the renewed movement to advance the
Gaelic language, making public speeches, encouraging the
production of plays in Gaelic, even having *The Untilled Field*
translated into the dying language before its publication in
English. From 1899 to 1901 he was making periodic trips to
Dublin to assist in the production of plays by Yeats, George
William Russell (AE), Douglas Hyde, Lady Gregory, and
Edward Martyn. In 1901 he set up residence at 4 Upper Ely
Place in Dublin and remained there until the end of the
decade. His enthusiasm, unfortunately, soon began to decline. His already established affinities with the realistic
theatre of Ibsen did not mesh with the symbolist techniques
of Yeats and the Irish Literary Theatre. His collaboration
with Yeats, most notably on *Diarmuid and Grania* (1901), was
strained by the different styles and by Moore's persistent
egoism, and when the Irish Literary Theatre folded Moore
was not asked to join the newly formed Abbey Theatre.

On top of Moore's failure with the Irish theatre came a
general disillusionment with the Irish renaissance. He saw
too clearly that the Gaelic language could not be revived and,
more importantly, he saw that the country was mummified
by priest-dominated Catholicism, by religion-haunted
zealots, by ill-founded dreams of opulence in America, by
the omnipresent alcohol, by never-to-be-tilled fields of smug
self-satisfaction. It is themes of this kind which characterize
the short stories of Moore's Irish period, most notably in *The
Untilled Field* and, to a less stringent degree, in the next
stories we reprint.

In ' "Emma Bovary" ' (1902) Moore examines Irish life-
denying provincialism by turning back to his French affili-
ations. Moore's critical attitude toward Flaubert was at best
equivocal, but as an emblem of notoriety the French novelist
would be useful at any time. In *Confessions* Flaubert is one of

the narrator's 'minor awakenings' who 'had astonished with the wonderful delicacy and subtlety of his workmanship' (Dick, X, 165). As late as 1897 Moore was lauding Flaubert in a review of *L'Education Sentimentale* ('A Tragic Novel', *Cosmopolis*, VII [July 1897], 38–59). He praises *Madame Bovary*, too, but at the same time finds grounds for stricture: 'there is an admixture of indiarubber in the characters in "Madame Bovary"; they are not all flame, like the characters in the "Comédie Humaine"; nor do they live with the same intense and volatile, unanalysable life as the men and women in Tourguéneff or Tolstoi' (p. 39). In *Avowals* (1919), Moore is regretting the excessive praise he had bestowed in the *Cosmopolis* review but compassionately adds that 'although Flaubert does not sit on the throne, he is entitled to a seat on the steps of the throne' (p. 262).

In the short story of 1902 we see Flaubert's famous heroine through the eyes of an aging, long-sheltered Irish spinster; clearly for her the fictional character could not be any more 'intense and volatile'. During her one trip out of Ireland, Letitia O'Hara is obliged for the first time in her life to occupy a separate room from her sister Ismena. She discovers a copy of Flaubert's masterpiece left by a previous tenant. Despite her faltering French, Letitia soon becomes absorbed in the 'passionate yearning' of this all-too-human heroine. Each page uncovers a whole new world, quite unlike anything she has read in Scott or Mrs Henry Wood, the principal literary diet of the two sisters. Unable to finish the book and fearful of confiding in Ismena, Letitia smuggles the book out of France and back to Dublin, only to die before she reaches the final page of Madame Bovary's sufferings. When, shortly after her sister's death, Ismena discovers the book in the garden, we learn that she (Ismena) has read the book years before but now muses, 'who ever would have thought this of Letitia!'

The rewriting of this story as 'Priscilla and Emily Lofft' (*In Single Strictness*, 1922) evinces two major points. First Moore wanted to emphasize even more strongly both the shock and fascination a novel like *Emma Bovary* can have on two Dublin old maids. In this version, neither of the two sisters, now twins, has previously read the 'immoral' book, and in the end Emily (Ismena) takes a righteous satisfaction in burning it. Secondly, Moore makes significant changes in the structure of the story, clearly showing a more sophisticated handling of narrative technique. The revision, nearly twice as long as the original, begins with Priscilla's (Letitia's) death, and the story of their drab lives, as well as Priscilla's finding of the book, is reconstructed through Emily's remembrances and conjectures. There is now an added element of suspense as Emily tries to understand her sister's dying unfinished utterance: 'In the garden.' The whole story revolves around Emily's reveries in her now lonely Dublin house immediately after Priscilla's death, shifting only near the close to several years later when Emily accidentally finds the forbidden book under a plank in the garden. The garden itself, used chiefly as a backdrop in the first version, now becomes a unifying symbol, expressing at once the fastidiousness of the two caretakers and the uncultivated fruit from a tree of life never allowed to flourish in the Puritanical inhibition and repressed desires of the two lonely women.

Despite the publication date of 'The Voice of the Mountain' (July 1904), it might well have been written earlier for possible inclusion in *The Untilled Field*. Again there is the criticism of uninspired Ireland, the overbearing influence of the parish priest, the exodus out of Ireland. Yet the tone is not as severe and there is less of the defeatist attitude which often overpowers the characters of *The Untilled Field*. This more positive attitude could reflect Moore's earlier impressions of Ireland when, between 1899 and 1901, he was making his frequent visits and becoming enamoured with the idea of a rejuvenated Ireland. Clearly, Moore's interests are reflected in the effect of Dan Coogan of the Druidical altar stone, the folklore, the stories of Irish myth, and the peaceful landscape. Unlike other 'wild geese', Coogan is not vitriolic in his criticism. He is willing to forgo America and marry his neighbour Mary Cronin; only his mystical experience on the mountain alters his resolve. But unlike the mysticism of, say, Biddy M'Hale in 'The Window' (in *The Untilled Field*), which stifles an already religion-intoxicated old woman,

Coogan's engenders a sense of philanthropic kinship. The barren hillside which was hitherto symbolic of his untilled Ireland now becomes the altar for a communion with his fellow-man. The mountain's voice prophetically tells him to go to Africa, significantly just before the priest arrives with the news that the Boer War has broken out. The optimistic tone of the story, with its emphasis on the much-needed sense of selflessness, is maintained until the end with his fiancée willing to await his return patiently and finding solace also in the voice of the mountain.

'A Flood' (March 1911) also belongs to Moore's Irish period, written while he was still living in Dublin. The revisionist's interest Moore reveals in converting ' "Emma Bovary" ' (1902) into 'Priscilla and Emily Lofft' (1922) is less striking in 'A Flood', albeit that the five separate publications, the two distinct versions, and the letter to Groff Conklin of 30 October 1928 quoted earlier may at first suggest otherwise. In fact, there was only one rewriting of the story, to which Moore first refers on 12 May 1928 when he wrote to Richard Best[19] asking him to send a copy of the story he inaccurately calls 'The Flood' from the first number of the *Irish Review*. He evidently finished the rewriting by October of the following year when he wrote to Conklin; in any case, the pamphlet version was published by Conklin's Harbor Press in 1930 and appeared in his *Smart Set Anthology* in 1934 as well.

The version printed in the present collection is that of the *Irish Review*, which is identical to the version reprinted in the *Living Age* (27 May 1911) and, with very minor changes in punctuation, to the *Smart Set* (November 1913) version. It is this version that Moore calls 'inferior' or 'inadequate' in his letter to Conklin. Yet only the first several pages of the 1930 version are significantly rewritten; the remainder he left substantially intact. The opening's revision, moreover, is chiefly stylistic, with a general concision of introductory material and some honing of language.

Both versions emphasize the same themes and portray the characters without extensive alteration. Of particular importance are the harshness of the peasant's life, the triumph of

44

superstition, the matter-of-factness with which the imminent deaths are treated, the note of recurrence. Both versions retain the surrealistic atmosphere with little if any authorial intrusion, making the story a *tour de force* chronicling the deaths of six persons in one very stultifying flood.

The story may well be based on a journalistic report of a flood or an experience told to Moore by the kind of oral narrator he often used in writing the tales that make up *The Untilled Field* and *A Story-Teller's Holiday*. In addition, Moore may also be recalling the personal experience with his brother which Joseph Hone briefly reports: 'One day the two boys, embarking on the reedy and dangerous lake in an improvised raft, were almost drowned' (p. 19). Such amalgamations of historical and autobiographical fact imaginatively treated were in any event Moore's common practice.

The sixteen-year period between 'A Flood' and the next story we include from 1927 was one of Moore's most productive, both in the short story and in the numerous other genres he was working on. He brought out *A Story-Teller's Holiday* in 1918, *Euphorion in Texas* and *In Single Strictness* in 1922, *Daphnis and Chloe* and *Peronnik the Fool* in 1924, and *Celibate Lives* in 1927. His reputation obviously was at such a high point that he could collect the many stories he wrote between 1911 and 1927 and get the volumes published. He was during this time continually interested in the various collected editions of his works, revising early novels and writing new ones. His interest in the theatre was renewed with *The Apostle* in 1911, the dramatized *Esther Waters* and *Elizabeth Cooper* in 1913, *The Coming of Gabrielle* in 1920, and *The Making of an Immortal* in 1927. Yet his most noteworthy works of this period are the three-volume autobiography, *Hail and Farewell*, the fictionalized account of Jesus in *The Brook Kerith*, the tales of *A Story-Teller's Holiday*, and the re-created romance in *Héloise and Abélard*.

We have already noted that 'At the Turn of the Road: An Irish Girl's Love Story' (July 1927) was probably one of the stories Moore had in mind for his proposed *In Minor Keys* volume. In it he concentrates on both the idea of a minor incident pregnant with larger consequences and on the anticlimactic ending. The story begins with the suicide of Cicely Wyatt; the unravelling of the story is built on an analysis of 'the crevice through which an idea enters the mind', later giving rise to a drastic outcome. For hitherto contented Cicely, an unscheduled meeting with the more travelled, more experienced Grigg, the piano tuner, provides sufficient awakening to cause the affianced young girl to forgo marriage with steadfast but unaspiring Sydney, to recognize the futility of her dreams of romantic adventure, and to take her own life. Moore does not dramatize Cicely's infatuation with Grigg but suggests the effect he has on her by the brief yet poignant interest she derives from the nomadic piano tuner in the sound of nightingales at midnight.

Beginning the story with Cicely's suicide makes clear Moore's interest in the anticlimactic ending. The bulk of the story is devoted to the distraught parents' piecing together of the circumstances surrounding the girl's death. By contriving the story in this manner, Moore shifts the emphasis to the parents and the effect their only daughter's death has on them. Moore changed the subtitle in the *Nash's Magazine* version to 'A Tragedy of the New Forest', thus acknowledging the more inclusive impact of the girl's suicide. Both lines of action are linked, however, by the growing awareness that this small-town life, tied down by the daily rigours of running a grocery store, is not fulfilling. The five pounds a week saved by the Wyatts for eighteen years to ensure their daughter's well-being now provides the parents themselves with the opportunity to escape the drabness of their provincial lives. With a calm, saddened resignation they leave their grocery store and, as the story closes, stand at the turn of the road on the outskirts of the hamlet, knowing only that some change is essential. Their plans are indefinite, and any speculation about the future seems unnecessary.

Interestingly, in 1920 or 1921 Moore had read John Freeman's 'The Harp',[20] in which the subject is a brother-sister suicide. In a letter to Freeman incompletely dated December, but probably 1920, Moore discusses the poem about suicide Freeman was then writing:

Now about your suicide. Will it surprise you to hear that I'd prefer a double suicide to a single, for then you would get the pathetic incident of a sister who will not leave her afflicted brother. And if the story be not formed on those lines I'd prefer the sister's marriage to lead up to the brother's suicide – it is the single unprepared suicide that jars. Like every other act suicide should have a poetic significance.[21]

At the end of 'The Strange Story of the Three Golden Fishes: A Comedy of a Man Who Always Was Lucky – Especially in Marriage' (September 1927) Moore calls his story a successful exemplification of what Henry James refers to as the 'irregular rhythm of life'. The phrase is extracted from James's 'The Art of Fiction':

Catching the very note and trick, the strange irregular rhythm of life, that is the attempt whose strenuous force keeps Fiction upon her feet. In proportion as in what she offers us we see life *without* rearrangement do we feel that we are touching the truth; in proportion as we see it *with* rearrangement do we feel that we are being put off with a substitute, a compromise and convention.[22]

Moore was fairly consistent in his praise of James's craftsmanship, but he regularly found other grounds for complaint:

I will ask him only why he always avoids decisive action? Why does a woman never say 'I will'? Why does a woman never leave the house with her lover? Why does a man never kill a man? Why does a man never kill himself? Why is nothing ever accomplished? . . . Mr James' people live in a calm, sad, and very polite twilight of volition. (Dick, X, 151)

The velleities of James's world were to him appropriate material for fiction '*without* rearrangement', but Moore, despite his agreement with James on the artistic supremacy of 'character-drawing', embraced the need both for decision and for the consequences of the enacted decision. Thus out of James's lengthy essay he locks in on this 'irregular rhythm of life', this acknowledgement of bizarre twists of fate, to lend artistic precedence to his unlikely tale.

'The Strange Story of the Three Golden Fishes' is framed by

a story-within-a-story as the narrator arrives in the dying port town of Sandwich, convinced that somewhere amidst the natives is a story to be found. The hopeful *shanachie* goes to the Royal George inn, saying to himself, 'An inn of story, the veritable inn of my imagination.' His search is not long, for his waiter at the inn is ably prepared to narrate the implausible connection between Mr Cather's fishing rod and the sixty thousand pounds he inherited from Trout, the 'third greatest butler in England'. What interests Moore is a story stripped of the usual literary demand for likelihood, too often ignoring the vicissitudes of the improbable, offering instead, as James puts it, 'a substitute, a compromise and convention'.

(v)

A final word about Moore's influence and his reputation as a writer. His influence on other short-story writers is difficult to measure because, as might be expected, there is little public record. His influence on other genres, especially on autobiography and the novel, is undoubtedly more general and more important. He provided brilliant examples in *Confessions* and in his remarkable *Hail and Farewell* of imaginative, creative, or fictional autobiography. There were precedents, of course, in such works as St Augustine's *Confessions*, Cellini's *Autobiography*, Rousseau's *Confessions*, Wordsworth's *The Prelude, The Recluse,* and *The Excursion*, and Cardinal Newman's *Apologia pro Vita Sua*. In Moore's autobiographical work there is even more candour than in that of his precursors, a similar emphasis on what Pater called mind-building, more revelation of multiple personae, and, above all, a comic self-view. He blends the essay, anecdote, poetry, straightforward factual narration, invented dialogue, and reverie to create a distinctive and original form of autobiography.

In the novel Moore's greatest influence, supported mainly by *A Mummer's Wife* and *Esther Waters*, is on realistic fiction. His importance as the chief proponent of French naturalism in England and, in his own practice, as one who modified the French naturalist mode to make it palatable to English tastes has been generally recognized. In fact, what Moore accomplished in the novel is much more complex than the preceding oversimplification suggests. He created a quite original blend out of what he learned not only from Zola but also from Turgenev, Balzac, Dickens, Gabriele D'Annunzio, and even Henry James. To this blend he added elements of what he discovered in Ibsenian drama, Wagnerian opera, and Impressionist painting.

His influence on the short story was more limited, for his work in this genre was not as widely known and not as flamboyantly advertised, either by himself or by critics and reviewers. The early reviews of *Celibates*, though rather mixed, do suggest recognition of Moore's candid exploration of the human psyche. More important, the stories of *The Untilled Field* and, to a lesser extent, those of *A Story-Teller's Holiday*, significantly influenced Irish writers. The influence of these works, however, does not seem to have been extended much beyond the Irish literary revival, perhaps because of the regional flavour of those works or because Moore did not sufficiently exploit what he accomplished in them. James Joyce's admitted indebtedness in *Dubliners* to Moore's *The Untilled Field* is well known. J.M. Synge also owes something to Moore's representation of Irish speech rhythms. Other Irish writers, such as Padraic Colum, Sean O'Faolain, and Mary Lavin may also have been influenced by Moore's work in a more general way.

Moore's reputation as a short-story writer, like his general reputation, seems to have suffered somewhat during the years following his death in 1933. A new generation of writers came into the forefront between the two world wars – Joyce, Lawrence, Conrad, and others – and attracted much attention among intellectuals and in the academic community. They were generally looked upon as more difficult and thus more interesting. Their works were inexpensively reprinted, appeared in university courses, and became the subjects of doctoral theses. Moore in the last twenty-five years of his career produced most of his books in expensive, limited editions, drastically changing his style and subject matter from those that had become familiar and that had originally led to his considerable reputation. This is not to say that Moore did not receive favourable attention but only that he did not have an effective 'bull-dog', in the sense in which T.H. Huxley was Darwin's bull-dog or the sense in which Henry James has had his dedicated and vocal supporters.

The last thirty years, especially since the publication of Malcolm Brown's excellent *George Moore: A Reconsideration* (1955), have seen a renewed scholarly interest in Moore, at least among serious students of the novel, of Anglo-Irish literature, and of cultural history of the late nineteenth and early twentieth centuries. Yet one is forced to conclude that Moore is more studied than read, an irony he might well appreciate, for, above all, he wrote to be read. He tells a good story and he tells it in a stylistically and technically interesting way. The range and diversity of his work may for some have done harm to his reputation, but it is also among its attractions. When he wrote in 1912 that he was one step nearer the summit of Parnassus, he was a little premature. Now that his wide-ranging accomplishments are on record, now that the most essential primary materials are available, and now that interested scholars have begun looking at Moore's work again, perhaps the summit of Parnassus is indeed nearer.

Moore has been much admired for the architectonics of his fiction, his flowing later style, his use of myth and symbolism, his sensitive studies of character, and his treatment of significant themes. He has been favourably viewed by major critics in America, England, France, Germany, Italy and elsewhere. His work belongs to world literature, for he absorbed something from most national literatures. Perhaps David Garnett, who once had considerable reservations about Moore, is not far off the mark when in reconsidering Moore in 1961, he wrote, 'I accept him almost at his own valuation. With the exception of Conrad and Henry James, he is the greatest writer I have known – at any rate the greatest artist.'[23]

Notes

1. *A Bibliography of George Moore* (DeKalb, IL: Northern Illinois University Press, 1970).
2. (London: Elkin Mathews and John Lane, 1894), pp. xv–xvi. Further references to the preface are given parenthetically.
3. *Impressions and Opinions* (London: David Nutt, 1891), p. 70; first published in *Fortnightly Review*, 1 February 1888.
4. *Ibid.*, p. 131.
5. 'George Moore à Paris', adapted in French by Philippe Neel, *Nouvelles Littéraires*, 21 May 1927, p. 6. In slightly expanded form, he said much the same thing in another interview about six months later: John Austin, 'Hail, My Farewell! By George Moore (in an interview)', *T.P.'s Weekly*, IX (12 November 1927).
6. *George Moore: Letters to Lady Cunard 1895–1933*, ed. Rupert Hart-Davis (London: Rupert Hart-Davis, 1957), p. 156n. Further references to these letters are given parenthetically as Hart-Davis.
7. Letter to Curtice H. Hitchcock, Vice-President of the New York firm of Macmillan, at the Humanities Research Center, University of Texas, to be included in Gerber's forthcoming *George Moore on Parnassus*.
8. Letter to Richard I. Best, at the National Library, Dublin, to be included in Gerber's forthcoming *George Moore on Parnassus*.
9. Letter to Groff Conklin, at Arizona State University, to be included in Gerber's forthcoming *George Moore on Parnassus*.
10. *Bat*, 4 January 1887, and *Hawk*, 12 August 1890, respectively.
11. See Joseph Hone, *Life of George Moore* (New York: Macmillan, 1936), p. 459. Further reference to this biography are given parenthetically as Hone.
12. The letters to Symons are located at Arizona State University and will be included in Gerber's forthcoming *George Moore on Parnassus*.
13. *Books on the Table* (London: Heinemann, 1921).

14. In the Henry E. Huntington Library and Art Gallery, this letter is to be included in Gerber's forthcoming *George Moore on Parnassus*. O'Sullivan's story, 'The Bookman', was published in *Common Adventures: A Book of Prose and Verse. Nicholas Flamel: A Play in Four Acts, From the French of Gérard de Nerval* (Dublin: The Orwell Press, 1926), pp. 22–9.
15. *Confessions of a Young Man*, ed. Susan Dick (Montreal and London: McGill-Queen's University Press, 1972), p. 130. Further references to this edition will be given parenthetically as Dick.
16. See Edmund Downey, *Twenty Years Ago* (London: Hurst and Blackett, 1905), pp. 9–11, 271.
17. 'The Influence of French Realism and Naturalism on George Moore's Early Fiction', New York University Ph.D. dissertation (1954), p. 103.
18. See n. 3 above.
19. In National Library, Dublin, to be included in Gerber's forthcoming *George Moore on Parnassus*.
20. In *Music: Lyrical & Narrative Poems* (London: Selwyn and Blount, 1921), pp. 111–35).
21. Letter to Freeman, December [1920], in the University of Kansas Special Collections and to be included in Gerber's forthcoming *George Moore on Parnassus*.
22. *Longman's Magazine*, IV (September 1884), pp. 502–21; reprinted in *Partial Portraits* (London and New York: Macmillan, 1888), p. 398 for our quotation.
23. 'Some Writers I Have Known: Galsworthy, Forster, Moore and Wells', *Texas Quarterly*, X (Autumn 1961), p. 200.

Under the Fan

Chapter I

Mrs Wallington White leaned her elbow on the crimson ledge of the private box, and pressed her large feather-made fan against her cheek. She was a little woman, about thirty, beautifully dressed in black satin. Her shoulders were too large, but her waist had not lost its symmetry. In the orange-coloured glare a fine dust floated softly downwards; the dazzling light caressed the milky whitenesses of arms and breasts, and the diamonds flashed around necks turned pensively to listen. The curtained boxes seemed like the luxurious nests of birds; and fans, like wings, wafted breaths of musk-perfumed lace to and fro. The stalls were filled with young men, varying in age from twenty to twenty-five; they almost seemed to be in uniform, so exactly did the suits of black, shirt-fronts, and gardenias correspond.

The black monotony was broken up here and there by groups of muslin-dressed young girls, with fair frank faces, and hair tied in a small knot behind the head, which Du Maurier loves to depict.

They were with their mothers, placid-looking matrons of forty-five, in lace caps, and their fathers of fifty, City looking, with mutton-chop whiskers. Here and there might be seen a journalist, whose Bohemian life slyly peeped through his dress clothes.

The finale of the first act had been reached. The young men levelled their opera-glasses in their white-gloved fingers; the ladies ceased fanning themselves and leaned to listen, for Miss St Vincent had stepped down to sing her famous song, 'They thought to nobble the horse'. Although possessing scarcely enough voice to sing the slight music allotted to her, Miss St Vincent knew how to intensify the effect of her song by a thousand little tricks, and she amply atoned for her musical deficiencies by her charming acting.

The piece was one of those modern comic operas now so much in fashion. It was trifling, whimsical, frivolous, and set to jingling tunes. The plot turned upon the fortune, in love and gambling, of an English nobleman, Lord Sidegirth, who had married an Arabian princess. He was obliged to resort to all kinds of disguises to escape the vigilance of his wife, who was as jealous of him as a lioness of her young. The scene was laid in Newmarket, and the slight story was garnished with choruses of betting-men, welshers, bookmakers, etc., written in correct slang to lively tunes. As the trainer's daughter, Miss St Vincent was charming, and in her song, which told how she defeated the horse-nobblers and saved her lover from ruin, to use the correct phrase, she nightly brought the house down. She was an amusing mixture of the French and English girl; she had the sparkling grey eyes and the general rumpled look of the French *grisette*; but there was in her face much Saxon sentimentality and frankness. She was dressed in her father's colours, pink and white. A short skirt, not long enough to hide her slender ankles and feet, in pale rose-colour, trimmed with a few large flowers, and garnished with a large white-cashmere scarf tied behind in the form of a pannier. The body was a jockey's jacket, and the pink and white cap did not hide the large masses of mustard-coloured hair which shadowed her clear white temples and little ears. She spoke the racing slang with such gusto, and seemed to understand so thoroughly the intricacies of stable life, that the young men of Pall Mall could not resist; they came night after night to see her, and spent their mornings talking of her. The stage-doorkeeper had made his salary twice over in half-crowns and half-sovereigns, paid for the safe delivery of letters, bouquets, and small cases containing jewellery. Yet, notwithstanding all their persistence and generosity, not one of these young men had succeeded in making her acquaintance. All their invitations to dinner and supper remained unanswered, and the rings and bracelets were invariably returned when they were accompanied with the sender's name. Morality of all kinds is generally a compromise. The best of us yield a little; and the pretty actress thought, and sincerely, that she was doing as well as the most scrupulous would demand if she returned a diamond ring when the sender enclosed his name; for then the jewel, she argued, was not a tribute paid to her art, but to her good looks. The reasoning may have been a little forced, but it perfectly satisfied her conscience; and is not that all that can be demanded of any of us?

Mrs White looked at Miss St Vincent with more than ordinary interest, and the actress had bestowed more than one searching glance at the fashionable woman who sat in the stage-box with Lord Wedmore. At the end of her song, as Miss St Vincent bowed her acknowledgements to an applauding public, Mrs White took a large bouquet of white flowers, which was lying on the ledge of the box, and adroitly threw it full at Miss St Vincent's feet. The actress picked it up, and the women exchanged a look fully as indicative of hatred as if they had drawn daggers from their skirts. The throwing of the bouquet, apparently a compliment, was one of those secret sneers which women know well how to give, and which they never forget.

These two women, although separated by immense social barriers as wide as the oceans which divide continents, were united by enmity in the closest bonds. They knew each other well by sight and name; they knew each other's intentions, and they knew they were engaged in a struggle where no quarter would be given or expected. It was one of those thousand duels which take place in our midst, whose collective force, although unnoticed by the historian, is certainly equal to the battles which decide the fate of empires. Men fight for many things, women fight only for *man*, and Mrs White's quarrel with Miss St Vincent was no exception to the rule. Lord Wedmore was the stake played for; the game was matrimony, and never were gamblers more absorbed in their play than these two women. Lord Wedmore was the young man who sat beside Mrs White; he sat there quite as unconscious of the cunning, the trickery, and the heartlessness that would be used to gain him as the pile of money on the green cloth is of the eyes watching the cards that will transfer it from one to the other.

Lord Wedmore was the man whom most women wish to marry, but whom none love. Yet he was tall and well built, and was not ill-looking, although his hair was fair and his face florid. He was unattractive to women solely because he excited their curiosity in nothing. He was a neutral tint, offensive for its monotony. He had been surrounded by actresses, match-making mammas, racing-men, yachting-men, all of whom had done their best, in different ways, to help him to spend his twenty thousand a year. But, after a short trial, he had shaken them all off one after the other, for the amusements they had to offer bored him. He had tried to flirt in drawing-rooms; he had bought a few worthless screws; he had lost money at cards; he had even travelled a year in Italy; but, unable to cultivate a taste for art, came home, and smoked cigars and drank brandies-and-sodas in despair.

After a time he grew very tired of this, and he inwardly blessed a friend who advised him to lend a few thousands to the manager of the Pall Mall Theatre, who allowed him to go behind the scenes when he liked, and make what presents he thought fit to the actresses. After some hesitation, Lord Wedmore's choice settled upon Miss St Vincent, partly because she encouraged him more adroitly than the rest; partly because every fellow he knew thought her charming, and was dying to know her. He was very proud of his acquaintance with her: it gave him a slight individuality in his club – he was the man who knew Miss St Vincent. Miss St Vincent allowed him to make love to her; but, in common with the rest of her sex, she thought him the greatest bore she ever met. His defects were doubly visible to her; for she liked very much (if she were not in love with) a young actor with whom she had once, in the provinces, played Juliet to his Romeo. Lord Wedmore had twenty thousand a year , and as dearly as she wished to play leading business in high-class comedy with Mr Shirley, she was aware that Lady Wedmore was the better part of the two. She therefore allowed Lord

Wedmore to take her home from the theatre occasionally, and make her presents of jewellery; but, always in the approved way, he left them at the stage-door anonymously. She put them on at night and showed them to him, saying, 'How kind it is of the sender, and how much obliged she was!' The deception was a thin one; but appearances were preserved, and that was all she wanted.

Mrs Wallington White, on the other hand, had met Lord Wedmore in society, and she at once fixed upon him as the most likely person she had ever met to realize her dreams of wealth, honour, and position.

Mrs White's opinion of herself was that she had only made one mistake in life – that she had married for love. The disagreeable result of this error was that, on her husband's death, she had been left with only five hundred a year to live upon. What she would have done if her father had not allowed her a few hundred extra was more than she could imagine. She just managed to dress beautifully, and keep a carriage and a house in Norfolk-street – a matter of no small difficulty – on something less than a thousand a year. Her drawing-room was a wilderness of delicate trifles. There was much old Saxony on the *étagères* and inlaid cabinets; between the fireplace and the window there was a little black sofa; and behind, a rose-shaded lamp, which threw a soft light over Mrs White's face as she leant back reading, one foot resting on the tiger's head whose skin was the hearthrug, and the other drawn up on the sofa. She was generally found in this position when visitors called. The walls were wainscoted with white painted wood, divided into panels by gilt mould-ings, and decorated with well-chosen porcelain and draw-ings. The piano stood in a corner, turned away from the wall, and was draped with a rich Indian shawl. The windows were curtained with mauve-coloured satin, with double-crossed lace blinds. From this sketch it will be seen that she was a woman, if not of natural, at least of acquired taste. She could talk of the fashionable pictures in the Academy, and attribute to them their accepted qualities. She knew what was thought about the latest novel, had seen all the new plays, and had always a criticism to offer, which; if sometimes a little commonplace, was never stupid. She had learned what she could of music and art, not because she cared for either, but because she knew that the woman of thirty had to conquer the girl of twenty by other means than dressing youthfully and putting a little rouge on her cheeks. She educated herself carefully and studiously for the drawing-room successes; of any other she knew nothing, cared nothing. In her dark bead-like eyes could be easily read her hard material nature, which could look neither into the past nor the future, but which found its joys and griefs solely in the present.

Not the least of Mrs White's social qualifications was her talent for keeping her friends.

In her service there were men whom she had known before she was married, and who were as loud in her praise as ever.

She had friends scattered over the whole of society, and was therefore in a position to command it. There was scarcely an invitation and no news she could not obtain. In twenty-four hours she could find out what was passing in the semi-detached villa in St John's Wood or the stately mansion in Carlton House-terrace. Lord Wedmore's wealth was, of course, known to everybody; in half an hour she had sounded exactly his character; and, after a few visits from old club-men, she knew all about the *opéra-bouffe* prima donna, and how vain the young man was of his acquaintanceship. It did not require much more investigation to discover how the racing, yachting, and card men had failed. In a word, Mrs White saw that they were now (to borrow a sporting phrase) in the 'run home', and that Miss St Vincent and she were left to fight the issue out by themselves.

Previous to going to the theatre, Lord Wedmore had spent the whole afternoon with her; and owing to the delicate tact with which Mrs White had started subjects of conversation for him, and at the same time suggesting to him appropriate answers, he thought he had never spent a pleasanter day. At six, when he took up his hat and prepared to go, he had been easily persuaded to put it down and stay to dinner. The champagne and the entrée, which had been sent for to Gunter's, were excellent; and Mrs White conversed so pleasantly, ever deluding him that it was he who was doing the talking, that he looked forward to continuing the conversation up-stairs. But she knew better than to risk it. Three hours is a severe strain upon anyone; and feeling afraid that he might bore himself, she wisely proposed to adjourn to the theatre. Ten years of London life had led Mrs White into a great many secrets. She knew well that where there is no intelligence there are still the senses, and she therefore tried to win him by tempting him through the flesh. She gave him nice dinners to eat and wines to drink, soft chairs to sit on, and, by a thousand artifices, contrived to engender the idea in his mind that she understood him, that he was not half the fool in her society that he was elsewhere. She flattered his self-love in every way; she spoke to him and quizzed him about Miss St Vincent; congratulated him on his good fortune; praised her beauty, her acting, her singing – for she knew that nothing would be gained by abusing her, that any opposition on her part would only have the effect of stimulating his passion. So she laughed, joked, and praised her; and when the time came to decide what theatre they should go to, Mrs White did not hesitate to say that she was dying to see *The Tinman*. By this means she would continue the pleasantness of Lord Wedmore's evening; it would flatter his vanity and humiliate Miss St Vincent, who would be forced to dance and sing, while she would do the grand lady in the stage-box, flirting and applauding as the humour came to her. Throwing the bouquet was the finishing touch to the picture designed by a master.

Before the curtain was rung down on the last act, Mrs White asked Lord Wedmore to give her her opera-cloak; and having wrapped herself well up, she took his arm, and went down to the vestibule of the theatre.

There was a slight fog; the pavements were slippery, and the house-tops could not be distinguished against the murky sky. The streets were full of people coming from the Strand and Haymarket. With bent heads they hurried along, trying to breathe as little of the foggy air as possible. They went by in groups. Dirty-dressed girls passed, gathering up their skirts; boys still shouted out the last editions of the evening papers, and offered to call cabs for those leaving the theatre. The hansoms and carriages stopped and whirled away every minute.

Refusing all invitations to supper, Mrs White got into her brougham, bade him good-bye, and lay back on the soft cushions and calculated the progress she had made as she drove home.

Chapter II

Lord Wedmore turned up a narrow street towards the stage-door. He was curious to see Miss St Vincent; he wondered if she were jealous, and what her comments would be on Mrs Wallington White. Two private broughams and three hack-cabs were standing before the low doorway, out of which a lot of seedy-dressed men were hurrying, buttoning up coats and wrapping thick comforters round their necks.

Lord Wedmore passed the stage-doorkeeper with a nod, wishing that the whole club could see him, and went down the narrow flight of steps leading on to the stage. The drop-curtain was drawn up, and all the lights in the theatre were out except a large iron gas-pipe in the form of a cross, which lit with a flaring uncertain light the auditorium, now empty of all but three or four servant-women, who were covering the seats in the upper boxes with large linen cloths. The stage was dim and deserted, and the scene-shifters piled the large side-scenes up in one corner, and pushed by the actors and actresses who stood about chatting. Mr Lendsell, the manager, was talking to Miss St Vincent in one of the wings, and he shouted to the girls who passed in groups up the narrow staircases leading to their dressing-rooms, that there would be a rehearsal at twelve to-morrow. The manager and actress shook hands with Lord Wedmore, and then withdrew, talking together in whispers. Mr Lendsell was a tall thin man, splendidly built. An immense shock of very dark frizzly hair gave him at first sight a look of an Italian; but his large blue-grey eyes betrayed his Saxon, or rather Celtic, origin. Owing to a few failures, he had the reputation of being easy with other people's money. Yet there was little of the swindler in his face; it was more that of the sensualist, who loves good living, and does not much trouble himself about the rights and wrongs of things.

At last Miss St Vincent ran upstairs to dress, and Mr Lendsell, with a hurried and anxious manner, looked about for someone. Meeting Lord Wedmore, he stopped to talk, forgetting the person he was seeking. He gave his very dirty hand to Lord Wedmore, and, drawing him aside, said,

'Look here, old man; I am rather short for treasury to-morrow. Could you advance me another fifty? With the new piece we shall get it back.'

'Certainly,' answered Lord Wedmore. 'I will send you a cheque to-morrow.'

'Could you not let me have it to-night?'

'I have not my cheque-book with me.'

'It does not matter; the stage-doorkeeper will give you a sheet of paper. It is just the same to give it me now. You would be sure to forget it in the morning.'

They went up-stairs together, where, while Mr Lendsell arranged with Mr Chapel for the rehearsal, Lord Wedmore wrote the cheque. These little matters having been arranged, he proposed a supper to the manager, who was preparing to dart down the stairs after somebody or something he had forgotten. Mr Lendsell consented, and asked who were going to be the guests. Lord Wedmore had no idea beyond that he would like to ask Miss St Vincent, and he was glad to shift the responsibility of the whole thing on the manager's shoulders. Mr Lendsell, seeing that he would have to 'boss' the affair, collected his thoughts, and said,

'Miss St Vincent, of course. I'll ask Lottie – Miss Powell is a nice girl. And then for the men: you don't mind my asking old Centreboard? He is a bore, you know; but I want him to advance me a little money for the new piece.'

This last phrase was purposely thrown in; for Mr Lendsell did not want the young lord to think he was the only 'mug'.

'But that will not be enough.'

'Ah, I forgot,' said the maager reflectively: 'I shall have to ask the two Miss Westerns for the old man, and we might ask De Bridet, and Oscalia is good fun. Have you a friend you would like to invite?'

'Ask Slaughter, he is not a bad fellow,' answered Lord Wedmore, suggesting the acting-manager; for he preferred to relate his adventures behind the scenes than that his friends should be eye-witnesses of them.

'All right, that will do, then,' replied Lendsell as he hurried

away. 'Stop the girls as they come up. I shall not be a
minute.'

Mr Lendsell's minute was a long one, and he left his friend
kicking his heels together in the cold narrow passage for over
a quarter of an hour. The chorus people had mostly all left,
but now and again a couple of girls in dark bonnets and
shawls would hurry away together, hoping that they were
not too late for their bus. At last the two Miss Westerns made
their appearance, and Lord Wedmore begged them to stop to
supper. The girls seemed embarrassed, they did not know
whether to accept or refuse; for the fact was that their father
and mother were respectively the stage-doorkeeper and
principal dresser. Mr and Mrs Western let their daughters do
pretty well as they wished, yet the girls would have liked to
quiet the old people with a word of explanation. However,
this was impossible: Lord Wedmore was there, and it never
would have done to betray their parentage. So the elder gave
her father a quick look and they went down-stairs to oysters
and champagne, leaving the authors of their being to go
home to a bit of bread-and-cheese.

They found Mr Lendsell in one of the wings, talking to Mr
Chapel, the pianist. Apparently he had forgotten all about the
supper, for seeing them he was seized with remorse, and
rushed up a rickety staircase, and was heard knocking for
admittance at Miss St Vincent's door, and the following
dialogue was the result:

'You can't come in, I am not dressed!'

'It is only me.'

'Ah, I didn't know. Wait a second. Mrs Jones, give me my
shawl.' A minute after, a door opened, and Miss St Vincent's
voice was heard asking what he wanted. After some whisper-
ing the actress promised something, and shut her door, and
the manager went to Mdlle Oscalia who dressed in the same
room with Miss Powell. When the dresser opened the door
there was heard the sound of wrangling voices. The mention
of the supper pacified them, and Mr Lendsell – or Dick, as
everybody called him – joined Lord Wedmore, who had met
De Bridet and Centreboard, and was inquiring after Mr
Slaughter. Mr Centreboard declared that he was delighted to

stay to supper, but that every place was shut up, and that they would find it impossible to get anything to eat at that hour. The news was disappointing, but Dick declared that he would get everything that was wanted – champagne, oysters, chickens, salads – and that they would sup up-stairs, which would be much better fun than going out. To put his plans into execution, it was necessary to take Lord Wedmore into one of the wings, borrow whatever loose sovereigns he had in his pocket, and tell him that there had been a seizure made up-stairs some time ago, which would account for the scarcity of furniture. This, Dick declared, did not matter; and having got ten pounds from his friend, and a couple of sacks from the property-man, he went off without giving any further explanation than to tell De Bridet to show everybody up-stairs, to light a fire, and that he would be back in a minute. The adjoining house was let always with the theatre, and there was a door of communication between the two. When the whole party had assembled on the stage, De Bridet led the way. After having passed into the front of the theatre, round the dress-circle, and up a couple of narrow staircases, he showed them into a large room without fire or light. When the gas was lit there was a general cry of astonishment. The room was absolutely empty; there was literally, with the exception of the piano, not a single piece of furniture in the place, not even a carpet on the floor. They asked De Bridet how they were to sup in a room without a table, a question he admitted he was unable to answer. Was there no other room? Was he sure he had made no mistake? He had made no mistake, and there was no other room, was all he could say; and he proceeded to light an enormous fire, which was sorely needed, for everybody was shivering with the cold. Undoubtedly the supper had been badly started, and seemed likely to prove a failure. Everybody was discontented and out of humour. Mdlle Oscalia declared the whole thing to be *une farce anglaise*; and Miss St Vincent said that if she were hoarse to-morrow night and could not sing, Dick would have no one to thank but himself. The ladies kept their wraps on, the gentlemen their greatcoats and hats, and stamped about the floor, trying to keep themselves warm. A gloom had fallen over them, and had it not been for De Bridet, who strove, with coarse joking, to keep their spirits up, it is not impossible that they would have gone home, and that Dick would have found no one to eat the supper he had gone to fetch: all prophesied that he would return empty-handed. They were a strangely-assorted company. There was De Bridet, a short thickset little man with a snub-nose, and the hair cut close over his high bumpy forehead. He spoke English with a vile foreign accent, and French with a still viler native one. There was old Centreboard, as he was called behind the scenes, a stout little man nearer sixty than fifty, with mutton-chop whiskers and a pompous manner. He made love to the two Miss Westerns, and it was impossible to tell which he preferred; his chief annoyance in life seemed to be that they occasionally treated him more in the light of a relation than an admirer. Mr Semper was a tall American with a hatchet-like face, who perpetually smoked cigarettes, and annoyed Miss Powell by ever telling her that he was utterly *blasé*, but that if he had met her ten years ago he doubtless would have admired her very much.

The fire at last commenced to burn, and the ladies took off their wraps, and began to talk of the new piece and the probable distribution of parts. A slight tiff had arisen between Miss St Vincent and Mdlle Oscalia for possession of the music-stool, both ladies being now anxious to entertain the company with a little music. Their slight wrangle was, however, cut short by the arrival of Dick. He had a large sack over his shoulder, and was bending beneath its weight, and he was followed by a pot-boy carrying an immense hamper. In the language of the theatrical critic, Dick's entrance was a great success; it aroused the house at once to a pitch of enthusiasm.

'Now then, you lazy beggars,' he cried, 'give me a hand – my back is broken. Here are twenty-four dozen of oysters. It is one o'clock. I had a devil of a job to get them.'

'But where are we going to sup?' asked half a dozen voices.

'Why, here, of course,' he said, wiping his forehead. 'Where do you think? Don't you know what a picnic is? Come, Wedmore, do you know how to open oysters? If you don't, Jack will show you. The supper is communistic. Everyone must bring his brick.'

All laughed at the sally, and the company seemed to wake up like birds in the bushes when the rain is over and the sun shines out. Miss St Vincent held up one of Wedmore's long, white, weak-looking hands, and asked if they thought that paw had ever opened an oyster. They were now beginning to think that the supper on the floor, which at first had so horrified them, was rather fun; and they jostled each other and crowded round to see Wedmore help the pot-boy to open the oysters. Dick and his aide-de-camp, De Bridet, in the mean time unpacked the hamper, spread the table-cloth on the bare boards, and covered it with knives, forks, plates, lobsters, cold chickens, and salad, which later Mdlle Oscalia seized on, and began to mix a dressing in a very learned way. Centreboard took the wrappers off the champagne, assisted by the Miss Westerns, who chaffed and flirted with the gay old gentleman to his evident delight; and Miss Powell accompanied Mr Semper, who sang a comic song with much gravity.

In half an hour twenty dozen of oysters had been opened, the salad was ready, the chickens were carved, and everybody was now in high good-humour. Miss St Vincent sat next Lord Wedmore, and even gave him her handkerchief to wipe his oyster-dirtied hands, his own not being now in a state fit to be touched. Old Centreboard sat between the two Miss Westerns; Mdlle Oscalia next to Dick, for whom she did not disguise her admiration; and De Bridet tried to make love to Miss Powell (a tall thin girl, with a lot of wavy flaxen hair, and a high aquiline nose), much to her disgust and Mr Semper's amusement, who aggravated the situation by pleading De Bridet's love-case in a low drawling voice.

'You don't love me at all now – in France it was so different,' said Mdlle Oscalia, looking tenderly at Dick.

A sudden silence had made her declaration audible, and a titter went round the cloth. As manager, Dick had to appear to be of austere virtue; so, to break the thread of Mdlle Oscalia's attentions and partly to create a laugh, he shouted brutally at Wedmore, 'Well, Wedmore, what about the little woman in black? I guess if she saw you now there would be a row.'

Wedmore at this moment was lost in admiration of Miss St Vincent. As she sat on the floor, with her legs tucked under her, sucking the oysters out of their shells with her coral lips, she appeared to him the realization of all that was charming. He had forgotten all about the afternoon in the shady drawing-room, and the little dinner in the oak-panelled dining-room; all was forgotten in the delight of the supper on the bare boards. Dick's question embarrassed him not a little. He tried to look annoyed, but inwardly he was pleased; it tickled his vanity and he hoped that the suspicion would make Miss St Vincent jealous.

'O yes, I saw him; he was flirting with her as hard as he could, and he pretends to like me,' returned the actress, trying to pout and trying to turn her back on her lover, a matter of no small difficulty, as she was sitting on the ground. With a shriek she tried to get up, but fell into Wedmore's arms.

'What is it?' he cried, assisting her to rise.

'O, I have the pins and needles!'

At this there was a roar of laughter, mingled with cries of pain, for more than one lady suddenly found she was a victim to the same affliction. For some time they had been vainly trying to hide their ankles, and enduring tortures in so doing.

'It is dreadful this sitting on the floor,' cried Miss Powell, recklessly changing her position. 'I am not going to bother any more about my skirts.'

Mdlle Oscalia followed her example, and took a stretch still more conspicuously.

'*Qu'est-ce que cela fait?*' she said; '*on voit à davantage quand nous sommes sur la scène.*'

After Miss St Vincent had walked about a bit and stamped her circulation into order, she was induced to sit down again, and persuaded to finish her glass of champagne and the wing of a chicken she was eating when the little accident took place.

The supper had now reached its height; cigars and

cigarettes had been lighted, and jokes, which would not have been dared before, became general.

Shaking off Mdlle Oscalia, whose black eyes were now melting with tenderness, and who was too desirous to talk about some long-past time in France, Dick determined to have his joke out about the lady in black; so, holding up a glass of fizz in one hand, he begged for silence. When this was obtained, he said,

'Ladies and gentlemen, in the absence of a chairman – ' the joke was received with shouts of laughter, and Mr Semper proposed to give him the piano-stool, which he, however, declined. 'I do not rise,' he continued, 'to propose Lord Wedmore's health, because there is no table before me.' ('Hear, hear.') Everybody looked at the young lord, who began to feel uneasy, and wondered what was coming. 'I propose Lord Wedmore's health, and that of the lady he loves best.' ('Hear, hear.') 'Now, as, according to an old proverb, present company is always excepted, I do not refer to anyone here, although I notice that one lady is beginning to look guilty.' Clamorous applause followed this sally, and Lord Wedmore's face beamed with delight. 'Now,' continued the manager, 'as I am not acquainted with the lady whose health I wish to drink, and as I do not know her name, she shall be nameless.' (Laughter.) 'I will only refer to her as the lady in black; whom you all saw in the stage-box tonight, and who was so appreciative of talent as to throw a bouquet to Miss St Vincent.'

Mrs Wallington White's health was drunk with much noise and applause; but Miss St Vincent could not conceal her annoyance, and Dick, not knowing the real cause, for a moment began to suspect that she were really in love with Lord Wedmore. Lord Wedmore noticed it too, and the discovery raised his spirits to the highest pitch of enthusiasm. He felt that it was necessary to explain. So, to Miss St Vincent's vexation, who saw how her face had betrayed her, and how it had been misinterpreted, he got up, and, in a long-winded and contradictory speech, solemnly declared he had no intention of marrying Mrs White, which denial evoked peals of laughter; and when he finally stated that the lady in black was his aunt, the merriment of the company knew no bounds; and, amid roars of laughter and sarcastic allusions, Wedmore sat down, bitterly cursing Dick's want of tact and insufferable impertinence. The joke of relationship having been started, Mr Slaughter applied it successfully to old Centreboard, who, he declared he had satisfactory proof, was the Miss Westerns' uncle. Centreboard looked up embarrassed. He had been enjoying himself highly between the two, and he evidently thought it cruel to have his age flung in his face. Mr Semper was sullen and silent; he seemed to have a difficulty in sitting upright, and he lolled against Miss Powell, who resented the familiarity, and complained bitterly to Miss Mure that three o'clock never saw him steady.

'I cannot understand what you find to like in him,' answered Miss Mure confidentially.

'He is not always so cold,' returned Miss Powell, who did not allow anyone but herself to find fault with Mr Semper.

'But he is so cynical. He is always laughing at love and sentiment.'

'Do you say in English, "We will dining on the grass", or, "We will going to dinner on the grass"?' asked De Bridet, who was deep in the agonies of composition, intensified by an imperfect knowledge of the English language. After having informed herself, with difficulty, of which tense he wished to use, Miss Mure, whom the champagne had rendered sentimental, turned to her friend, interested in her love-story. But De Bridet, having at last satisfied himself on the idiomatic construction of his phrases, rose to his feet, and, with a full glass of champagne, half of which he spilled down Miss Mure's back, said:

'Gentlemens and Madams, this supper having been so grand a success, I propose that next week we do all repeat it over again on the grass in the country, and in this order: Lord Wedmore with Miss St Vincent; Mr Dick with Mdlle Oscalia; Mr Centreboard with the two Miss Westerns.'

Old Centreboard, who was pleading, in low tones, so as not to attract attention, mercy of the younger Miss Western, who, pulling him over by the whisker, was making him beg pardon for some past offence, evoked peals of laughter. The old gentleman only maintained his equilibrium by clinging to the other sister, who was angrily trying to disengage herself from his grasp. He declared that he could be quite satisfied with either. Upon which the elder sister took hold of the other whisker, and would not release him until he sang the song, from the beginning to the end, 'How happy could I be with either, were other fair sister away!' De Bridet, elated at the success of his joke, paired himself off with Miss Mure, and assigned a bottle to Mr Semper at the proposed picnic next Sunday.

The hilarity was here unfortunately cut short by Mr Semper struggling to his feet, with the aid of the piano, and declaring he was going for the Frenchman. A disagreeable scene might have ensued, had it not been for the timely intervention of Dick, who precipitately left Mdlle Oscalia, and placed himself between the combatants.

'My dear fellow,' he argued, 'he can't pronounce English, you know. He meant Powell, and not bottle.'

The assurance somewhat pacified Mr Semper; but he, nevertheless, demanded an apology. Nothing would appease him but this, till suddenly he felt that a little fresh air would be a still greater boon. The room was full of smoke. They had been breathing the same atmosphere for hours. The ladies put on their cloaks, and declared they were suffocating. When the blinds were drawn a cry of amazement broke from all. Heavy snow had fallen during the night, and the clear rose-coloured sunrise shone against the glittering house-tops. A wind, as cold and as piercing as steel, blew briskly, and the ladies drew their shawls and cloaks round their shoulders, and shivering, spoke unanimously of getting home.

The supper was over now; everyone was tired and pale; and the bare room, covered with oyster-shells and empty bottles, looked horrible in the yellow flaring gaslight and the bright morning air. Heedful that the early bird catches the worm, Miss St Vincent told Lord Wedmore to go and see if he could find a cab. He stole away unperceived, and ran, shivering in his thin dress-slippers, through the cold snow towards the Haymarket. He was lucky enough to find a four-wheeler coming from the Strand; and, bribed with a sovereign, the half-frozen cabman consented to take them to Kennington Oval. When Miss St Vincent heard the cab was at the door she took a hasty adieu of her friends, and hoped that they might be equally lucky in getting cabs.

Lord Wedmore and Miss St Vincent drove away together.

It was piercingly cold, their feet were like ice, and they drew together, instinctively seeking warmth. Miss St Vincent was a little sleepy; the champagne had gone to her head, but the cold kept her well awake. She had long studied the man by her side, and she now felt sure that, before they reached Kennington, she would have to decide if she would or would not be Lady Wedmore.

To any third person hesitation would seem impossible; yet Miss St Vincent's reluctance was rational enough, when you knew what was passing in her mind.

Twenty thousand a year, a title, and a possibility of being received later on by the *élite* of Vanity Fair, was doubtless a wonderful dream; but it was not her dream – that was its only fault. Hers was more simple, but not less dear to her. She had dreamed of marrying Mr Shirley, and playing high-class business with him on the boards of a first-class London house, where she would make love to him from eight till half-past eleven, and be called before the curtain at the end of each act; and none of these things could she do with Lord Wedmore. Miss St Vincent was not a girl who thought that to eat, drink, be beautifully dressed, and rush from one amusement to another, was the sole aim and purpose of living. She loved her profession, and was devoured with ambition. She disliked Lord Wedmore as much as she liked Mr Shirley. Looks had nothing to do with it. Lord Wedmore was not ugly. He was stupid; but he might have been clever enough to have filled the office of Prime Minister, and she would not have loved him any better. She disliked him because he knew nothing of the life she lived; her thoughts and prospects were not his. She found in him no echo of her own desires and sentiments. The greatest and most enduring love is self-love; the next best is in proportion to the similarity between the being on whom we have bestowed our affections and ourselves, mentally and physically. It is true that we may love, for a time, some person who is the direct opposite to ourselves; but this is only a caprice, and cannot last: love that endures is based on similarity of colour, form, taste, and education.

Miss St Vincent drew her cloak round her, and leaned back against the boards of the clattering cab. Lord Wedmore spoke but little. He was determined to come to the point, and was waiting for an occasion to speak the fatal phrase.

He had offered horses, carriages, country and town houses, spoken as rapturously as his meagre elocution would allow him of a cruise in the Mediterranean, and vaunted the delights of love pure and free, untrammelled by social laws, and found, if a slang phrase be permissible, that it was not good enough. Lord Wedmore's love for the pretty actress originated in idleness, chance, and vanity. It was stimulated by the difficulties which lay between him and its attainment. His love for Mrs Wallington White was of precisely the same character, with the slight difference that the widow imposed herself upon him by sheer strength of will – forced him, as it were, to admire her; whereas he was really a little attracted by Miss St Vincent's beauty, independent of other people's opinion.

The cab plodded slowly through the snow. The windows were frozen over, but through the blurred panes Lord Wedmore could see the outlines of the Houses of Parliament, the long wharfs and quays. They were passing over Waterloo Bridge. For the hundredth time since they left Pall Mall he asked her if she were cold. Apparently there was no need to ask, for poor Miss St Vincent's little nose was red, her teeth chattered, and she beat her feet on the cab-floor, trying to warm them.

She had drawn her fur-trimmed cloak around her tiny ears, and looked like the fantastic figures of Winter seen upon Christmas-cards. She had forgotten her muff, and complained bitterly of Lord Wedmore's negligence in leaving it behind. He took her hand in his; she did not withdraw her frozen fingers, and, not guessing the real reason, he ventured to put his other arm round her waist. She could not resist, for the warmth of his arm was so grateful in her half-frozen condition that she had not the courage to consider proprieties.

'I never loved anyone until I saw you,' he said. 'I never cared for anything – I could not amuse myself like other fellows. I have lots of money, but I don't know what to do with it. I do not care for betting and racing like other men; it only bores me to spend money. Last year I could not get through more than five thousand pounds, and I have twenty a year. Now, if you would only love me a little, all this would be so different; for you would know how to get through all this money properly, and I should have something to live for; it would be such a pleasure to make you happy!'

This was not very eloquent, but it had a flavour of sincerity which Miss St Vincent did not fail to recognize. There was something so piteous in the statement of the poor swell, who felt so lonely with his twenty thousand a year, not having any of the tastes necessary to enable him to spend it, that the actress felt really sorry for him, and, in a way, began to like him.

The two nestled together in the cold cab, the lord pleading and the actress listening, as they drove through the narrow streets leading to Kennington Oval. For a long time he took Miss St Vincent's silence as a favourable augury; but at last its duration began to frighten him.

Suddenly the cabby drew up before a shabby two-storeyed house, and Miss St Vincent made a movement to rise; but Lord Wedmore put his hand on the door, and said,

'No, I may not see you again alone; I must know my fate. Do you love me? Can you ever care for me?'

Miss St Vincent did not know well what to answer. She was anxious, she was determined that he should ask her, in so many words, to be Lady Wedmore, although she did not really know if she would accept him or not; so she said evasively,

'I do not know if I ever might grow to love you as you want to be loved; but I like you well enough.'

'What must I do, then, to make you love me?'

73

This was a difficult question for her to answer. She could do nothing but say that love was an involuntary emotion, and that it came and went of its own accord. This led, of course, to a prolonged discussion as to what love is and is not, much to Miss St Vincent's discontent, for her teeth were chattering and her cheeks were violet with cold. The cabby sat as if petrified on his box; and through the frozen panes the white snow was seen extending on every side.

Several times Lord Wedmore nearly said the wished-for words, and as often the conversation slid away into some trifling discussion. She waited and waited, thinking that every phrase would be the phrase of phrases, till at last the cold became so intense that she could stand it no longer, and she begged him to let her get out.

'No,' he said at last, 'not until you say you will be Lady Wedmore.'

The actress sank back into her seat. The words were said, and Lord Wedmore drew her towards him and kissed her. Yet she could not make up her mind to throw over Mr Shirley and the profession she loved, nor yet to say 'No' to a title and twenty thousand a year.

'Yes or no?' he asked, taking her hand.

'What is the use of my answering you now?' she said, annoyed at herself for not being able to say yes. 'I am too cold, too miserable. Pray let me out; if you don't, I shan't be able to sing tonight.'

'Say yes, and I will tell cabby to drive to Victoria, and in a few hours we shall be out of this hateful London.'

With a little more pressing she might have accepted him, if it were only to get out of the cab; but the idea of driving back to Victoria was too fearful. It was not the impropriety of the runaway match she thought of; she could think of nothing but the cold, and the fire she knew was burning in her room. How often are our gravest steps in life decided by some trifling incident!

'No, no, I could not. It would kill me. Already I am beginning to feel the effects of the cold. I have waited here too long as it is.'

'When shall I see you?' he asked imploringly; 'when will you tell me?'

After a few moments, during which time it was clear, from the fixed calculating look that came over her face, that she had suddenly thought of some way out of the embarrassing situation in which she found herself –

'To-morrow,' she said, getting out of the cab, 'I will come and see you at your house.'

'At what time?'

'Between two and half-past four,' she answered quickly. 'Wait for me; I shall come.'

'Shall I help you? Take care or you will fall,' said Lord Wedmore, preparing to get out of the cab.

'No, no, I shan't. Don't get out, I beg of you,' she replied, holding on to the railings, and climbing up the snow-covered steps with difficulty. Kissing him a good-bye, she let herself in with her latch-key, the door closed, and Lord Wedmore, with a sigh, told the nearly half-frozen coachman to drive to Maddox-street, Regent-street.

Chapter III

When Miss St Vincent got up to her room she stirred the fire, which had been carefully slacked by Mrs Clark herself, who always verified with her own eyes that nothing was wanting in her daughter's room before she went to bed. The actress warmed her cold hands, and set her alarum for nine. 'Only four hours' sleep,' she thought, looking wistfully at her bed. 'Shall I ever be able to get up? I never was so tired in my life.' But Miss St Vincent was a woman of purpose, and when the clock sent forth its rattling sound, she jumped out of bed without a moment's reflection, and was down to breakfast at a quarter to ten. Mrs Clark was astonished at seeing her daughter so early, and she said, as she poured out the tea,

'My dear, you will kill yourself! You were not in till five. I heard you open the door.'

'I am very sorry, Mamma, if I disturbed you; but there was a supper last night at the theatre, and I had to stay. Give me a cup of tea; I am dying with thirst.'

'But why did you get up so early? The rehearsal is not until half-past twelve.'

'I have business in the City, and I am going to take Emma with me.'

'And what, in the name of goodness, are you going to do in the City?'

'O, nothing of consequence,' said Miss St Vincent, drinking greedily her cup of tea, but refusing all her mother's pressing offers of eggs, kidneys, steaks, chops, etc. She could scarcely touch a bit of dry toast. 'Ring the bell, Mother, and tell Emma to get ready and fetch me a cab.'

Mrs Clark had been left a widow some seventeen or eighteen years ago, with two hundred a year, and her daughter to bring up. This sum proved more than sufficient until Miss Nellie announced her intention of going on the stage, and demanded lessons of the most expensive masters. Mrs Clark knew not how to say 'No' to her daughter, and she spent uncomplainingly the economies of past years, without ever dreaming of the magnificent return they would

76

bring in. Miss St Vincent worked hard. It was her nature to
see life seriously; and in a couple of years she got a small part,
and before she was two-and-twenty, stepped into leading
business at fifteen pounds a week.

Mrs Clark rang the bell; having implicit confidence in her
daughter's good sense, she let her conduct her affairs in her
own way. Emma soon put on her bonnet and shawl, and, in
a few minutes, maid and mistress were whirling away in the
direction of Holborn. Emma occupied a special position in
the little household. She had been with them for many years,
and, from a girl of all work, had, with the family fortunes,
been promoted to the position of lady's-maid. She was
invaluable to Miss St Vincent, for she knew she could trust
her implicitly.

The cab drove over Westminster Bridge, through
Trafalgar-square, then on through Oxford-street, and at last
stopped before a door in Gray's Inn.

Looking at the names painted on the wall, Miss St Vincent
said, 'Yes, here it is, on the third floor – Messrs Fox &
Seaward, Solicitors.'

For two long hours the cab waited, until the driver began
to feel afraid that his customers had given him the slip. At last
the two women came down, and Miss St Vincent told him to
drive in all haste to the Pall Mall Theatre. The rehearsal had
begun. It was for an under-study, and was a very wearisome
affair for everybody except the one who lived in the hopes
that coughs and colds would overtake the principal whose
part he had to learn. Everybody idled in the wings, and
inwardly cursed the unfortunate under-study.

Miss St Vincent was so absentminded that she could not
give the proper cues; she looked at her watch every few
minutes, and at last told her manager that she could wait no
longer, that he must do without her.

She was evidently absorbed by some project which she
was dying to put into execution, and could think of nothing
else.

She ran up the steps to the stage-door, and called a
hansom. Emma asked her if she was to accompany her.

'Of course, yes. Yes, jump in,' was the reply.

'Where to?' asked the cabby.

'27 Norfolk-street, Park-lane.'

During the short drive from Pall Mall to Mayfair, Miss St Vincent did not speak. From her thoughtful appearance, Emma supposed that she was studying some new part. When they arrived, Miss St Vincent told her maid to wait, that she might want her.

The smart footman who opened the door, in answer to the query if Mrs Wallington White was at home, said, 'Mrs White does not receive before three.'

This was what Miss St Vincent wanted to know. So, handing him her card, she said, 'Give my card to Mrs White, and say that I should like to see her on important business.'

The footman showed Miss St Vincent into the dining-room, and sent the card up by the maid.

Mrs Wallington White was still *en peignoir*. Her maid laid down the tress of hair she was going to twirl and pin up, and went to answer the knock. Mrs White sat before the large toilette-table, which resembled a ball-dress in its thousand folds of muslin garnished with coquettishly-tied blue and pink bows. The carpet was soft and delicious underfoot; there was nothing else in the dressing-room but the bath, from which came an odour of *eau de Lubin*, a very voluptuous sofa, and looking-glasses of all kinds.

When Annette handed her mistress Miss St Vincent's card, Mrs White looked at it in amazement, and said, 'Miss St Vincent! Impossible! There must be some mistake!'

'No, Ma'am, I don't think there is. The lady asked for Mrs Wallington White, and said she wanted to see you on business.'

'See me on business! What can this mean? What is the lady like?'

'I don't know, Ma'am; I have not seen her.'

'Very well, go down-stairs and ask her if it is not a mistake.'

'Will you see her, Ma'am, if she does want to see you?' asked Annette, as she went towards the door.

'Yes; show her into the drawing-room. I will do up my hair myself,' said Mrs White, holding a tress of hair with one hand, and searching for a hairpin with the other amid the ivory nick-nacks that covered the dressing-table.

'Can it be?' she thought, as she looked in the glass sideways, and pinned up her hair, and then put a little colour on her lips and some powder on her cheeks. Rouge she did not yet use in the morning. Mrs White was very handsome in her grey-silk dressing-gown. She scented her hands with some white rose, and impatiently awaited for her maid to return. In her heart she hoped that it was not a mistake, for she had nothing to look forward to the whole afternoon except a series of visits each more monotonous than the other; whereas to meet in her own drawing-room her rival, a burlesque actress, was full of novelty, and promised excitement. In a few minutes Annette came back.

'Is she young or old?' asked Mrs White, before her maid had time to speak.

'She is quite young, Ma'am – not much over twenty, I should think.'

'What does she look like? Is she a lady?'

'Well, Ma'am, since you ask, I think she looks like an actress.'

'You have shown her into the drawing-room?'

'Yes, Ma'am.'

'How extraordinary!' thought Mrs White, as she walked from her dressing-room through her bedroom. She hesitated a moment before the drawing-room door, thinking how she would receive her unexpected visitor. Making up her mind that studied coldness would probably embarrass her more than anything else, she opened the door, and stood face to face with Miss St Vincent, who was examining the daintily-furnished room. Mrs White bowed to the actress, asked her to sit down, covered herself with a cloak of stiff frigidity, and sat down on the little black sofa out of the light.

'You are, doubtless, surprised at my visit?' said Miss St Vincent, by way of opening the conversation.

It never was Mrs White's plan to answer questions directly, so she remarked that she had heard that Miss St Vincent had come to see her on important business.

'I have, otherwise my visit would have been an imperti-

nence,' returned Miss St Vincent, determined to show her
rival that such sneers as that would not discountenance her.
'My business,' she continued, 'is so important that I will ask
you half an hour of your time.'

Mrs White raised her eyebrows to express her astonishment at the request; but she bowed an assent. Yet this did not
seem to satisfy Miss St Vincent; for, after a moment of
embarrassment, she said:

'The matter on which I wish to speak to you is strictly
private, and it would be awkward if we were interrupted
before we had come to a conclusion. May I ask you to give
word that you are not to be disturbed during the time you
kindly consented to give me?'

Mrs White's curiosity was roused to the highest pitch; she
almost trembled with excitement; and she so far forgot
herself that she neglected to make any affected movement or
remark, and answered simply,

'Certainly; nothing is so annoying as to be disturbed when
one is talking of anything serious.' She rang the bell, and,
when the servant appeared, said, 'John, mind I am not at
home for anyone – mind, for anyone – until Miss St Vincent
leaves.'

When the door closed Mrs White bent forward to listen,
and waited for her visitor to begin. Miss St Vincent was
embarrassed. She knew very well what she had come to say,
but a preparatory sentence was difficult. However, there was
no time for choosing, so she said, 'I hope you liked the piece
last night. You were sitting in a box with Lord Wedmore.'

Mrs White smiled, and she thought, 'Ah, of course; it is of
him you have come to speak with me! I might have guessed
it, but what you have to say I can't for the life of me
imagine.'

'After the piece was over there was a supper given by the
management.'

Mrs White smiled, and thought, 'What can the suppers of
ballet-girls and actors have to do with me? However, I can't
do better than to remain silent; it will embarrass her more
than any questions.'

The smile was not lost on Miss St Vincent, who thought,

'Ah, you want to play the indifferent; we will see if we cannot wake you up.' 'After the supper,' she continued, 'which lasted till five in the morning, Lord Wedmore drove me home.'

'Ah,' thought Mrs White, 'so you have come to tell me that, in order to try to have some revenge on me for the bouquet last night! I am surprised, for you do not look the little fool that you are.'

'During the drive from Pall Mall to Kennington Oval he asked me to be his wife.'

The news was so unexpected that for once in her life Mrs White lost her self-possession; she nervously grasped the arm of the sofa and turned pale. Out of sheer malice Miss St Vincent waited to watch the effect, and she thought, 'Ha, ha, my fine lady, you would throw bouquets and sneer! I wonder who has the best of the game now?'

Quivering with rage, Mrs White rose to her feet. There was no doubt the actress had trumped her trick, but, mastering her emotion with a supreme effort, Mrs White said,

'And how do you suppose that your intrigue with Lord Wedmore in a cab can interest me?'

'I know that you want to marry him.'

'Your impertinence obliges me,' said Mrs White, rising and moving towards the bell, 'to – '

'But it depends upon you, Mrs White, whether I shall accept him or not,' replied Miss St Vincent.

Mrs White's arm dropped by her side, and she looked wonderingly at the young girl before her. Not for years had Mrs White made any outward manifestation of her real sentiments; she had looked glad and sorry when it was necessary, as the well-educated butler will hand round sherry and claret, and uncork the champagne in the right places; she had carefully laced her mind as she had her body, and the breaking of the strings of the former changed her as much morally as an accident to the latter would physically. Her naturalism seemed the height of mannerism; and none of those who knew her well would have believed that it was not a highly worked-up part she was playing, when she said boldly,

'It depends upon me if you will refuse or accept him? What do you mean?'

'Merely this,' the actress answered, laying her hand on Mrs White's arm: 'Lord Wedmore has twenty thousand a year; he is the richest prize in the market; his fortune is still intact – racing-men have failed, card-men have failed, women, up to now, have failed – it is left for you and me to fight out the battle!'

'You say he proposed to you last night: why don't you accept him and win the battle?'

'I will tell you. I am only two-and-twenty. At my age, as you know, women have their illusions. Life is before them, and it is a hard thing to give up all they have dreamed of. I speak practically enough, but I am not made of stone.'

'You love someone else,' said Mrs White, looking sneeringly at the young girl, in whom she now began to recognize her equal, if not her superior.

'Quite so. I like someone far better: one with whom I hope to succeed; one in the same position as myself; one with whom I might be happy.'

'And you would like to effect a compromise?' said Mrs White, who now began to guess vaguely at what the actress was trying to arrive at.

'I would,' returned Miss St Vincent; 'and will, if you will assist me.'

'But how?' asked Mrs White, feeling a little ashamed at seeing herself fairly beaten by one at least ten years her junior in experience.

'As I have told you, it lies between us two. He proposed to me last night; so far the advantage is on my side. But pray do not let any foolish jealousy prevent us from arranging matters to suit our mutual interests,' said Miss St Vincent; for she noticed an expression of annoyance pass over Mrs White's face, from which the mask being torn was now as transparent as a child's. 'I only go over the facts,' continued the actress, 'so as more perfectly to explain the case. But although Lord Wedmore asked me to be Lady Wedmore last night, and is now waiting to hear my decision, I know, as a fact, that he is nevertheless very much under your influence;

and I assure you that there is no doubt that if I withdraw you will succeed in marrying him.'

'And you will withdraw upon what conditions?' asked Mrs White somewhat feebly, for she found herself completely beaten by the little actress, whom she had determined to snub as she thought only she knew how to snub.

'On this: that you will sign a bond, promising to hand me over twenty thousand pounds, say three months after you are married.'

'You are certainly a wonderful girl,' said Mrs White, forgetting her animosity in her admiration for the tact displayed by Miss St Vincent; 'and when shall I sign this bond?'

'Why not now?' answered Miss St Vincent. 'Can you depend on your maid?'

'I can. But we shall want two witnesses.'

'Mine is waiting in a cab at your door. Will you kindly ring, and tell your servant to ask her to come up-stairs?'

As in a dream, Mrs White touched the bell, and gave John the requisite order.

'But the bond?'

'I have it in my pocket,' returned Miss St Vincent, smiling. 'Did you think that I was so foolish as to come unprepared? These affairs are done at once, or not at all.'

'True; but one question more. How in the world am I to get twenty thousand from Lord Wedmore without an explanation?'

'I do not think you will find any difficulty. Something whispered, between two kisses, about debts. I think I could easily get forty.'

'And what are you going to do with the money when you get it, if it is not an impertinent question?'

'Marry the man I love, drop *opéra bouffe*, and play high comedy in a first-class London house,' was the prompt reply.

'Well,' said Mrs White, taking the actress's hands, 'you are a fine, brave, clever girl. I hated you yesterday, and I like you to-day; and if you play always as well as you have done to-day, you will conquer London as you have conquered me.'

The deed was signed and witnessed between mistresses and maids, and in that womanly conclave Lord Wedmore's future life was decided.

The rest of the story is easy to guess; it ran on the lines Miss St Vincent predicted.

Lord Wedmore came round to the theatre, and after having bitterly reproached Miss St Vincent for having kept him waiting all day, heard his fate with sorrow; but he consoled himself with the fact that the dreaded interview, in which he would have to tell his mother that he had married an actress, would not, after all, have to take place.

Two days after, he received a note from Mrs White, asking him to dinner; and a month later they were married. Lady Wedmore chose well her moment between the two kisses, and her husband gave her the twenty thousand without a murmur. It was at once handed over to Miss St Vincent, who married Mr Shirley, renounced *opéra bouffe*, and played the love scenes in high-class comedy for many years to fashionable London audiences. Lady Wedmore made her husband very happy, probably far happier than Miss St Vincent would have ever done. He did not appear to wish for anything; his cup of happiness seemed to be quite full. But no, there was one little worry – one little desire – that always remained ungratified. But ah, in what life is there not some one little ungratified desire? Lord Wedmore's was not a large one; it was merely a vexatious bit of curiosity; but at times it proved troublesome enough. It was this – that although he tried hard to fathom the mystery, he never found out how Mrs Shirley and Lady Wedmore became, and always remained, such dear and constant friends.

A Russian Husband

Madame Ardloff was a slender, blond-haired little Parisian, who once used to dance lightly in the ball-rooms of the Champs Elysées, and chatter gaily of the things of the boulevard; but she now no longer felt interest in anything. Paris was to her a vanished dream, Siberia an unchanging reality. Nine months out of every year of blank, mournful snows, white silence, extending from horizon to horizon; then a brief respite, when the fields caught flower, and colour rushed through every valley and over every hill, and innumerable insects buzzed in the green underwoods of the steppes: such is Siberia.

She had married Count Ardloff, the Governor of Tobolsk, to save her father from ruin; but this child of the asphalt thrived but poorly in the desert, and her husband saw, and with fierce anger, that she could not endure her present life; saw there was nothing in common between them but the chain of marriage by which he held her. 'Scratch the Russian and you will find the Tartar.' Nothing can be more true. Primitive races can but ape the sentiments and refinements of feeling which make bearable our lives, and Count Ardloff could not pass the gulf – the impassable gulf – the gulf made by centuries of civilization which lay between him and his wife. He could hold her to his bosom, but even then she seemed nearer to Vanca, a young Polish officer, than to him. He could tell her to do this and that, and force her to obey him, and that was all. They were separate beings that marriage could not join together. They had to walk through life with linked arms, but their spirits remained unblended.

But when Vanca was present all was different. Then Madame Ardloff's eyes would fill with regretful tenderness, that was akin to happiness, and it was clear that the mystic union of souls which we all seek and yearn for as the highest of contentments was at once accomplished. A haze of dream and poetry arose around them, enveloped them, and the beautiful Pagan fancy of a cloud lover seemed to be realized. And yet no friendship could be purer; they were merely exiles who talked of their distant homes, their lost friends, and their abandoned dreams.

But such sentiments are little understood in Siberia, and ugly little rumours concerning Madame Ardloff and young Vanca had begun to be whispered – the end of a phrase hissed slightly and a concluding smile was turned somewhat serpent-wise – that was all. The Siberian hostesses, in their mock French fashions, could not, although trembling for their own safety, resist a little innuendo. Count Ardloff watched and waited as suspicious and fierce as a wild cat. He was a man about fifty, his beard was strong and grey, and he stook like a Hercules. Five years passed in Paris had lent him a disguise which, in his ordinary moods, perfectly enabled him to hide his Tartar character, and when she married him the bright French girl little thought that a few glasses of champagne or a slight contradiction would transform the elegant gentleman on whose arm she leaned into a savage Cossack. Now a cold gleam shot from his cold eyes as they fell upon his wife, who, lying back in her easy chair, sat languidly listening to Vanca's clear voice. It mattered not to the Count what they were saying. He did not stay to consider whether they were planning an elopement or talking of the emperor. He merely hated her for appearing to be so intimate with one of his officers. She belonged to him – she was his property – a property he had acquired because it had pleased him to do so. What, then, did she mean by thinking of or concerning herself about anyone else? These were the Count's thoughts as he took the cards that had been handed to him and shuffled them through his strong fingers. Some eight or a dozen gentlemen in the uniform of the Russian army were grouped around him, a lady in a clear dress sat at the piano, and couples were seated under the greenery of the exotic plants with which the recesses of the room were filled. There was not much conversation, the interest of the company being apparently centred in the Count. Every now and then someone passed across the room, and, after watching the cards for a few minutes, would cringingly murmur some words of adulation. Every phrase began or ended with 'Your Excellency', and was rounded off with a bow or a modulation of voice betokening the social inferiority of the speaker.

But the Count paid very little attention to his flatterers. When he had finished dealing, as he threw down the last card, he glanced again in the direction where his wife was sitting. As she listened to the young Pole her attitude grew more and more abandoned. He spoke to her of his past life, of a lost love; and the accents of regret with which he narrated his experiences reminded her of how she had suffered similar deceptions; of how her aspirations and glad visions had, like his, perished. They spoke of those sad eternal truths which each pair of lovers fancy they alone have discovered, but which have moved all past generations, as they will, doubtless, move all those which are coming to birth, till man's soul has ceased to be what it is.

So absorbed were Vanca and Madame Ardloff in the contemplation of the past that they were only so much conscious of each other as each helped the other to realize their separate lives. The outer world had faded from them, and in the insinuating emotion which drew them together she leaned her hands over the edge of the chair, and, following the movement instinctively, he took up the glove she had laid down and played with it. At this sign of intimacy the Count's eyes flashed vindictively, and he called to his wife impatiently:

'Marie, will you order me some champagne?'

Without answering, she told Vanca to ring the bell. Instantly rising, he complied with her request, and then, forgetting he had not returned the Countess her glove, stopped to speak to a friend. His friend tried to warn him with a look, but, before a word could be said, the Pole had walked across the room, still twirling the fatal glove in his fingers. He did this with a certain nonchalance that would have angered a better-tempered man than Count Ardloff. A grim scowl passed across his face, and he whispered something to an aide-de-camp who stood near him. The officer left the room. It was a terrible moment, full of consternation and silence; but before the unfortunate Pole had time to realize his danger two Cossack soldiers entered the apartment. The company gave way before them, withdrawing into groups and lines. Vanca had his back turned to them, and he still wrapped the fatal glove round and round his fingers. He stood as if lost in reverie scanning a marble bust of the Countess. At last the stillness of the room awoke him, and, as the Cossacks were about to seize him, he turned. His frightened eyes met theirs; he started back precipitately, but, with a quiet movement, the soldiers laid hands upon him. In a low voice the aide-de-camp said:

'You are arrested by order of His Excellency.'

Dazed and bewildered, Vanca pushed the soldiers from him, and, stretching forth his hands, appealed to the Count.

'How is this, Your Excellency?' he cried, wildly. 'I am guilty of nothing. There must be some mistake.'

Count Ardloff stood broad, tall, and vindictive, with the light of the lustre shining full on his high, bald forehead; an iron-grey beard concealed the lower part of his square face. Vanca cried one more word of appeal, and then stopped puzzled. Madame Ardloff arose, pale and trembling, but her husband motioned her away. The guests remained in rows, still as the figures of a frieze, and, at a sign from the officer, with a movement of shoulders the Cossacks forced the Pole from the room. The scene was very short.

Immediately after the Count spoke of indifferent things, and glasses of champagne were handed round. Madame Ardloff stared vacantly, unable to collect her thoughts; till, suddenly seeing the glove which Vanca had dropped, the reason of his arrest dawned upon her, and she trembled violently, and so agitated was she that she could scarcely say good-bye to her guests. The Count, however, dismissed them rapidly, speaking all the while of the approaching summer, the number of convicts that had escaped from the mines, and the Emperor.

When husband and wife were alone, the Count picked up the glove and handed it to the Countess, with an ironical smile, and, without alluding to what had happened, said that it was very late, and advised her to retire to her room. She obeyed without answering. She knew something horrible was going to happen, and, stupefied with fear, she mounted the staircase. He stayed behind to give an order, and, mastering her fears, she listened.

He was talking in the hall below to his aide-de-camp, and she heard him say that Vanca must be at once degraded to the ranks; and her heart beat with joy at the prospect of his escaping with so slight a punishment. Her emotion was so great that she did not catch the next phrase, and when she heard again her husband was telling his officer to have all in readiness, that he would be at the barracks at nine next morning. There was something strange in this, and Madame Ardloff went trembling to her room. The shadows seemed livid, and the lamp burnt luridly; and, oppressed with the horrors of the evening, she sat in the silence, afraid to go to bed. Through the frozen window-panes she could see glistening the wide snows of the Siberian winter. Wearily she asked herself why she had been condemned to live in these impassable deserts. The howl of a dog broke the stillness of the night, and it sounded in her excited mind like the last dying cry of some poor one unjustly done to death. What was to become of Vanca? Why could she not save him? Save him! Was there need for that? Starting to her feet, she strove by an effort of will to rid herself of her terrors. Then, shaken with forebodings and regrets, she undressed; but a hundred fancies assailed her imagination, and gave life to the figures on the tapestry, to the shadows on the floor, and, white, like a ghost in a tomb, she lay restless in her large bed.

Sleep fled from her, until at last she fell into a deep, dreamless torpor, from which, towards morning, she was awakened by a heavy tramping of feet in the corridor. A moment after her husband entered. He was attired in the Russian military cloak, and his hand was on his sword.

'Get up,' he said, impatiently. 'I want you to come out with me. I have ordered the sledge.'

'Why should I get up at this hour? It is only just daylight, and I am very tired.'

'I am sorry you are tired, but I want you to come to the barracks.'

Remembering the order she had heard given over-night, Madame Ardloff turned pale at the mention of the word barracks. Twenty times she felt an infinite desire rising up within her to throw herself into his arms and beg him to be merciful; but he looked so implacable that her courage died away, and she feared that any interest she might show for Vanca would only still further prejudice his chance of escape.

Wrapping her long blue-fox-fur mantle around her, she told him she was ready. He looked to see if she had forgotten anything. Her handkerchief lay on the table, and as he handed it to her his attention was attracted by a *flaçon de sel volatile*.

'We may want this,' he said, and slipped it into her pocket.

'What do you mean?' she said, turning suddenly. 'Are you going to murder me?'

'To murder you!' he replied, laughing cynically. 'What nonsense!' And, half pushing her before him, they descended the staircase. She tried several times to resist him, but he got her into the sledge.

'To the barracks,' he cried to the coachman, as he sat down beside his wife and arranged the rugs. During the drive neither spoke a word. His face was clouded in a sort of sullen moodiness, and, terrified, she looked down the dazzling perspectives of the outlying streets. The barracks were siutated at the further end of the eastern suburb. The horses cantered briskly, and soon a large building appeared. It stood alone; all round stretched the white expanse of the steppes, and the sledge passed a large gateway into the barrack square, which had been cleared of snow.

The officer who was waiting to receive them helped the Count to descend. Madame Ardloff was told to remain seated. Immediately after a trumpeter blew a call, and a file of men marched to within a few yards of the sledge, and formed themselves into a double line. 'Front rank, quick march,' cried the officer. When they had gone eight paces, he cried, 'Halt!' and then gave the order, 'Right about turn.'

Vanca was then led forth. He walked between two soldiers. He was naked to the waist, and behind him came the executioner. He carried in his hand the barbarous knout, and over his shoulder dangled its seven cruel lashes.

In Russia, an officer in the Army cannot be flogged, but he can be degraded to the ranks in twenty-four hours. This is what happened in the present case. Vanca was now a common soldier, and was waiting to receive the fifty lashes to which he had been sentenced. And the fashion of administering the knout in Russia is as follows. The condemned man is forced to walk between two files of soldiers; before him, holding a sword pointed at his breast, is an officer, who steps backward with a slow and precise pace, which regulates the strokes that the executioner administers. So terrible are the loaded thongs, armed at the end with sharp iron hooks, that at the tenth or eleventh blow, even the most robust fall fainting to the ground. Sometimes, however, the executioner is merciful, and kills the victim outright, but more often he is forbidden to strike with his full force, and the mangled being is carried to a hospital and cured of his wounds; and this is repeated until he has received his full punishment.

Such is Russia; and for Vanca all was now prepared – the soldiers stood in line, the executioner twirled his lashes, only an officer to lead the way remained to be appointed. It was for Count Ardloff to do this. He looked around; there were half-a-dozen men standing round him, any one of which he might have chosen. As he glanced from one to the other, his attention was attracted by a man who, from a doorway at the other end of the barrack yard, was eagerly watching. 'Who is that man?' asked the Count. The man was called to. It was Vanca's brother. 'What are you waiting about that doorway for?' 'I was waiting to see if your Excellency would pardon my poor brother,' replied the Pole.

'Pardon your poor brother,' said the Count Ardloff with a bitter sneer. 'I will show you how I pardon. Draw your sword and lead the way, and take care you don't walk too fast.'

After one deep, questioning look, which told him that the Russian meant to be obeyed, he broke his sword across his knee, and said, as he hurled the pieces scornfully aside: –

'Do with me as you will, but I will not serve a country inhabited by barbarians, and governed by fiends.'

Even the Cossacks exchanged glances of sympathy, and had they known the whole truth, it was not improbable that they might have revolted. Suffice to say, that for a moment Madame Ardloff feared for her husband's safety. But his fierce brutality dominated his soldiers, and the elder Vanca was manacled, and a guard placed over him.

The scene that then presented itself was this: – Two files of soldiers, Count Ardloff commanding, stern and implacable; one brother half-naked and bleeding, the other in irons; a pale woman with agony written on her face, wrapped up in furs, and a pair of horses, munching in their nose-bags, unconscious of ought else.

The officer took another step back, the seven thongs whistled in the air, and again tore into red furrows the lacerated flesh. As Vanca staggered forward, his face convulsed with pain, his eyes were fixed on Madame Ardloff, and they asked, with a terrible eloquence – 'Oh, why did you thus betray me?' Her hands were clasped, and in her emotion, having lost all power of utterance, she strove to send forth her soul to tell him of how innocent she was. Then another blow fell, and the blood squirted horrible, and the flesh hung ragged. It was sickening, and from sheer horror and nausea Madame Ardloff fainted. But it was her husband's intention that she should witness, to the end, the revenge he had so carefully prepared, and diving his hand into the pocket of her mantle, he produced the bottle of *sel volatile*. With this he quickly restored her to consciousness, and then she heard him saying: 'Awake, awake, for I wish you to see how I punish those who insult me.'

Vanca had now received nine strokes. He was but a raw mass of quivering flesh. Helpless and faintly, like one in a nightmare, Madame Ardloff strove to speak, until at last the words long denied her rose to her lips, but they came too late, and, mad with pain, the tortured man, with a whirling, staggering motion, precipitated himself on to the drawn sword, and fell to the ground a corpse.

This was unexpected. There were hurried words, and a trampling of feet, and a deep silence, but Madame Ardloff remembered little. The imprecations the elder brother hurled after her as she was driven away sounded dim and indistinct in her ear during the long days of delirium which followed this double tragedy, for on arriving home she saw her husband make out the order for Vanca's transportation to the mercury mines. She pleaded and prayed wildly, but the Count only smiled grimly in reply to her hysterical supplications. It seemed to her that the heavens should fall to crush, that the earth should open to receive so inhuman a monster. She raised her hands, she screamed madly, her thoughts danced before her, faded, and then there was a blank, and during several weeks, for her, Time stood still.

Slowly her senses returned to her, slowly through a dim mist, through a heavy torpor, that held her powerless and inert; they returned to her, and with them came the ghastly remembrance of a terrible crime. The subject was never alluded to. The affair was hushed up; but time could neither blot nor tear this cruel page out of Madame Ardloff's life. Her only consolation was the certitude that no pain was in store for her greater than she experienced, when, years after, in a ball-room at St Petersburg, Count Vanca, an old man with long white hair, and a life's sorrow on his face, said to her, 'Madame, I hope your children are very well.'

Dried Fruit

The patient tranquillity of West Street, Thurlow Square, was rarely disturbed by hansom cabs, and the only sounds the ear took note of were the cries of the butcher-boys, the jangling of a belated barrel organ, and the measured tramp of the policeman. At seven o'clock in the morning, as if acting on one inspiration, the Venetian blinds were raised: all revealed meagre strips of red or green curtains, and in each drawing-room window there were a couple of thin chairs, with antimacassars hung over the backs. Immediately after, servant girls appeared and began scrubbing the steps. Their dirty print dresses and frayed boots were an epitome of English middle-class poverty; and as they knelt with their heels in the air they were proclamations of lodgings to let.

About the fashionable end of the street, – the corner that commanded a view of the square, several familes knew each other and were on visiting terms. At undetermined periods Mrs Wilson was in the habit of calling, and stopping to tea with, Mrs Smith; the hospitality was of course invariably returned, and sometimes both went to partake of that meal at Mrs Lewis's. Landlady jealousy made them often refer to Mr Barnwell, who was admitted to be the oldest inhabitant in the street, although the date of his arrival was somewhat problematic. Mrs Lewis had inherited him twenty years ago on the death of her mother, Mrs Stokes, with the house and furniture; and as Mrs Wilson said to Mrs Smith, whenever they caught sight of the old gentleman at his window: 'He 'as been as good as a little fortune to them at twenty-nine. Thirty shillings a week for the dining-room set, not counting what she makes out of his breakfasts, dinners, and teas, and that is, I'll be bound, a pretty penny.'

Thus it was that Mrs Lewis's good luck made her a source of envy to the rest of the street. She seemed to her neighbours to be exempt from all the ordinary cares of West Street. Trade might be depressed, bad seasons might follow each other in intolerable succession, but they did not bring cards to her window: her house remained ever free of the ominous signs; and had it not been, indeed, for her difficulties with a naval officer who occupied her top front bedroom, and broke her candlesticks when he tumbled up stairs as late even as two o'clock in the morning, she would have been able to pose as quite a superior being at Mrs Smith's tea parties. And it was to this mote in her neighbour's happiness that Mrs Wilson invariably alluded when she as much as suspected her friend of thinking of the two young ladies who had lately been staying at 43. Mrs Wilson could attack Mrs Lewis in no other way. The tipsy naval officer was the one assailable point in Mrs Lewis's household. Nothing could be said against Mrs Lavington, the middle-aged lady who for the last ten years had occupied the drawing-room set; and as for Mr Barnwell, was he not a kind of advertisement of respectability for the entire street? His respectability was, as it were, a common wealth; his person and his purse belonged to 29, but his influence extended nearly as far as the Fulham Road. No doubt the worthy gentleman was quite unconscious of his benedictine reputation; but certain it is that his leaving West Street would have been regarded as a calamity almost equal to the establishment of shops, and as a forewarning of a not far distant depreciation of house property. Nor can it be asserted that this confidence in Mr Barnwell was altogether misplaced. Seeing him at his window in the morning vaguely gazing at the trees of the square, it was impossible to mistake him for anything but what is known as a 'safe man' – the most imaginative would not suspect either face or window of any desire for change. The grey dust of time, that makes all things look alike, had effected a curious likeness between them: the fat, round, colourless cheeks, slightly pitted with the small-pox, the double chin, the forehead covered with a brown wig, harmonized perfectly with the lustreless window. Both looked as if they were meditating a problem that neither would be able to solve.

And yet Mr Barnwell could not be called a melancholy man. During twenty years of intimacy he had never failed to exchange a pleasant word with Mrs Lewis when he met her in the passage, or when she came into his study to settle his weekly account. This little business transaction was performed every Wednesday evening, punctually at five o'clock, and it varied in amount but a few shillings from year's end to year's end.

Nevertheless, his life had not always been so methodically arranged. Mrs Lewis remembered when he used to have friends who came to dine with him, and when he used to go to the theatre; but for the last ten years he had gradually given up going out in the evening. At first he used to complain of Mrs Lewis's cooking. He gave a good deal of trouble by asking for special dishes; but habit grew upon him, and he had learned to content himself with what she could do. Now he never grumbled at even the plainest of food, whereas she, ashamed of her lack of culinary imagination, and presuming on their long acquaintanceship, would sometimes inveigh against his extreme seclusion and advise him to go up to town and 'get a change'. Smiling, he would assure her that he was satisfied with her dinners, and he would urge that he must get on with his work: that he had his books to arrange. Nobody knew what his work was, and his books were a perpetual source of terror to the servants. When they were touched, Mr Barnwell complained; when they were left untouched, Missus said the dust was something shocking. Shelves had been put up in every available corner of bedroom and sittingroom; but even then the space did not suffice, heaps and single volumes encumbered table, chiffonier, and mantelboard. There were histories of all countries, of all times reaching to within three hundred years of the present day – then there was a blank unbroken, save by Macaulay's History of England. Above the ponderous tomes dealing with the political constitutions of Egypt, Greece, Rome, Spain, and France, there were volumes on volumes of

travels – travels in South Africa, in Sweden, in North
America. The comment of every parlour-maid on these
books had been: 'I suppose he was brought up when he was
young in those foreign countries, and he likes to read about
them now.'

But, although little was known about him, Mr Barnwell
did not give the impression that he had anything to conceal.
He spoke often and freely about himself, and Mrs Lewis
constantly thought she knew as much about her lodger as she
did of herself. It was only when she was questioned that she
began to suspect that she knew no more than that his father
and mother were dead, that he had lived in London nearly all
his life – facts that, considering he was obviously over sixty
years of age, and had lived in 29, West Street, for more than
half that time, were sufficiently patent to everybody. Therefore, a certain glamour of mystery hung about Mr Barnwell
– hung about this old man, who, with his money safely
invested in the funds, was living his life calmly and soberly to
the end. He breakfasted at nine, wrote or read for three or
four hours, had some lunch, went out for a walk if it were
fine, dined at six, and spent the evening in reading, rejoicing
in that only happiness which does not disappoint us –
habitude.

Like us all, he had had his love affair. When he was one and
twenty an invitation to a fashionable ball had been procured
for him. It was his first introduction to the world. There he
had met Julia Gaythorn, the belle of the season of 1850. She
was surrounded by admirers, and young Barnwell was
surprised when she accepted him for a waltz. Afterwards he
met her at other balls, in the park, and at theatres, and
eventually he was asked to call. He was shy and timid before
this beautiful girl. She treated him good-humouredly, but
without seeming to pay attention to what he said. Nevertheless, before the end of the season, as they were looking over
an album of photographs, he asked her for her portrait. She
gave him one. Then two years passed without him seeing
her, and during this time she became engraven on his heart –
became, as it were, part of himself. He thought of her as a
vision of wonderful sweetness that had floated across his life,

that was now to him irretrievably lost; and when he met her unexpectedly at an archery party in Sussex it was with difficulty that he spoke without betraying his emotion. Never did he think he had seen such exquisite elegance, and as he watched her drawing her bow to shoot at the mark he thought of a statue of Diane la Chasseresse. Towards the end of the day, when the tournament was over, she talked to him almost as an old friend; and, leaving the company, they walked side by side through the evergreens. It was a clear autumn evening, and as they passed round each turning a clapping of wings was heard in the trees, and a flock of rooks flew over the sloping meadows into the gleam of a sunset that faded.

Exactly how it came to pass he could never say; and, afterwards, he could only think of what had happened as of a half-remembered dream. He remembered that the horror of losing her had suddenly overcome him, and that awkwardly and abruptly he had said, 'Miss Gaythorn, I love you; I can't help saying so.' She made no answer; but a swift look of surprise was enough: he saw his mistake and apologized.

Two years after he heard she was engaged; then that she was married. Some men would have sought oblivion in dissipation; he sought it in books. He read deeply and profoundly, the taste grew upon him, and gradually, without any violent transition, he gave up society and devoted himself to study. His disappointment in love had fallen upon him heavily, and, as the years went by, it seemed more and more to have dried up the sap of life within him, and to have made of him a reserved, if not a taciturn, man. Once, more than a quarter of a century ago, he had said to Mrs Stokes that he could never love anyone again, and a former servant maid declared that she had caught him kissing, with tears in his eyes, the photograph of the lady in white that stood in the little gilt frame upon the mantelboard. The tale, after having been the subject of kitchen jokes for years, was now forgotten, and West Street gossiped only of Mrs Lewis's luck with her lodgers. During the last year the chief events that had disturbed its peace were that Mrs Smith had had her drawing-room floor unlet nearly all the summer, that Mrs

Wilson had been cheated out of fifteen pounds by a runaway lodger; but the monotonous murmur of suburban life was not fairly broken until Mrs Lavington electrified Mrs Lewis by saying that she intended giving up her rooms, and was going to live in the South of England. The news was not considered displeasing by the rest of the street, and Mrs Lewis had difficulty in forcing her friends to acquiesce in the explanation that Mrs Lavington was leaving, not because she was dissatisfied with the attendance or the price of gas, but merely because she had come into a little property in the Isle of Wight, and was going to live there.

Then came troubles and trials, and Mrs Lewis at length learned to appreciate the difficulties her neighbours had so long laboured under. Single ladies, with very blond hair, had the impertinence to attempt to bribe her with an extra half sovereign a week. There were also young gentlemen who came and stipulated for latch keys and other liberties still more objectionable. Indeed, there was no lack of offers – offers that both Mrs Smith and Mrs Wilson would have gladly accepted, but which the respectability of twenty-nine could not think of considering. Mrs Lewis had saved money, and was now not going to deny herself the luxury of choosing her customers. Nevertheless, the pride of being the successful landlady of her street burned in her bosom, and she continued to torture all the house agents and clerks within a radius of three miles. Emma and the cook were fairly worn out showing people up and down stairs.

'Who's that, I wonder?' said cook, the third Saturday of the second month after the immemorial departure of Mrs Lavington, as she leaned over the table finishing her dinner with a piece of bread.

'Someone come to look at the drawing-rooms, most like,' Emma replied, without moving from her chair.

'Then why don't you go up and open the door?'

'Where's the use since Missus won't 'ave any of them?' returned Emma; and she went upstairs grumbling something to the effect that she couldn't expect to have all her lodgers made to order like Mr Barnwell.

On opening the street door, the servant girl found herself

99

facing a tall, ladylike woman, too youthfully dressed in a
fashionably-cut, dark-cloth dress.

'Can I see the apartments?' she asked, in a clear, distinct
voice.

Having – to use her own expression – 'taken stock of 'er',
and seen that she was quite respectable, and of the sort they
wanted, Emma replied:

'Certainly, Ma'am. Will you walk upstairs.'

On arriving on the first floor, after much shaking of
woodwork, and rattling of door-handles, it became clear that
the rooms were locked, and, as cook hadn't the key, it was
conjectured that it must be in Missus's pocket. What was to
be done? Would the lady be so kind as to call again? But the
lady declared that to be impossible – at least for some time –
and, in Emma's experience, some time meant going over to
Mrs Wilson's or Mrs Smith's, and taking rooms there. What
was to be done?

Missus was expected home every minute, but it was
difficult to ask the lady to wait; there was no room to show
her into. Emma did not think she could well offer her a seat
in the 'all, so respectable did she look; so after a consultation
with cook, it was decided that, as Mr Barnwell was not
expected home before evening, it could be no harm to make
use of his sitting-room. Emma pulled up the blinds, wheeled
forward an armchair, and after apologizing for not having a
daily paper to offer her, left the lady, who gave her name as
Mrs Woodville, to her reflections.

She was a woman that a close observer would declare to be
on the wrong side of fifty; he would also detect in her face the
indefinable something that so eloquently bespeaks an unrest-
ful life. She was evidently the heroine of a hundred adventures; and there was about her an unmistakeable air of supper
parties, of jewels, of divorce, of Nice. Sitting in Mr Barnwell's armchair she made a strange contrast with her sur-
roundings; an eight-buttoned glove found in a hermit's rocky
cell could not suggest a more incongruous association of
ideas. The May sunlight came floating into the room, the fire
burned low in the grate, and the books in the high cases
seemed to be dreaming of the many long years of quiet that

they had been the givers of. Mrs Woodville, too, was
dreaming of rest, of peace from the world. She was weary of
it, but the tightly-fitting astrakhan-trimmed jacket attested
that it was not yet entirely forgotten. Her figure remained to
her, and she had not learnt to despise its graces, although she
was now determined to devote herself to the education of her
sons. It was to be near them, and that, in their behalf, she
might eke out her jointure, to the last penny the dressmaker
did not demand, that she had come up to London and was
seeking quiet suburban lodgings.

And she thought of her sons until the silence of the place
awoke her from her reveries. Then, raising her head from her
hand, she looked around the room, seeing in its tranquillity
and dust the ideal life which she was now so eagerly sighing
for. The calm and peace of years that the apartment, as it
were, exhaled, interested her; she began to wonder who the
owner was, and to ask herself if he had been happier in his
solitude than she in her dissipation. The idea getting the
better of her she got up, and walking about, sought for traces
that would reveal his individuality to her.

She examined two engravings after portraits painted by Sir
Joshua Reynolds. One represented an admiral in his cocked
hat, the other a bishop in his white lawn sleeves. Neither
however interested her, and her eyes wandered until they
were arrested by two volumes, entitled 'Travels in Sweden
and Norway'. She would have liked to have taken the books
down. They recalled her mind a season she had spent amid
pine forests in the north. A journey through Barbary and
scenes in Spain affected her in the same way and for similar
reasons.

She asked herself, had this man visited all these places, or
had he stayed at home and only read about them? Possibly he
had dreamed his life; she had lived hers! Which was the better
plan? With a sigh she crossed the room to regain her chair;
but, as she did so, her attention was attracted by the
photograph of the lady in the small gilt frame that stood on
the mantelpiece. At first she looked at it languidly, but
suddenly her face opened in an expression of great surprise,
and the portrait slipped out of her hands. She was evidently

reasoning with herself, and, as if ashamed of the emotion she had been betrayed into, she picked up the photograph and examined it a second time and more closely. But there could be no mistaking it. Although much faded, the outlines were still distinct enough. It was a picture of herself taken thirty years ago, when she was young and a beautiful English girl.

If so, where was she? To whom had she given the picture? Out of the past three or four faces instantly detached themselves, but she repulsed them petulantly. It was none of these she wanted. Then, striving to recall her admirers of the time when this *carte de visite* was taken, she looked through the pages of her life. She racked her brain, skipped from reminiscence to reminiscence, missing the right person now as she had done before. She looked back to the officer she had married when she was the belle of the London season, whom, after three years of miserable life, she was obliged to leave. Then came another face! and she remembered a duel, years of pleasure and amusement; debts and much misery; she remembered seasons spent in Paris, Nice, and Vienna; travels undertaken on the plea of acquiring knowledge in different countries. And so ten, fifteen years had passed like irritating dreams, until worn out she had fallen into the arms of an old man whom she had consented to marry for the sake of acquiring a little peace – a little rest. All this she remembered; she had only forgotten the awkwardly worded proposal of marriage made to her by a timid young man on a Sussex lawn. Such was her fate, such was his. The life sorrows of men and women are inherent in themselves, and the fashionable woman is not to blame because she passes a John Barnwell without seeing he is there! Nor is it John Barnwell's fault that he is ever powerless to express, in equivalent words, the lasting and noble affection that he, and he alone, is capable of giving. In the rough the greatest love is worthless, the diamond must be cut, polished, and befittingly set; the simplest woman demands a little charlatanism of the truest man.

And now, the excitement of finding this old photograph, taken thirty years ago, made this withered cosmopolitan beauty almost look young again; it was new to her, to whom all else was old, to find that at least one admirer had remained faithful. For he must be an admirer – she would not admit that he was not – and, as she considered the question, her curiosity went to her head like wine; and with a flush in her thin cheeks she determined she felt she must find out who was the occupant of the rooms. But how? Surely there must be some letters about – an envelope addressed to him! No sooner had her brain conceived the idea, than, without thinking a second time, she commenced searching amid the papers on the table. But there was nothing there except manuscripts bearing philosophical headings. She removed them, at first carefully, but, as her impatience got the better of her, she threw them petulantly on one side, one on the top of the other. Her nerves were working; and in a few moments she was opening drawers and shutting them with a series of bangs; pulling down books, creating, in a word, a frightful disorder. And quite regardless of danger, she proceeded with her reckless search until suddenly startled from her dreams by the grating of the latch-key in the street door. The brief interval passed as the hat-stand gave her time to get back to her chair, and, immediately after, without knocking, an old man entered the room. His short, fat neck was encased in a high collar, and a blue cravat was passed twice round, after the fashion of old time. He was about the medium height – five feet seven or eight – and his movements were slow, like those of studious people. On seeing his visitor, his face betokened so much amazement that she had no difficulty in concluding he was the owner of the apartment. With the calm indifference of the woman of the world, she explained that she had been asked to wait in the study until Mrs Lewis, who was expected back every minute, returned. Mr Barnwell asked her to sit down. A still further expression of distress passed over his face when he noticed the disorder of his table; but attributing it to a mistaken display of zeal in the cause of dusting, he strove to recall the polite phrases with which social chasms are successfully bridged. His very visible anxiety forced the woman of the world to smile, and it suggested to her a way out of her difficulty. In a moment she had decided to face the matter boldly, and looking him

103

straight through with her slate-coloured eyes, she said:

'You will be astonished when I confess that I have been searching amid your papers.'

The effect produced was equal to the intention; the old gentleman looked positively thunderstruck. Had she given him time to recover himself, he might have rushed to the door, thinking he was closeted with a mad woman; but smiling blandly, she continued: –

'I have known Julia Gaythorn all my life. I knew her thirty years ago, when that photograph was taken, when she lived down in Sussex; therefore, you will understand my curiosity to know your name, and even daring to look amid your papers for an envelope, for a card, for something that would reveal it to me.'

Mr Barnwell did not answer her. At the mention of Julia Gaythorn he had turned pale, and staring like a dead man, he sat grasping with both hands the arms of his chair.

Fearing he was going to have a fit, Mrs Woodville rose to her feet; but, with a sign, he motioned her to be seated again. Then he walked up and down the room twice without speaking. She followed him with her eyes, every feminine fibre in her nature strained to the utmost. Why, she asked herself feverishly, was this man so deeply moved at the mere mention of her name. He did not recognize her! Was it credible that he had remained faithful to her memory through all these years. Then real truth and affection did exist in the world! There was much mingled sweetness and bitterness in the doubt that had so suddenly presented itself to her mind. She waited for him to speak, until the silence became intolerable to her.

'Perhaps,' she said, her voice trembling a little, 'I was wrong to speak to you of her, but I have known all her friends; my life was intimately bound up with hers, and, as the existence of that photograph proves that you value her memory, I was curious to learn your name: you will forgive a woman her curiosity.'

'You are right,' he said, speaking as if out of a dream. 'I do cherish her memory; but it is now more than thirty years since I have seen her. My name is John Barnwell. Did you ever hear her speak of me? I suppose not, it is not probable,' he added, as he resumed his walk up and across the room.

Julia Gaythorn – now Mrs Woodville – hesitated. The name did not enable her to see, through the old man, the youth who had loved her; and wishing to learn more concerning him, and the love affair she had forgotten, before admitting her identity, she said:

'Yes, I think I have heard her speak of you.'

Like a wintry gleam of sunlight in an autumn forest, a flush of pleasure for a moment animated his withered cheeks.

'Did you?' he said, stopping in his walk, and looking fixedly at his visitor. 'I knew Julia when that photograph was taken. I used to see her at Molesworth Manor; I met her there once at an archery meeting. Do you know the place?'

Then she recalled everything. She remembered the young man who had taken her by surprise, by suddenly telling her that he loved her. She saw the shrubberies, and heard the cawing of the rooks in the tall and spreading evergreens.

'I would not have . . . but since you have spoken of Julia Gaythorn – you may – I shall be glad if you will tell me something about her. Mine is no idle curiosity, and although not given to speaking of my sentiments, I may tell you that she was the only woman I ever loved: but she did not love me. It may have been my fault, or perhaps she may have been to blame. To some men such slights make no difference; I do not mean to reproach her, I am merely telling you a fact when I say that her refusal to marry me spoilt my whole life. I never got over it.'

Mrs Woodville bent her head. The truth came upon her now, as it comes upon us all sooner or later, that we, to put it colloquially, have muddled away our lives. What had she striven for? What had she achieved? Nothing! Where were the lovers who had sworn to love her for ever? As well might she ask where were last year's roses. What had the vows she had made, the vows she had listened to, brought her? Nothing. All had forgotten her but this poor old man; and in a poignant moment of retrospect she felt her life would have been a satisfaction, a joy to have looked back upon, had she chosen the quiet felicities of home, the certain friendship of such a man as now stood before her, rather than the nervous delights of fashionable life, the excitements of admiration. It seemed to her that she had never lived at all. But thank heaven this old man – this terrible evidence of her folly – did not recognize her. Thank heaven, she was spared at least that.

Getting up to go, she strove to think of what she would say to him.

'There is little to tell,' she said, speaking rapidly as she moved towards the door, 'about Julia. She left her husband, and was divorced; she married again, and is now a widow; her life was neither successful nor happy.'

Mrs Woodville tried to draw down her veil as she spoke, but the sunlight came streaming through the dusty window, defining every line of her features. She felt Mr Barnwell's eyes were upon her; nervously she tried to pass him; but, laying his hand on her arm, he stayed her firmly, yet gently –

'I think I can recognize now her whom I have been speaking to. Julia! Yes, you are Julia Gaythorn.'

'Yes; I was once Julia Gaythorn; now an old woman fills the place of the lighthearted girl you loved. But we must not speak of the past; I did not know you loved me better than the rest. If we had met again: but now we are too old.'

'I never loved but you, and I have remained faithful to the memory; but, as you say, our time is past.'

'Yes, yes,' she answered, 'our time is past' – words to pause on. 'But we shall be friends I hope; we shall be sincere, loyal friends.'

He held out his hand to her, and, to conceal his emotion, turned his face aside. We may spread our joys over a series of years, or they may be concentrated within the limit of a moment, and John Barnwell's life was lived, and lived completely, in a single touching of hands.

The soft May sunlight came streaming into the room, the embers died out in the grate. The silence was deep and intense; it was not broken until Emma's dirty face was suddenly thrust in at the door; and, in a hard, jarring voice, she announced that Missus had come in, and the lady could come up stairs and see the rooms if she liked. The 'if she liked' was an addition suggested by the sight of Mr Barnwell,

106

whom she had supposed to be still out walking. Seeing what was going to happen he cut short the apologies 'for having come in without knocking', which it was clear that Emma was desirous of giving expression to. He explained curtly, so that Mrs Lewis, who was probably outside, might hear, that 'the lady' was a very old friend of his, and that no excuses were necessary for having asked her to wait in his room. For this display of tact Mrs Woodville thanked him with a look, and thus encouraged, he resolved to decide the situation by introducing her himself to Mrs Lewis.

'This lady,' he said, 'is a very old friend of mine. We had not seen each other for many years, but accident, you see, has brought us again together. I do not think you will find a more satisfactory occupant for your rooms; and you,' he added, turning to Mrs Woodville, 'I do not think will have any fault to find with Mrs Lewis; and I can speak authoritatively on the subject, having lived twenty years in her house.'

After so distinguished an introduction, Mrs Lewis could but say that she would feel highly honoured, and looking from Mrs Woodville to Mr Barnwell, as if trying to read the secret on their faces, she showed them over the drawing-rooms. They were pronounced to be perfectly satisfactory, and were engaged for the season. But this assumption of indifference was only maintained by a supreme effort of will: and it was a relief to the old couple, after promising that the morrow should again bring them together, to wish each other good-bye. To escape from Mrs Lewis, whom he knew would follow him into his study and question him, Mr Barnwell went out for a long walk, and did not return home until late.

Such irregularities did not pass unnoticed in West Street; very significant indeed were such proceedings considered to be; and that evening, at a tea-party given for the occasion in Mrs Lewis's parlour, all the side issues and attendant circumstances of this adventure were thoroughly sifted and discussed. The most different opinions were advanced. Mrs Wilson invidiously hinted that they ought to have been married long ago, until Mrs Lewis, indignant at hearing the morality of her lodgers called into question, alluded to keeping up the respectability of the street, and the letting of rooms to young ladies wearing straw-coloured hair. The quarrel was beginning to wax warm, but Mrs Smith smoothed the troubled waters by suggesting that they were married, and that after years of separation had again agreed to live together. For a moment the ingenuity of this idea almost obtained its acceptance, but Mrs Lewis, being romantically inclined, insisted that the banns would soon be published, and that there would be a wedding breakfast at her house. She, however, seemed disposed to modify her view of the case when Mrs Wilson maliciously insinuated that 'if so, the 'appy pair would go off on a 'oneymoon.'

But the days came and went without Mr Barnwell and Mrs Woodville announcing their intentions of entering the holy bonds, and after having gossiped longer than it had done before on any one subject, West Street relapsed into its normal state of indifference, absorbed by its own little affairs and troubles. Sometimes when Mrs Smith and Mrs Wilson went out shopping in the morning, they would stop to look into the square, and, watching the old couple, would again discuss the possibility of a marriage, and enviously expatiate on Mrs Lewis's luck with her lodgers.

But the old people never married; they knew they felt their time for love was over, and, contented with friendship, they were seen constantly sitting together in the shade out of the warm August sun. Nor did they often speak of what might have been; they rarely alluded to the past. They were glad to dream, letting life glide gently away to the end, amused the while with the thousand and one little incidents of suburban existence. For the interests of life, Mrs Woodville had still to look to her sons and Mr Barnwell to his books; and the only change the neighbours could make note of was, that a few autumn flowers, taken from the balcony overhead, now bloomed cheerfully in the philosopher's window.

Two Men

A Railway Story

The stoker, James Hall, gave the brake a last twist, and the engine stopped. John Nixon, the driver, took up an oil-can, and made his way along the boiler. Hall watched him hungrily, counting his movements as he passed underneath, in front of the wheels, to oil an axle. Hall trembled, he struggled with himself, but temptation stole through his veins, and, like gravitation, the regulator drew his hand to it. Now, he knew that, with a touch, he could crush his rival for ever out of all interference in his aims and desires. The thought was imperious, but the hand slipped slowly from the steel bar; he could will the deed, but he was powerless to execute it. He saw the crowd rushing to seize him; he heard the judge condemn him to be hanged by the neck till he was dead; he saw the hangman coming to meet him at the end of the long passage, with the fatal straps. Then he recalled the many opportunities that had presented themselves during the day, all of which, yielding to an uncontrollable weakness, he had let pass. He remembered how, descending the incline, at the rate of fifty miles an hour, to the lonely, marshy land, Nixon was standing with his back towards him, and one determined push would have precipitated him from the engine. He remembered how, in the tunnel, red in the glare of the furnace, Nixon had looked over the side: in that moment he might have sown the seeds of a new life. Now, from reveries of what might have been, Hall was roughly awakened by the voice of his mate, crying –

'Now then, leave off dreaming, mate; look to your fire.'
For Nixon had returned from beneath the engine, and with

the oil-can in his hand he said, 'What are you dreaming after? Wake up, wake up; I wouldn't mind betting sixpence you have forgotten to take your brake off. I believe you're in love,' he added, with a coarse laugh.

'Am I? And what's that to you if I am? You can't say as much, leastways regarding your own wife.'

The train was backed out of the station, the pointsman let the carriages into a siding, and the engine was sent into the engine-house. The day's work was over, and driver and stoker made their way to the station, where they would see in their room, marked on a card, the hour they would be expected to commence work to-morrow. 'Two o'clock, London Bridge, Tunbridge Wells, and Dover train. We shall not be finished before one o'clock to-morrow. I do like getting done early, and having the evening to myself.'

'Are you going down to the Stag and Hounds this evening?'

'I don't think so, my wife is too ill; I don't think I can leave her.'

The stoker fell into the trap; his face grew glad; his fair, innocent, rosy face – an oval face, with a weak chin covered with a fair, thin beard; a slight moustache shadowed, but did not hide, the red lips. His eyes were light blue, the glance was winning; he was not more than five feet seven in height, but was stoutly built. The driver offered a marked contrast. A dark, handsome man, about five feet nine; a square and almost intellectual face. The black eyes were piercing and bold, the black hair curled over the broad forehead, a scanty, but well-shaped beard set off the lower part of the face, which was prominent and massive; and it was not difficult to see that there was cruelty and much pure and defiant animalism in this man's nature. Now he watched, and with a good deal of amusement, the artless expression of satisfaction into which Hall had been so easily betrayed.

'Yes,' he said, after a pause, 'My wife is very ill indeed – I doubt that she will pull through the winter.' Hall fell into the second trap as easily as the first. A grey cloud passed over his face, and, unable to contain himself any longer, Nixon roared with laughter.

' 'Pon my word, mate,' he said, holding his sides, 'you are as good as a play; my word, mate, you'll be the death of me one of these days if you make me laugh like this.'

'What do you mean? Don't make a damned fool of yourself, Nixon.'

'You would like to stand by a regulator and arrange my wife's health just to suit your own convenience – shut off steam just when a danger signal is up, put the brake on, and now when the line's clear, set her going again. You would like her to be ill, so that I might not be able to get down to the Stag and Hounds; but you would not have her die. Oh, dear no, that wouldn't do at all, for then I should be free to go in and marry the widow.'

'I wasn't thinking of the widow.'

'Weren't you, indeed? Well then, you were thinking of the back parlour, so nice and cosy. How pleasant it would be to sit there, lord and master; no more shovelling of coals on the engine fire; slippers warmed, glass of hot toddy on the table, pipe in its place, only to say, "Lucy dear, will you be good enough to hand me down my pipe?" Very pretty business is the Stag and Hounds. I would not mind betting a sovereign it doesn't bring in less than two hundred a year to Mrs Heath.'

Hall writhed under Nixon's words, like a dog under the lash.

'I tell you, I wasn't thinking of Mrs Heath,' he said; 'but if you ask me, I tell you straight that if I had a wife, and a poor sick wife, I would stay at home and mind her, and not go after another woman, and spend the money that should go to support a family in a public-house.'

'And who told you what I spent at the Stag and Hounds? Come, now, I'll take you a bet that I haven't spent a half, nor yet a quarter, of what you have within the last fortnight, and Mrs Heath shall decide the bet.' Hall understood. Nixon did not pay for his drink. 'But never mind, mate,' continued the driver, 'I'll take your advice, and stay at home this evening and look after my wife.'

The men parted. 'I wonder if he believes me,' thought Nixon, as he hurried home. 'I shall see by his face when he comes into the bar. I wish I could get there before him. The

111

missus will kick up a row, but I shan't stand much of her jaw to-night – I am in no humour for it.' Nixon lived about half-a-mile from the station, in one of a long line of cottages that stretched into the country. The moon was shining with dazzling brightness on the snow, and the stars glittered in the blue heavens. Lights in the windows twinkled, but Nixon's cottage was in darkness. 'I wonder where the missus is?' he asked himself. A neighbour told him that she had gone to meet him at the station.

'Here is the key, Mr Nixon. Your children are sitting with me by my fire.'

He took the key, and thanked the woman. He begged her to allow his children to remain where they were till their mother came back. He had an appointment to keep, and was only running in to change his coat.

'Tell her,' he added, 'that I shall be back in an hour's time.' 'Nothing could happen more fortunately,' he thought, as he washed himself free of the daily dirt and grime. 'I shall be in for a scolding match. She will guess where I am, but I don't think she will come after me; she got enough of that the last time.' Then he slipped on his Sunday coat, and in a moment was hurrying along the frozen roads.

The Stag and Hounds was situated at the end of a small street leading from the station. It looked like a small villa residence that had been transformed into a hostelry. Red-lettered boards hung in the large windows, on either side of the swinging door, announcing that the best Old Tom was sold on the premises, and that sausages and potatoes were always kept in readiness. The bar-room occupied all, save a small triangular space in one corner; the floor was strewn with sawdust, and there were a few high stools. Behind the zinc counter there were shelves reaching to the ceiling. These were lined with bottles of whisky, brandy, and gin, decanters of port and sherry, white, green, and pink glasses of all shapes and sizes. At the back there was a door curtained with a piece of red silk; and when it was open or ajar you could see a bright fire, a small leather sofa, and a couple of comfortable arm-chairs. The table generally showed that a meal of some sort or kind was in progress.

Two Men, A Railway Story

There was no one in the bar when Nixon entered; but at the sound of footsteps, the door of the little back parlour opened, and Mrs Heath appeared. Her face lighted up with that look of tender, charmed voluptuousness which is instinctive in women at the sight of a man they love. Looking round to make sure no one was nigh, they leaned over the bar and kissed each other fervently.

'What will you take, dear? How cold you are. Shall I mix you a glass of hot brandy and water?'

'No, I'll take whisky. You'd be cold if you had been on an engine since seven o'clock in the morning. I am pretty nigh frozen. How snug you are in there by the fire. You don't know what we poor devils suffer.'

'My poor dear,' murmured Mrs Heath, throwing a bit of lemon-peel into a glass; she added two lumps of sugar, a large measure of spirit, and then filled the glass up with hot water from an urn which steamed at the far end of the bar. Nixon stirred his liquor and told stories of Hall, with an intention of making him ridiculous; but the widow evidently saw nothing absurd in the fact that a man should be madly in love with her, and the stories fell somewhat flat.

Now the bar began to fill. Children of thirteen and fourteen came in with jugs and cans, and demanded pints and quarts of porter, beer, and half-and-half; a vagrant, who had probably just earned a few pence for fetching a gentleman a cab, shivered in his thin jacket, and demanded something 'ot – 'Two-pennoth of gin 'ot, marm, please'; a couple of women in battered bonnets and worn shawls whispered together; a long soldier twirled his moustache and looked at Mrs Heath, who had been obliged to ring for the barman to assist her, so numerous were her customers. Outside, three children were heard, singing 'Fairy Voices', and they rasped out the tune agonizingly on two fiddles and a violoncello. The voices sounded deathlike and hollow in the frosty air.

Hall started on seeing Nixon in the bar; his face clouded and he withdrew to the opposite corner.

'You did not expect to see me here, mate, did you?'

'Well, you said you were going to stop at home and look after your sick wife.'

Both men spoke loudly, and there was an intonation of anger in their voices. Mrs Heath, fearing a dispute, went over to Hall, and, smiling pleasantly, asked him what he'd take. A little mollified, he gave his order, and she remained speaking with him a few minutes. But when she went back to Nixon, Hall said, as if resolved to come to conclusions with his mate, 'I met your wife as I was coming along here, Nixon. She asked me if you had told me where you were going to spend the evening. I said you had, that you had said that your wife was ill, and that you were going to stay at home and nurse her. She said she knew better than that, and that if it cost her her life she'd show you up. It won't be long before she is here.'

'What the devil has my wife got to do with you?'

'Nothing; I only tell you what she said. You had better look out for squalls; she said she'd show you up.'

'Show me up! I'd like to see her. If she dares to come down here, messing about after me, I'll show her what's what. I am not going to let any woman bully me. Things have come to a pretty pass if a man cannot go and have a drink at his pub without his wife coming down after him. Let her try it. But I don't think she will try it on.'

'You had better not hit her too hard. It is a bad habit to get into. One doesn't mean it, of course; but the time comes when one hits a bit too hard, and then . . . (Here Hall made a movement with his hand, indicative of a man being hanged.)

Nixon flushed crimson: but at that moment two persons entered the bar. The first was a small child of four, with a fiddle in her hand; the second was a tall, gaunt woman, holding an infant to her breast. One side of her face was disfigured by great yellow and dark blue stains, the result of a recent blow. The little musician held out a cap for halfpence, but at the violent words withdrew frightened into a corner.

'I don't care if you kill me for it, but I will let the people know how you treat me. Look 'ere; that's what he gave me last week, because I asked him not to go to the public-house. It is that woman there . . . Oh, you beast you; why do you not get a man for yourself, and not go after other women's husbands? I'll do for you one of these days.'

114

'Now then, no more of this, out you go; I'll show you I am not to be made a fool of,' said Nixon, seizing his wife by the arm and forcing her towards the door.

'No, I won't go home without you . . . Yes; strike me, you brute, I dare you do it; strike me and I'll have you locked up for it. Yes; kill the innocent child.'

Threatening to do for her, Nixon forced her out of the bar room; but she returned frequently, and, thrusting her head inside, she screamed violent abuse. Finally she retired; her voice grew fainter and fainter in the distance. The singing was heard again. The little one collected a few halfpence, and Hall took advantage of the occasion to whisper to Mrs Heath that if he had a wife he would not treat her like that. Mrs Heath laughed, and replied that all men were very nice till you married them. Nixon drank and smoked in stolid silence; his glass had been replenished several times. But Mrs Heath, who was by no means pleased at the accusations that had been brought against her, whispered something to him; he nodded in assent, and jamming his hat over his eyes, he left the house without bidding anyone good-night.

At these signs of intimacy Hall was influenced to frenzy, and he resolved – he swore to himself – that he would throw Nixon from the engine.

At two o'clock next day they met at the station. They took a train to Hastings. They worked up to the Rotherhithe Road, and on to Cannon Street. It was then five o'clock in the afternoon; they were bound for Tonbridge. The signal whistle sounded, Nixon answered. With the left hand he touched the regulator, with the right he turned the wheel that brought a pressure of steam on the engine. A slight whiff, and the engine started. Snort followed snort. Nixon's hand never left the regulator, and he used it like a rein. Through the round window he viewed the labyrinth of iron ways; he took note of the signs in the constellations of green, white, and red lights. The pointsmen could be seen in their glass boxes, tugging at the handles. The engine capered in and out of this and that set of rails, and the inanimate life of the creature of steam and steel throbbed and palpitated. She was speeding now along a high embankment, but had not yet

115

fairly settled into her stride. The brown wilderness of brick that is London spread far away; through it the great brown and ornamental Thames rolled by: barges moored in mid-stream, barges a-row, with long yards pointing, drawn up on its slimy banks. The roofs were white with new fallen snow, there was snow in heaps in the gardens of the outlying streets; and soon appeared the fields, ghostly under the rays of the moon. Then a road and bridge silhouetted across the sky; the whistle shrieked, and the train rushed into the red glare of the tunnel. Overhead, the steam floated away in great white clouds, and the men in darkness and flame were as demons. It was here that Hall had thought of precipitating Nixon from the engine. Now a unique occasion presented itself. The driver, one hand laid on the rail, was looking over the side, a determined push would send him crashing against the brickwork. 'But if they picked him up alive, I might hang for it; better settle him with a shovel first.' The stoker turned to draw the shovel out of the coals, but at that moment Nixon turned round; Hall hesitated, and the train passed out of the tunnel. Then the end of a long silence, speaking like a man who has had something on his mind for a long time, Nixon said –

'Now, look here, mate, I would sooner play fair with you. I have chaffed you a bit, it is true, but there is not much good going on with that game. I'd sooner play fair. Take my advice and turn it up.'

'What up? What's it to do with you?'

'Not much; I don't mind, but I'd sooner play fair and tell you straight that you haven't a ghost of a chance. If my wife died to-morrow I would marry the widow.'

'I know nothing about that, but your wife won't die to-morrow, leastways, if you don't murder her.'

'Now then, keep a civil tongue in your head. It doesn't make much difference whether my wife dies or not. I am the widow's man. There you have it straight.'

'It is a lie!' cried Hall, overcome with passion. He lifted his shovel suddenly and brought it down on Nixon's head. The driver fell back stunned; Hall prepared to repeat the blow, but before he could do so, Nixon had closed in on him. They seized each other by their throats. At the moment of the attack, Nixon was about to turn the wheel and relieve the engine of some pressure of steam, for they were now descending the incline towards the low-lying marshy lands. The engine snorted violently, and in ribbons of iron the miles fled beneath the wheels of the locomotive. The blow of the shovel had rendered Hall more than a match for his mate, and he dragged him forward; but seeing the fate that awaited him, Nixon made a tremendous effort and almost succeeded in throwing the stoker into the tender. But his grasp relaxed at the last, and Hall forced him at a run right back against the furnace, and held him there. The regulator was shifted right over, and now, like a race horse that has got the bit fairly between his teeth, the engine rushed along the plain, entering a deep cutting at fearful speed. The train rocked as if it were going every minute to pitch over, and more than one terrified passenger leaned out of the window, unable to imagine what was happening. The danger signal was up, but without a warning shriek the train plunged into the tunnel. Now the little blond face of the stoker was demonized with rage and red light. He had thrown Nixon over, and was striving to batter his head against the iron work; and, far away, the end of the tunnel gleamed like a white star, growing gradually larger, until at last the line of the ground, a tree, the high structure of the signal-box were visible. Then suddenly the train rushed past, out of the red flame into the blue light. The signalman threw up his arms in terror. A few hundred yards further on, at Tonbridge Station, the line was blocked by a cattle train. The station-master turned aside, the night echoed with the roar of sixty miles an hour, the yellow eyes gleamed fiercely, the pebbles flew from the route with a sharp sound, and, ah! with a horrid crash, the cattle trucks telescoped one into the other – disappeared as if in an earthquake. For a moment it seemed as if Nixon's engine would pass triumphantly after all; but suddenly it turned over, and, helplessly as a giant done to death, fumed out its life of steam and fire. Then, hurling their great weight of iron and wood forward, the carriages came on, mounting one on top of the other like acrobats in a show, and they fell back, pounding out the lives of those within. The flying wood-work shrieked, and the whirling wheels broke with a grating sound. Between two awful moments of destruction, a tiny cry was heard. Was it that of child, or man, or beast, or woman? Impossible to say. It sank out of memory in the ocean-like cry of suffering which engulfed the night. O, beautiful and bountiful night, thou hidest so much misery beneath thy dark and shadowy garments. Why dost thou not close our ears to the heart-rending cries: to this groaning of married men and women, to this bleating of mangled sheep, to this moaning of lacerated bullocks, to this most awful tumult of pain and desperate agonies?

The line is like a wreck-strewn shore. Men with lanterns and implements arrive. But with the removal of each fresh heap of débris a new object of horror is discovered. This broken carriage is full of crushed human beings; this truck over-thrown, with wounded and dead animals; under the carcass of a sheep you find the body of a man, a bullock stands breathing in your face, and you see that one leg has been torn from its body; every runnel flows with blood, and the smell is the soft sickly smell of the shambles. A child is heard crying, and many lanterns flash through this long scene of bewildering confusion.

The townspeople came running and breathless. They asked the cause of the accident. None knew, but a stout woman about five-and-thirty. Her face was round and pale, her chin was slightly doubled, and she wore her hair parted, and it was looped up over her ears. It was very cold. She shivered, for she had left her bar without waiting to snatch up a shawl. She asked if the engine driver and stoker were killed, and she murmured nervously – 'Oh, I knew those men would get a fighting over me.'

A Strange Death

Chapter I

Charmandean was a lonely and ugly village in an ugly and lonely district.

The station – a dot on a high embankment which crossed the valley – attracted village idlers; and every evening half-a-dozen assembled on the little platform to view the arrival and departure of the five o'clock train. It often brought an acquaintance, and, like the weather, afforded an unfailing subject for gossip. But on May 6th, 1889, not a door was opened, not a parcel was thrown out. Presently the guard was called, and a curiously well-dressed man got out of a first-class carriage. He wore a long, green overcoat with a fur collar and fur cuffs. Stopping occasionally, leaning on his cane, he looked round with a weary and apprehensive air; and, avoiding the eyes of the station-master, who advanced to take his ticket, he said he would send for his portmanteau, and passed hurriedly out of the station. The station-master, his admirers, and his underlings turned the portmanteau over. It had evidently travelled far, and was covered with labels of strange, foreign towns, the very names of which were unknown to those present.

'Bucharest! I wonder where that is?' said one. 'Algiers; I think I have heard the name, but for the moment I can't remember.'

'I wonder,' said a young idler who always spent the afternoon on the platform, 'what a man who goes to such places wants down in this little out-of-the-way hole?'

'And isn't he a toff!' said a second idler. 'Plenty of money, I should say.'

119

'Never judge a book by the cover,' said the station-master, a bluff, middle-aged man, with a pair of small, ferret-like eyes set in a rugged, red face. He stood with his legs apart, his heavily-booted feet set firmly on the ground, his hands thrust deeply in his pockets. 'He may have money or he may not, but he do look unhealthy.'

'Fellows that travel in foreign parts always has livers.'

'Yes, I dare say,' replied the station-master, testily; 'but that is not telling us what he has come to Charmandean for. Didn't you notice the way he spoke to us, and didn't you notice how fast he walked? A man doesn't walk fast in a place he has never been in before.'

All were moved by the profoundness of the observation. The porter and both idlers looked admiringly at the station-master. Why hadn't they been struck by the suspicious circumstance of the stranger's gait?

'Then you think he has been here before?'

'I don't know; but when I see tramps walking about I say look out for your knives and forks, and when I see lords walking about villages I say look out for your politics or your daughters, or both.'

'Come, I don't think it is as bad as that,' said the first idler, whose name was Jim Smith.

'I don't say it is, and I don't say it isn't, but he is not here for nothing, you may depend on that. Look at his portmanteau, it has been all over the world. He is not a farmer, nor a commercial traveller, nor a visitor to the Hall.'

'How do you know?' said one, Bob Birket by name, and the inseparable friend of Jim Smith.

The conversation was here interrupted by the reappearance of the stranger.

'I find,' he said, 'that there is no hotel in Charmandean; can you tell me where I can put up?'

'There is the "Bell and Horns", Sir; they can let you have a bed there if it is only for the night.'

'I shall stay here more than one night.'

Jim Smith and Bob Birket exchanged looks, and they noted the evident and increasing embarrassment of the stranger.

His glance wandered nervously from one to the other. 'I should not care to lodge at the "Bell and Horns". Does anyone let lodgings in Charmandean? But, I beg your pardon, I am intruding – wasting your time.'

The station-master looked at the stranger sharply, and was evidently unfavourably impressed, for he made no reply.

'Farmer Jones, he that lives at the Grange,' said Jim Smith, 'might let you have a room, Sir. I know he did once before let a room to a gentleman who came here to fish. Perhaps you have come to fish, Sir. If so, the Grange would suit you very well – you'd be near the river.'

'It is very kind of you. Thank you; no, I have not come to fish, but if you will kindly direct me to the Grange I shall feel obliged.'

'You can't miss it, Sir; it lies at the end of the village, facing the river.'

When the stranger had left the office, the station-master turned sharply on Jim Smith.

'You are always in a great hurry, Smith. Couldn't you see that I had my reasons for not sending him to Farmer Jones? I suppose you thought I had forgotten him.'

'Why didn't you wish to send him there?'

'Your memory doesn't seem to grow longer. I say just now that people didn't walk fast in a place they've never been in before. He starts off as if he knew all about the place as well as we; then he comes back and asks if there is an hotel in the village. I say these are suspicious circumstances, and you have no right to send a man you know nothing about to lodge at Farmer Jones's. Jones is an old man; he lives alone with his old wife in the Grange. I say it isn't fair. Jones is a very unsuspecting man; he should have been warned; once he was warned – well, then it was his look-out, but he ought to have been warned.'

There was much that was resolute and emphatic in the station-master. Impossible not to see that his beadlike eyes, his well-planted feet, his hands thrust deep in his pockets, bespoke resoluteness and decision of character.

'You can think what you like. I say his manners and his appearance are both suspicious.'

'So do we. There is no doubt that he is a suspicious sort of character. But I don't think he is a lord, for did you notice that although he wore a beautiful coat his trousers were shabby? I'll find out what his little game is. I shouldn't be surprised to find there was a woman in it.'

'Or a burglary,' said the station-master.

'He doesn't look much like a burglar. Anyhow, there isn't much to rob at Farmer Jones's.'

'I don't know so much about that.'

'He can't be after a girl and a robbery both at the same time.'

'I don't know too much about that. You haven't been reading the papers lately.'

The conversation was presently interrupted by the arrival of a messenger from the farm house. He asked to have the gentleman's portmanteau pointed out to him; he tossed it on his shoulder, and the idlers dispersed, for it was close on tea time. Several trains passed, rushed through the little station, through the fir trees, into the echoing hills. Along the river lands a gentle mist was drawn, and there the kine and a single figure of a girl were full of such dim beauty as Corot would have loved. The Grange stood a hundred yards beyond the last cottage, and its grey stones were defined upon the picturesque colour of the hillside.

This gaunt Grange had been built from the walls of a castle of eldertime, and now outside the cottage doorways the housewives sat sewing as their husbands smoked; and all were talking of the stranger. Having heard of his probable character, the young girls lowered their eyes, and those who had money at home felt for their keys. And it was noticed that he passed nearly half-an-hour in the church and churchyard.

'Well, what do you think of him now?' said the station-master, planting himself in the middle of the roadway in front of Bob Birket.

'He's a puzzler, and no mistake. There's no doubt that he's after something, but it is hard to say what.'

'What does Farmer Jones say about it?'

'He agrees with you. He wished he had never had anything to do with him.'

'No, he didn't say that,' pleaded Jim Smith. 'Here is Mr Jones.'

'Well, Jones, what do you think of your new lodger?'

'I don't much like the looks of him, and my old missus is dead frightened. I don't know that she'll sleep in the house to-night.'

'You needn't have him there if you don't like.'

'Well, you see, I have taken his money. I have no good reason for turning of him out.'

The villagers drew aside, the stranger passed, and his scared face was noticed.

The harvest moon rose, a thin yellow crescent; and when the village crouched in the darkness the Grange loomed like a phantom above the hill-side, the light continuing to burn in the casement.

'I wonder what he be doing – it is nearly midnight.'

'Oh, Thomas, hasn't he gone to bed yet? I told you not to let him have the room.'

'Yes, after I had let it to him; you thought he was a very nice man at first.'

'Oh, Thomas, how can you say so? You know how opposed I am to sleeping in a house with strangers. I shall not go to bed – no, no, you'll not alter me – I shall not go to bed to-night. You must tell him to-morrow that we are not accustomed to such hours; it will be a good reason for getting rid of him. What can he be doing?'

'Reading or writing, perhaps.'

'Supposing we were to steal upstairs and listen.'

'He'd hear you – the stairs creak dreadful. I might go though, I know where to tread. But supposing he were to spring out on me?'

'Thomas, don't go! I forbid you. We'll sit up, and to-morrow he must go.'

Without answering her, Farmer Jones drew off his boots and went slowly up, treading where the stairs made least noise; the others listened with bated breath, expecting every moment to hear the stranger spring out and seize Jones by the throat.

'What's he doing?' they asked eagerly, as the old man crept down the stair by the wall, his face blanched.

'I dun no – I dun no. He is walking up and down the room; suddenly he stopped, and then I come away. I be afraid he was going to go for me.'

Next day, the village was full of rumours concerning the stranger, and the events of the past evening were debated. Bob Birket and Jim Smith lingered about the Grange, in hopes of seeing him. He ventured forth once, but seeing he was watched, he retreated to his room; and, upon inquiry, they learned that he was writing letters. The station-master held out vague hopes that he might send these letters to the post, if so they would find out at least who were his correspondents.

It was a quarter to eight before he left the Grange and walked with his letters to the post. All eyes were on those letters, and a little boy came running with the news that he had posted five. To the surprise of everyone, instead of entering the Grange, he went towards the river.

'Come on, Bob, let's follow him! I'll bet he's going to meet a pal over yonder.'

It was now dusk, and by keeping along the lower ground they thought they would be able to escape observation. The difficulty was how to cross the little bridge without being seen.

'Now then, take care, Bob, keep close along the wall or else you'll crab it.'

From the bridge they saw the stranger pass round the edge of the shaw into the darkness that the branches threw over the long wet grass. Determined to surpise him at his work, evil or good, whatever it might be, they ran forward, and, entering the shaw from opposite sides, they groped for him in the wet stillness.

'That's where I last saw him,' said Bob.

'Well, I never!' said Jim. 'He must be hiding; he cannot have got round by the river; he wouldn't have had time.' At that moment they noticed a tanny smell, and a fox escaped from the rushes. This incident deepened the mystery; for how was it, as Bob Birket put it, that he, the stranger, had not started the fox? A little troubled by the turn their adventure had taken, the young men returned to the Grange,

A Strange Death

and to a group of five they told their story. As a possible
explanation, Bob Birket suggested that he had committed
suicide; but the sound of footsteps put an end to this theory,
and the five villagers listened in awe to the stranger quietly
ascending the stairs.

'Well, he do come and go mysterious like. I didn't hear the
front door open, did you? Did you, Jim?'

'No, I didn't, but I'd give sixpence to know what his little
game is. What can have brought him to Charmandean?'
said Bob.

The farmer and those whom the untoward lodger had
made his guests, continued to debate in the parlour, interrupted at intervals by Mrs Jones regarding the various means
they might adopt to rid themselves of their lodger. From
time to time, one of the party would step outdoors, and
return with the news that his light was still burning. At last
the clock struck midnight.

'Thomas, I can stand it no longer, you must go and speak
to him. He had better leave the house. Go and see what he is
doing. We may be burnt in our beds. Go and see what he is
doing.'

Jones prepared to draw off his boots.

'No, no, go upstairs boldly. You are in your own house,
man. Our friends here will see that no harm comes to you.'

'I bain't afraid,' muttered Jones.

'He'll try to kill my poor husband! Oh, Mr Smith, do go
upstairs and see that all is right.'

'I don't know what he is about,' said Jones, over the
banisters, 'but he is moving the furniture.'

'He'll set fire to the house – that's what he's about!'

'I think that one of you had better come up.'

Jim Smith volunteered.

'Listen! He is pulling the table across the room. He is
blocking up the door. Are you sure? Certain! I can't open it.'

The farmer called Bob Birket and the station-master, and
they came clattering up.

'Now, Bob,' said Jim Smith, 'one! two! three!'

But the door was a stout one, and they could not move it
until they got a large beam of wood from the kitchen.

Chapter II

A man of forty-five sat alone in his library; the clocks were striking eleven. He sat alone thinking; he sat alone with his misfortunes. It was one of those hours when all our feebleness, all our failures, and all our vain efforts, terrible as monsters passing through the shadowy depth of some ocean way, come upon us out of the gulf of the past.

Edwin Harrington passed his hand over a thin, bald brow; it was a thin, sad face, whereon was written a tale of disappointment and ill-health. But for many a year success and failure had seemed to him alike, and he had desired only quiet from bodily pain. But maladies had accumulated in him, and his doctor had lately told him he must put by all work; and that with change of scene and air his spirits might revive. Harrington felt the will wanting in him to leave London: for days he had not even quitted his library. But one day London grew more than ever intolerable, and he said:

'Anything for a change, I can bear this no longer;' and he referred again to the newspaper that described Charmandean as one of the most rural spots in England. 'I will go there. I will only take a few things with me. I will stay there a week. The name is strangely pretty. I am a fool, no doubt, to allow the fascination of a name to lead me. But what matter? What does anything matter?'

He had pictured the conventional village basking in sunshine and shade; a village full of gardens where sunflowers flamed, creepers reddened, and where there were gables, and where there was an inn with nut brown beer, and a maid with nut brown eyes. But the railway line afforded only a view of a grey village, a marshy plain, a long hill, and some meadows where cattle grazed by the river. The little bleak station impressed him unpleasantly; and the rubicund station-master with eager black eyes set in a red, rugged face, and a manner of speaking that made, as it were, of each word a hook wherewith he could tear out some secret, jarred the nerves of this morbid man.

Harrington wondered why the station-master had watched him so suspiciously, and the looks of the slovenly idlers had filled him with alarm. He walked rapidly away, but he had not gone far when he stopped, and, looking round, he thought, 'This is absurd. I had better – indeed, I must ask where I can put up.' After a long pause, tremulous with irresolution, he succeeded in quelling his fears, and he braced himself to meet the stare of the idlers and the searching questions and glances of the station-master. As he ascended the steps he heard them talking of him, and was taken with an access of fear.

'Bucharest, Algiers – so they know me – how can this be? I don't remember.'

The morose village in grey stone and the dreary plain where the river gleamed like a knife whetted the edge of his fears, and as he proceeded down the jagged street towards the Grange, he more than once decided to return to town. He was, however, apprehensive the train service did not furnish the possibility, and was taken by the honest face of the farmer.

'There being no proper hotel in the village,' he said, 'I was advised at the station to ask here if you could let me have a room for a week.'

'We did once let a gentleman have a room who came here to fish. I suppose that's what you be after too?'

'No, I have not come here to fish,' Harrington replied, a little nettled at what he deemed unnecessary curiosity. 'Of course if you can't – '

'I didn't say we couldn't,' said the farmer good humouredly; 'on the contrary, I think we can if you don't mind the old place.'

'On the contrary, I am much interested; it seems to me a real old place.'

'They say it was lived in several hundred year ago by mighty rich folk. This way, please, Sir.'

Stopping to admire the great rafters and the hewn corner stones, Harrington followed the farmer up the rambling stair way.

'We don't often use this room; leastways we seldom sleeps

in it; my wife uses it occasionally as a store room; but she'll
see the bed is well aired, trust her for that!'

The tapestries had long since rotted, but the latticed
windows and some heavy oak furniture remained, and
preserved the medieval character of the room. Harrington
declared himself satisfied, and having partaken of supper he
said he would stroll through the village and visit the church.

It was a fine September evening, the last rays glinted on the
red tiles and the old grey stonework. Only a fragment of the
original church remained, and the ruins of the transept and
the nave extended through the grass of the graves. It was a
fine symbol of the spirit of old time; and Harrington had
forgotten all in contemplation of the arches and windows,
and life was beginning to appear to him in a less hideous
light, when turning, he met the prying stare of one of the
men whom he had overhead talking of him at the railway
station. Clearly he was being watched, and now, thoroughly
annoyed, he left the church. He could see as he passed down
the street that the ferret-eyed station-master was talking of
him to Farmer Jones. Everywhere half averted faces and
surreptitious glances.

'What can they be saying about me? I wonder if they know
me. Bucharest, Algiers – I could not quite distinguish what
they said.' And as his thoughts brooded, the mystery grew
stranger and darker; it seemed to him that the farmer and his
wife, who had spoken so pleasingly a couple of hours before,
now eyed him with suspicion. Or was it his nerves – those
cursed nerves! What a source of worry they were to him. To
what mad act might they not prompt him.

He took a book from his portmanteau and tried to read.
His mind was perturbed and his hand trembled. 'I shall not
close my eyes to-night,' he said, and he looked round the
room despairingly. The four massive pieces of oak furniture
it contained were veiled in shadows that the light of his
candle did not penetrate. He sat with the light of the candle
and the moon upon his face. Again he took up his book and
strove to read. Had he been dozing? He started – he listened.
He felt his flesh grow cold. A low stealthy shuffle moved on
the staircase. He grasped the arms of his chair. Was it a

dream? Was he mistaken? Surely not! The river gleamed amid the reeds and silent hills; the lonely plain, where the river gleamed, seemed pregnant with misfortune.

He did not sleep until morning, and then he slept so heavily that he made no inquiries about leaving until the afternoon – too late to catch the last train. The prospect of spending another day at Charmandean was not pleasing, and to avoid its inquisition he remained in his room and wrote letters. His dislike of the place had grown into such a fear that he avoided, as much as possible, looking on the landscape, and the posts of the great bed often startled him. It was with difficulty he summoned courage to take his letters to the post. He had hoped by a detour he might escape the observation, but he was unsuccessful, and had to run the gauntlet of all eyes. The little black eyes watched him out of the red, rugged face – that face was now an obsession, and held him like a nightmare; and he strove to drop his letters into the box so that they might not be counted, but his hand trembled, and he felt that they had been counted.

The evening was beautiful and calm; even the prying villagers could not utterly destroy the sweetness of the twilight; and for a moment he hung between his fears of being followed and his inclination to linger in the fading light. He yielded to his fancy; but he had not gone far before he repented his indiscretion, for as he was about to cross the bridge he perceived two forms crouching in the dusk, and he fled across the meadow, now thick with aftermath; he hid himself in the darkness of the trees, and the dew sank through his shoes. Then hearing the voices of his pursuers nearing him, he crept through the shaws that grew along the hill-side almost to the edge of the stream, and sustained by an obtuse instinct, he ran along the edge, sometimes falling into the water, but saving himself by catching at the grass and reeds. How his heart beat when he gained the bridge and ran along the road leading to the Grange! The stairs creaked beneath his rapid feet, and he closed the door, dreaming madly of escape. The casement was high; but perhaps when all was still he might escape by the window. He looked out, scanning the great walls, and, seeing three men watching in the moonlight, he hastily withdrew, and sat quaking in the dark. Presently his fears seemed exaggerated, and he argued that, perhaps, there was no real cause for alarm; and out of this calm of mind came a sense of his condition. He took off his wet clothes, and lay down in bed. But sleep fled from his eyelids, and the events of the last two days silhouetted across his mind in a long procession, and in the insomnia each insignificant detail became terrible, and all that could be taken in proof of death and doom crowded upon him – monstrous and deformed, scarcely like life. And it was when such fancies were at their highest, when the silence was deepest, that sounds of feet on the staircase crept into his ears. Then the sounds grew distinct. Tramp, tramp came heavy treads, and the staircase groaned. Rigid he sat in the great bed, his thin hands moist with perspiration, clutching the sheets.

'They may have passed my door – no, they have stopped!'

He heard further steps on the rambling staircase, and then, seized by blind terror, he sprang out of bed and pushed the oak table across the doorway. He strove to move the wardrobe, but his poor strength was not sufficient, and he uttered the little cry that animals utter when death is nearing them. Then, in the confusion of death and despair, he dimly distinguished that they were breaking through the door, and that its panels were falling one by one. He clung to the bed; his eyebrows were raised, his mouth was open, his skin was as white as a dead man's, he was an embodiment of the idea of terror, and when Jim Smith pushed down the door, he raised his arms, and, as if falling from a cross, he fell, quite dead.

A Faithful Heart

Part I

It was a lovely morning, and Major Shepherd walked rapidly, his toes turned well out, his shoulders set well back. Behind him floated the summer foliage of Appleton Park – the family seat of the Shepherds – and at the end of the smooth, white road lay the Major's destination – the small town of Branbury.

The Major was the medium height; his features were regular and cleanly cut. He would have been a handsome man if his eyes had not been two dark mud-coloured dots, set close together, wholly lacking in expression. A long brown moustache swept picturesquely over bright, smoothly shaven cheeks, and the ends of this ornament were beginning to whiten. The Major was over forty. He carried under his arm a brown-paper parcel (the Major was rarely seen without a brown-paper parcel), and in it were things he could not possibly do without – his diary and his letter-book. The brown-paper parcel contained likewise a number of other papers; it contained the Major's notes for a book he was writing on the principal county families in Buckinghamshire. The Major had been collecting information for this book for many years, and with it he hoped to make two or three hundred pounds – money which he stood sorely in need of – and to advance his position in the county, a position which, in his opinion, his father had done little to maintain, and which, to his very deep regret, his sisters were now doing their best to compromise. That very morning, while packing up his brown-paper parcel, some quarter of an hour ago, he had had a somewhat angry interview on this subject with his

131

sisters. For he had thought it his duty to reprove them for keeping company with certain small London folk who had chosen to come to live in the neighbourhood. Ethel had said that they were not going to give up their friends because they were not good enough for him, and Maud had added significantly that they were quite sure that their friends were quite as good as *the* friend he was going to see in Branbury. The Major turned on his heel and left the house.

As he walked towards Branbury he asked himself if it were possible that they knew anything about Charlotte Street; and as he approached the town he looked round nervously, fearing lest some friend might pop down upon him, and, after some hestitation, decided to take a long *détour* so as to avoid passing by the house of some people he knew. As he made his way through a bye-street his step quickened, and at the corner of Charlotte Street he looked round to make sure he was not followed. He then drew his keys from his pocket and let himself into a small, mean-looking house.

Major Shepherd might have spared himself the trouble of these precautions; no one was minded to watch him, for everyone knew perfectly well who lived in 27, Charlotte Street. It was common talk that the tall, dark woman who lived in 27 was Mrs Charles Shepherd, and that the little girl who ran by Mrs Shepherd's side on the rare occasions when she was seen in the streets – for it was said that the Major did not wish her to walk much about the town, lest she should attract the attention of the curious, who might be tempted to make inquiries – was the Major's little daughter, and it had been noticed that this little girl went forth now and then, basket on her arm, to do the marketing. It was said that Mrs Shepherd had been a servant in some lodging-house where the Major had been staying; other scandal-mongers declared that they knew for certain that the Major had made his wife's acquaintance in the street. Rumour had never wandered far from the truth. The Major had met his wife one night as he was coming home from his club. They seemed to suit one another; he saw her frequently for several months, and then, fearing to lose her, in a sudden access of jealousy – he had some time before been bitterly jilted – he proposed to marry

132

her. The arrival of his parents, who came up to town beseeching of him to do nothing rash, only served to intensify his determination, and, losing his temper utterly, he told his father and mother that he would never set his foot in Appleton Park in their lifetime if they ever again ventured to pry into his private affairs; and, refusing to give any information regarding his intentions, he asked them to leave his lodgings. What he did after they never knew; years went by, and they sighed and wondered, but the matter was never alluded to in Appleton Park.

But the Major had only £400 a year, and though he lived at Appleton Park, never spending a penny more than was necessary, he could not allow her more than £3 a week. He had so many expenses: his club, his clothes, and all the incidental expenses he was put to in the grand houses where he went to stay. By strict economy, however, Mrs Shepherd managed to make two ends meet. Except when she was too ill and had to call in a charwoman to help her with the heaviest part of the work, she undertook the entire housework herself: when times were hardest, she had even taken in a lodger, not thinking herself above cooking and taking up his dinner. She had noticed that her economies endeared her to the Major, and it was pleasant to please him. Hers was a kind-hearted, simple nature, that misfortune had brought down in the world; but, as is not uncommon with persons of weak character, she possessed a clear, sensible mind which allowed her to see things in their true lights, and without difficulty she recognized the unalterable nature of her case. It mattered little whether the Major acknowledged her or not, his family would never have anything to do with her; the doors of Society were for ever closed against her. So within a year of her marriage with the Major she was convinced that her marriage had better be kept a secret; for, by helping to keep it a secret, she could make substantial amends to the man who had married her; by proclaiming it to the world, she would only alienate his affection. She understood this very well, and in all docility and obedience lent herself to the deception, accepting without complaint a mean and clandestine existence. But she would not allow her little girl to carry up a jug of hot water, and it was only rarely, when prostrate with pain, that she allowed Nellie to take the basket and run round to the butcher's and buy a bit of steak for their dinner. The heiress of Appleton Park must be brought up free from all degrading memory. But for herself she had no care. Appleton Park could never be anything to her, even if she outlived the old people, which was hardly probable. What would she, a poor invalid, do there? She did not wish to compromise her husband's future, and still less the future of her darling daughter. She could only hope that, when dead, her sins would be forgiven her; and that this release might not be long delayed she often prayed. The house was poor, and she was miserable, but any place was good enough to suffer in. So she said when she rose and dragged herself downstairs to do a little cooking; and the same thought came to her when she lay all alone in the little parlour, furnished with what a few pounds could buy – a paraffin-lamp, a round table, a few chairs, an old and ill-padded mahogany arm-chair, in which it was a torture to lie; not an ornament on the chimney-piece, not a flower, not a book to while away the interminable hours. From the barren little passage, covered with a bit of oil-cloth, all and everything in 27 was meagre and unimaginative. The Major had impressed his personality upon the house. Everything looked as if it had been scraped. There was a time when Mrs Shepherd noticed the barrenness of her life; but she had grown accustomed to it, and she waited for the Major in the terrible arm-chair, glad when she heard his step, almost happy when he sat by her and told her what was happening 'at home'.

He took her hand and asked her how she was. 'You are looking very tired, Alice.'

'Yes, I'm a little tired. I have been working all the morning. I made up my room, and then I went out to the butcher's and bought a piece of steak. I have made you such a nice pudding for your lunch; I hope you will like it.'

'There's not much fear about my liking any beefsteak pudding you make, dear; I never knew anyone who could make one like you. But you should not tire yourself – and just as you are beginning to get better.'

Mrs Shepherd smiled and pressed her husband's hand. The conversation fell. At the end of a long silence Mrs Shepherd said: 'What has happened to trouble you, dear? I know something has, I can see it by your face.'

Then the Major told how unpleasantly his sisters had answered him when he had ventured to suggest that they saw far too much of their new neighbours, who were merely common sort of Londoners, and never would be received by the county. 'I'm sure that someone must have told them of my visits here; I'm sure they suspect something . . . Girls are very sharp nowadays.'

'I am sorry, but it is no fault of mine. I rarely leave the house, and I never walk in the principal streets if I can possibly help it.'

'I know, dear, I know that no one can be more careful than you; but as people are beginning to smell a rat notwithstanding all our precautions, I suppose there's nothing for it but to go back to London.'

'Oh, you don't think it will be necessary to go back to London, do you? The place suits the child so well, and it is so nice to see you almost every day; and it is such a comfort when you are not here to know you are only a few miles away; and from the top of the hill the trees of the park are visible, and whenever I feel well enough I walk there and think of the time our Nellie will be the mistress of all those broad acres.'

'It is the fault of the busybodies,' he said; 'I cannot think what pleasure people find in meddling in other people's affairs. I never care what anyone else does. I have quite enough to do thinking of my own.'

Mrs Shepherd did not answer. 'I see,' he said, 'you don't like moving, but if you remain here all the trouble we have taken not to get found out these last ten years will go for nothing. There will be more worry and vexations, and I really don't think I could bear much more; I believe I should go off my head.' The little man spoke in a calm, even voice, and stroked his silky moustache gravely.

'Very well, then, my dear, I'll return to town as soon as you like – as soon as it is convenient. I daresay you are right.'

'I'm sure I am. You have never found me giving you wrong advice yet, have you, dear?'

Then they went down to the kitchen to eat the steak pudding; and when the Major had finished his second helping he lit his pipe, and the conversation turned on how they should get rid of their house, and how much the furniture would fetch. When he had decided to sell the furniture, and had fixed the day of their departure, Mrs Shepherd said –

'There's one thing I have to ask you, dear, and I hope you won't refuse my request. I should like to see Appleton Park before I leave. I should like to go there with Nellie and see the house and the lands that will one day belong to her.'

'I don't know how it is to be managed. If you were to meet my mother and sisters they would be sure to suspect something at once.'

'No one will know who I am. I should like to walk about the grounds for half an hour with the child. If I don't see Appleton now I never shall see it.'

The Major stroked his long, silky moustache with his short, crabbed little hand. He remembered that he had heard the carriage ordered for two o'clock – they were all going to a tennis-party some miles distant. Under the circumstances she might walk about the grounds without being noticed. He did not think any of the gardeners would question her, and, if they did, he could trust her to give an evasive answer. And then he would like her to see the place – just to know what she thought of it.

'Won't you say yes?' she said at last, her voice breaking the silence sharply.

'I was just thinking, dear: they have all gone to a tennis-party to-day. There'll be no one at home.'

'Well! why not to-day?'

'Well; I was thinking I've been lucky enough to get hold of some very interesting information about the Websters – about their ancestor Sir Thomas, who distinguished himself in the Peninsular – and I wanted to get it copied under the proper heading, but I daresay we can do that another day. The only thing is, how are you to get there? You are not equal to walking so far – '

'I was thinking, dear, that I might take a fly. I know there is the expense, but . . . '

'Yes; five or six shillings, at least. And where will you leave the fly? At the lodge gate? The flyman would be sure to get into conversation with the lodge-keeper or his wife. He'd tell them where he came from, and – '

'Supposing you were to get a two-wheeled trap and drive me yourself; that would be nicer still.'

'I'm so unlucky; someone would be sure to see me.'

The Major puffed at his pipe in silence. Then he said, 'If you were to put on a thick veil, and we were to get out of the town by this end and make our way through the lanes – it would be a long way round; but one hardly meets anyone that way, and the only danger would be going. We should return in the dusk. I don't care how late you make it; my people won't be home till nine or ten o'clock at night, perhaps later still. There will be dancing, and they are sure to stay late.'

Finally the matter was decided, and about four o'clock the Major went to the livery stable to order the trap. Mrs Shepherd and Nellie joined him soon after. Turning from the pony, whose nose he was stroking, he said –

'I hope you have brought a thick shawl; it will be cold coming back in the evening.'

'Yes, dear, here it is, and another for Nellie. What do you think of this veil?'

'It will do very well. I do hope these stablemen won't talk; let's get off at once.' The Major lifted in the child, tucked the rug about them, and cried to the stableman to let go. He drove very nervously, afraid at every moment lest the pony should bolt; and when the animal's extreme docility assured him there was no such danger, he looked round right and left, expecting at every moment some friend to pounce down upon him. But the ways were empty, the breeze that came across the fields was fresh and sweet, and they were all beginning to enjoy themselves, when he suddenly espied a carriage following in his wake. He whipped up the pony, and contrived to distance his imaginary pursuer; and having succeeded, he praised his own driving, and at the cross-roads he said: 'I dare not go any farther, but you can't miss the lodge gate in that clump of trees – the first white gate you come to. Don't ask any questions; it is ten to one you'll find the gate open; walk straight through, and don't forget to go through the beech-wood at the back of the house; the river runs right round the hill. I want to know what you think of the view. But pray don't ask to see the house; there's nothing to see; the housemaids would be sure to talk, and describe you to my sisters. So now good-bye; hope you'll enjoy yourself. I shall have just time to get to Hambrook and back; I want to see my solicitor. You'll have seen everything in a couple of hours, so in a couple of hours I shall be waiting for you here.'

Part II

It was as the Major said. The lodge-keepers asked no questions, and they passed up the drive, through the silence of an overgrowth of laurels and rhododendrons. Then the park opened before their eyes. Nellie rolled on the short, crisp, worn grass, or chased the dragon-flies; the spreading trees enchanted her, and, looking at the house – a grey stone building with steps, pillars, and pilasters, hidden amid cedars and evergreen oaks – she said, 'I never saw anything so beautiful; is that where the Major goes when he leaves us? Look at the flowers, Mother, and the roses. May we not go in there – I don't mean into the house? I heard the Major ask you not to go in for fear we should meet the housemaids – but just past this railing, into the garden? Here is the gate.' The child stood with her hand on the wicket, waiting for reply: the mother stood as in a dream, looking at the house, thinking vaguely of the pictures, the corridors, and stair-cases, that lay behind the plate-glass windows.

'Yes; go in, my child.'

The gardens were in tumult of leaf and bloom, and the little girl ran hither and thither, gathering single flowers, and then everything that came under her hands, binding them together in bouquets – one for mother, one for the Major, and one for herself. Mrs Shepherd only smiled a little bitterly when Nellie came running to her with some new and more splendid rose. She did not attempt to reprove the child. Why should she? Everything here would one day be hers. Why then should the present be denied them? And so did her thoughts run as she walked across the sward following Nellie into the beechwood that clothed the steep hillside. The pathway led by the ruins of some Danish military earth-works, ancient hollows full of leaves and silence. Pigeons cooed in the vast green foliage, and from time to time there came up from the river the chiming sound of oars. Rustic seats were at pleasant intervals, and, feeling a little tired, Mrs Shepherd sat down. She could see the river's silver glinting through the branches, and, beyond the river, the low-lying river lands, dotted with cattle and horses grazing, dim

139

already with blue evening vapours. In the warm solitude of the wood the irreparable misfortune of her own life pressed upon her: and in this hour of lassitude her loneliness seemed more than she could bear. The Major was good and kind, but he knew nothing of the weight of the burden he had laid upon her, and that none should know was in this moment a greater weight than the burden itself. Nellie was exploring the ancient hollows where Danes and Saxons had once fought, and had ceased to call forth her discoveries when Mrs Shepherd's bitter meditation was broken by the sudden sound of a footstep.

The intruder was a young lady. She was dressed in white, her pale gold hair was in itself an aristocracy, and her narrow slippered feet were dainty to look upon. 'Don't let me disturb you,' she said. 'This is my favourite seat; but I pray you not to move, there is plenty of room.' So amiable was she in voice and manner that Mrs Shepherd could not but remain, although she had already recognized the girl as one of the Major's sisters. Fearing to betray herself, greatly nervous, Mrs Shepherd answered briefly Miss Shepherd's allusions to the beauty of the view. At the end of a long silence Miss Shepherd said –

'I think you know my brother, Major Shepherd.'

Mrs Shepherd hesitated, and then she said: 'No. I have never heard the name.'

'Are you sure? Of course, I may be mistaken; but – '

Ethel made pause, and looked Mrs Shepherd straight in the face. Smiling sadly, Mrs Shepherd said –

'Likenesses are so deceptive.'

'Perhaps, but my memory is pretty good for faces . . . It was two or three months ago, we were going up to London, and I saw my brother get into the train with a lady who looked like you. She really was very like you.'

Mrs Shepherd smiled and shook her head.

'I do not know the lady my brother was with, but I've often thought I should like to meet her.'

'Perhaps your brother will introduce you.'

'No, I don't think he will. She has come to live at

140

Branbury, and now people talk more than ever. They say that he is secretly married.'

'And you believe it?'

'I don't see why it shouldn't be true. My brother is a good fellow in many ways, but, like all other men, he is selfish. He is just the man who would keep his wife hidden away in a lonely little lodging rather than admit that he had made a *mésalliance*. What I don't understand is why she consents to be kept out of the way. Just fancy giving up this beautiful place, these woods and fields, these gardens, that house for, for – '

'I suppose this woman gives up these things because she loves your brother. Do you not understand self-sacrifice?'

'Oh yes, if I loved a man . . . But I think a woman is silly to allow a man to cheat and fool her to the top of his bent.'

'What does it matter if she is happy?'

Ethel tossed her head. Then at the end of a long silence she said: 'Would you care to see the house?'

'No, thank you, Miss; I must be getting on. Good-bye.'

'You cannot get back that way, you must return through the pleasure-grounds. I'll walk with you. A headache kept me at home this afternoon. The others have gone to a tennis-party . . . It is a pity I was mistaken. I should like to meet the person my brother goes every day to Branbury to see. I should like to talk with her. My brother has, I'm afraid, persuaded her that we would not receive her. But this is not true; we should only be too glad to receive her. I have heard Father and Mother say so – not to Charles, they dare not speak to him on the subject, but they have to me.'

'Your brother must have some good reason for keeping his marriage secret. This woman may have a past.'

'Yes, they say that – but I should not care if I liked her, if I knew her to be a good woman now.'

To better keep the Major's secret, Mrs Shepherd had given up all friends, all acquaintance. She had not known a woman-friend for years, and the affinities of sex drew her to accept the sympathy with which she was tempted. The reaction of ten years of self-denial surged up within her, and she felt that she must speak, that her secret was being

141

dragged from her. Ethel's eyes were fixed upon her – in another moment she would have spoken, but at that moment Nellie appeared climbing up the steep bank. 'Is that your little girl? Oh, what a pretty child!' Then raising her eyes from the child and looking the mother straight in the face, Ethel said –

'She is like, she is strangely like, Charles.'

Tears glistened in Mrs Shepherd's eyes, and then, no longer doubting that Mrs Shepherd would break down and in a flow of tears tell the whole story of her life, Ethel allowed a note of triumph to creep into her voice, and before she could stop herself she said, 'And that little girl is the heiress of Appleton Park.'

Mrs Shepherd's face changed expression.

'You are mistaken, Miss Shepherd,' she said; 'but if I ever meet your brother I will tell him that you think my little girl like him.'

Mrs Shepherd pursued her way slowly across the park, her long weary figure showing upon the sunset, her black dress trailing on the crisp grass. Often she was obliged to pause; the emotion and exercise of the day had brought back pain, and her whole body thrilled with it. Since the birth of her child she had lived in pain. But as she leaned against the white gate, and looked back on the beautiful park never to be seen by her again, knowledge of her sacrifice quickened within her – the house and the park, and the manner and speech of the young girl, combined to help her to a full appreciation of all she had surrendered. She regretted nothing. However mean and obscure her life had been, it had contained at least one noble moment. Nellie pursued the dragonflies; Mrs Shepherd followed slowly, feeling like a victor in a great battle. She had not broken her trust; she had kept her promise intact; she would return to London to-morrow or next day, or at the end of the week, whenever the Major wished.

He was waiting for them at the corner of the lane, and Nellie was already telling him all she thought of the house, the woods, the flowers, and the lady who had sat down by Mother on the bench above the river. The Major looked at his wife in doubt and fear; her smile, however, reassured him. Soon after, Nellie fell asleep, and while she dreamed of butterflies and flowers Mrs Shepherd told him what had passed between her and his sister in the beechwood above the river.

'You see, what I told you was right. Your appearance has been described to them; they suspect something, and will never cease worrying until they have found out everything. I'm not a bit surprised. Ethel always was the more cunning and the more spiteful of the two.'

Mrs Shepherd did not tell him how nearly she had been betrayed into confession. She felt that he would not understand her explanation of the mood in which his sister had caught her. Men understand women so little. To tell him would be merely to destroy his confidence in her. As they drove through the twilight, with Nellie fast asleep between, he spoke of her departure, which he had arranged for the end of the week, and then, putting his arm round her waist, he said: 'You have always been a good little woman to me.'

Parted

Lincoln-lane was a last remnant of a purlieu that had once thriven about one of the Inns of Court. It stretched like a drain from the bright thoroughfare, disappearing in shadows of old decrepit houses. Its single gas-lamp sufficed only to accentuate its mystery and its blackness. Opposite was a dead wall, yellow and crumbling, and beyond it the back windows of the inn and some back yards.

The tower clock had clanged the first hour of morning. A pause, then the rumble of a cab far away in the Strand, and before it had quite died out of the ear, an altercation was heard coming in the direction of the lane. It grew louder, it grew distinct; and when it turned into the lane the sleepers murmured in their beds, 'Dale trying to get that drunken wife of his home.' But the woman refused to come in, and the argument was continued under the windows. It concerned fourpence which Dale had taken from his wife.

'You stole my money; I want my money; give me my money.'

'Your money; my money, you mean. What did you raise it on?'

'You took it out of my pocket. I want my money.'

'What for? Aren't you drunk enough already?'

'Who says I'm drunk? I'm not drunk. I want my money.'

To the folk yearning for sleep the dispute seemed as it if never would end. Since eleven o'clock they had been kept awake by drunkards, angry, jovial and pathetic, and now prayers were offered up beneath every coverlet that Mr and Mrs Dale would settle their differences and go up to bed. At

144

last a window was raised, and a large night-dress was thrust forth.

'Make less noise there, please; we want to go to sleep.'

'Oh, it is you, Mrs Temple – you and your daughter, Miss Temple, the two ladies of the lane. I spoke to you this morning and you didn't deign to answer.'

'I'm not bound to speak to you; I never stoop where there's nothing to pick up.'

Immediately after another window was raised, and a lean shirt and a red beard appeared.

'I've to be at my work at half-past five; it is one o'clock, and not a wink of sleep yet, and every night the same thing since the beginning of the week.'

Then window after window was raised, and heads and shoulders, hanging arms and craned necks seemed like a bas-relief, the whiteness of the apparel lending itself to the deception.

'Leave me alone, you're killing me,' cried Mrs Dale, and her husband's strength failed to get her through the doorway.

With a gesture of shame and despair Dale let her go. Involuntarily his eyes went to Mrs Temple's window, where Annie stood behind her mother in the shadow of the room. Mrs Dale noticed the direction of her husband's eyes, and she turned upon him fiercely.

'It is easy to see that you are gone on her. A dear little thing, never touched a drop of liquor in her life; wouldn't touch it, of course not. I never seed her slip into the private bar of the Feathers with a lot of other girls from up the Strand when she thought no one was about. Oh, dear no! A very artful little minx is Miss Annie Temple; she wouldn't be her mother's daughter if she wasn't.'

The lane was proud of Annie, the best conducted girl in the lane, and Mrs Dale's accusations against her character filled the windows with numerous disapproval and protest. To better defend her daughter, Mrs Temple leaned still further out of the window. But Dale begged of her to desist; she would only make matters worse, and he would never get his wife upstairs.

'The two ladies of the lane!' reiterated Mrs Dale, as if the phrase alone expressed the completeness of her disdain. Suddenly her thoughts went back to her money. 'Give me my money. I must have my money; just enough for another drink. I want my – my – '

'Now then, mate, do try to get her upstairs,' said the red-bearded man, who had come down in his shirt sleeves and trousers. 'You've woke up my babies; I can't get them to sleep, and I've to be up myself at half-past five, and it is after one. If you don't get her upstairs I must go after the "copper".'

'I don't care; go after the "copper". It don't matter to me. Complain to the landlord if you like. I've had enough of it. I wish I was dead.'

The red-bearded man looked at Dale compassionately, and then hitching up his trousers, which were falling over his naked feet, he entered his house two doors up the lane.

'Now, Liz,' said Dale, 'come upstairs. We shall get turned out of this.'

Drunken obstinacy gives way unexpectedly, and Mrs Dale allowed her husband to push her up the broken staircase. But she recovered herself somewhat when they got into their room, and the neighbours could hear things being thrown about, and now and then a shuffling of feet as if a struggle was in progress. At last silence came, and for a few hours the tired folk forgot the drudgery of their lives. A few hours of rest, and then the window-panes grew grey with day, and preparations for work began. They had heard Mrs Dale screaming in the street, and now they could hear her declaring that she was too miserable to live, her husband all the while moving about the room dressing himself quickly. He buckled his strap round his thick waist, he tied his comforter round his neck. His wife lay on the bed, half dressed, moaning and throwing her brown hair back from her pale, plump face.

They had had a nice home once, but she had taken to drinking, and then things had begun to disappear. Two years ago the home had been sold up. Dale had been obliged to leave his wife, but she had come after him, and though he did

not believe much in her promises never to touch liquor again
he had been induced to take her back.

There had been hardly any attempt at reformation. Life
had gone steadily from bad to worse, and for the last two
years his wife, as he himself expressed it, had made a pig-sty
of his home. He was disheartened, but still he went to his
work regularly. Notwithstanding the inconvenience and the
neglect of the room they lived in, Dale managed to keep
himself clean, and in spite of his coarse clothes, his manner,
bearing, and tone of voice indicated a certain refinement of
nature. There was despair and disgust on his face when he
looked at the heap of rubbish in the grate. He knew he would
find the room when he returned in the same state as when he
left it, and that he would again have to hunt up his wife in the
public-houses; she'd be getting drunk again in some quiet
corner. But what had she pawned to get drunk last night?
Dale thought of his Sunday clothes. No, the lock had not
been broken. Then he remembered his Sunday shirt which
she had promised to wash for him. They were going next
Sunday to Hampstead for a blow on the Heath. He taxed her
with having pledged it, but instead of answering she continued to bemoan her miserable condition. It was jealousy
that drove her to it. He had never cared for her, and now he
wanted to get rid of her so that he might marry Annie
Temple. He knew very well that she did not believe what she
was saying. Annie was not the cause of her drunkenness; she
used to get tipsy long before they came to live in the lane –
long before he laid eyes on Annie Temple. Curious, there
was a likeness, yet how different they were. He lathered his
face and had cleaned off a stubble growth from half one
cheek, when he stopped shaving. He remembered how she
was always threatening to make away with herself. She had
once tried to kill herself. But he had till now kept things out
of her way. Often it was his razors that she begged for, and
when she had a fit of blue devils he never left the house
without asking one of the neighbours to keep an eye upon
her. She was just in the mood to do it. Why should he
prevent her? He would leave the razors where she would be
sure to see them, and slip away to his work without saying a

word. It would be a happy release for both of them. Why should he lock up everything? Nothing obliged him to. It was her own look-out if she chose to kill herself. His hand trembled as he began shaving again. He cut himself and was vexed, for he thought that the sight of blood might alter her resolution.

'What's the matter?' she said, seeing him holding his handkerchief to his face.

'Nothing; got the toothache.'

'Oh, Bill, don't go yet. I'm so miserable; I can't stay here all alone. I'm afraid I shall do some harm to myself.'

'I've heard that story before; not much harm will come to you except the public-house.'

'Oh, Bill, don't leave me. I'm so miserable; I'm so ill. You'll never see me alive again. I can't bear up any longer. I'm so miserable. When will you be back?'

'Back! I feel like never coming back; I've seen about enough of this.'

'Oh, Bill, don't say that. If you knew how ill I am; how miserable I feel.'

He heard her throw herself back on the bed; he heard her scream as he closed the door, and he went downstairs thinking: 'Well, if she does do for herself it's her own look-out. I ain't obliged to lock up everything. Besides, I can stand no more of it. We shall be turned out of that crib to-morrow.' . . . . He quickened his pace, and to rid himself of unpleasant thoughts, he forced himself to notice the morning's aspect of the town.

He wondered whether the day would turn out wet or dry. The tall Embankment buildings showed like shadows on the morning sky, and in the middle of the brown river little whiffs of fog trailed along the edges of the barges. The pavement echoed with the clink of hob-nails, and Dale bade a cheery good morning to the gangs of workmen hurrying to catch their early train. His work was in Westminster; there was no need for him to hurry, so he stopped, and leaning on the parapet, looked out on the river. When he left the razors on the table it seemed to him that he was merely forgetting to lock them up. But he was already beginning to find that he

could no longer see the matter in so easy a light. He turned
from the river and some of its gloom seemed to have caught
on his face, and the cut he had given himself while shaving
had opened afresh, and it was bleeding when he laid his hand
on the ladder and mounted the scaffolding. The blood
frightened him: it seemed to him like a warning and a sign;
his mates, who knew of his wife's failing, whispered,
'Poor Bill, she's been a-knocking of him about again. He
stands it like a hangel; if she was my wife I'd have strangled
her long ago.'

Dale was popular on every scaffolding he had ever worked
on. His voice was cheery and his laughter hearty. He knew
dozens of songs and his singing made the time pass pleasantly. So when his face was overcast his mates cursed Mrs Dale
for their own sakes. He sang no song that morning, nor did
he whistle or speak or notice the jests with which his mates
sought to divert his thoughts from his home troubles. In a
moody silence he worked steadily at the chimney he was
building. When he had done a couple of hours' work he laid
down his trowel, and leaning against one of the scaffolding
poles he looked into the void of the crowded street. The
hauntings of his wife's gashed neck were too much for him.

'This is about the time,' he thought, 'she'll be getting out
of bed, and once she sees them razors she'll go for them at
once.' Then whether he looked up or down he could see
nothing but running blood. The white plaster he had taken
from the board, and that was now drying in the chimney-
stack, seemed to have a faint reddish tinge. There seemed to
be red in the street below, on the necks of the passers by, and
the white clouds sailing past seemed no longer white. His
thoughts paused and turned suddenly in a different direction.
Whether she was alive or dead his fate was equally wretched.
If she were alive he would find her in some public-house, and
would take her back amid the jeers of the neighbourhood, as
he had done last night. It was beastly. He had borne with her
as long as he could; he could put up with her no longer, and
still less with the idea that he had murdered her. 'There isn't
much difference,' he thought, 'between putting a razor into a
drunken woman's hand and cutting her throat from ear to

149

ear.' Escape, whether from sight of her, dead or alive, was necessary, and the way of escape lay down there. He wouldn't feel it; it would be all over in a moment. A giddy, irresistible impulse to throw himself over besieged his brain.

'What is it, Dale? not feeling well?' said the foreman. 'Come, pull yourself together and follow Smith down the ladder. There's work for you below.'

Dale stared hard at the foreman. He wondered if he had guessed what was passing in his mind, or if the interruption had been entirely accidental. However, he followed Smith down the ladder, and when they got into the foundation he said – 'I'm in a bit of trouble, Sir; could you spare me for an hour or two? – I dare say I could be back in less.'

'We are very behind-hand, and I expect the contractor round to-morrow. I was thinking of asking you if you'd like to do some overtime. You live close by; you can slip round during the dinner-hour.' Dale did not dare to leave his work without leave; work was scarce, and if he fell out of employment he mightn't get any again. So once more he tried to stifle his conscience with the reflection that if she cut her throat it was her own look-out. The wall he was building ran up at a prodigious rate; the hodman could hardly keep him supplied with bricks, and his mates said, 'What is Bill a-getting at? Do 'e want to run up that 'ere ten foot of wall before the dinner-hour?' Dale had resolved to slip round to see how she was getting on, and he was out of the building almost before the clock had finished striking; but he was followed by three or four of his mates. They knew of his trouble; he must think no more about it, but come along with them. Fearing troublesome questions if he refused, Bill went with them, and a couple of tankards of strong ale soon made him forget his wife. The clock struck one, and, very pleased with themselves, Bill's mates brought him back to work as jolly as a sand-boy. Never, they said, did Bill sing better than he had done that afternoon.

It was not until about three or four o'clock that he began to look sad again. For as the fumes of the beer began to evaporate, his conscience began to take hold of him: his regret grew deeper, until at last it overpowered him, and he covered his face in his hands, unable to restrain his tears. She was gone from him; he would never see her again. He had begun to remember the days of his courtship. She was a pretty girl then, not unlike Annie, only not quite so tall; the same nose and the same look in the eyes. He thought of the evenings they spent sitting side by side, holding each other's hands, in the gardens near the Embankment. It was there that they had planned out their future. How she used to talk, to be sure, about the home they would have. But things hadn't planned out as he had expected. He thought of the evenings they had spent together at the theatre. She used to remember the plays they saw wonderful well, near as well as Annie. He had been twice to the theatre with Annie – her mother had had tickets given her, and had asked him to come with them. Coming back he had had Annie all to himself, Mrs Temple having met a friend on the way home. What a nice good girl she was! What a good wife she'd make! What a nice, clean, comfortable home she'd keep for a man! It would be pleasure to come back to a home that she had the looking after. He had always liked talking to her, and she had always had a nice, civil, pleasant word to say when he met her; a pretty girl, too, not unlike what Liz used to be. Poor Liz, it wasn't her fault; she couldn't help it. He found excuses for her; the wrong she had done him began to appear trivial and insignificant. Again he threw himself into his work, and hardly ceased to call to his hodman until work-time was done. His mates gathered up their tools, and swinging their baskets over their shoulders they left the building in gangs, hurrying to catch their trains. Two of his pals took Bill by the arm, but he asked them to let him be. They looked at him suspiciously, and then left him. Bill returned home alone along the Embankment. The twilight was just beginning to gather, and was fashioning the city and its river into a mystery of mist and starry light. Bill watched the brown tumbling water, hardly thinking at all, his mind crossed every now and then with a sensation of funeral flowers, and a quiet grave which he would not fail to visit. He was infinitely sad, and yet without the desire of suicide which had possessed him in the morning. Poor dear Liz, with all her faults, she was gone from him for ever. There couldn't be much doubt about it; he knew her; she had gone and done it. Then suddenly a strange thought tumbled into his mind – he might be accused of murder. He was the last person who saw her alive. There had been a dispute overnight, and she had accused him of wanting to get rid of her, so that he might marry Annie Temple. He turned away from the Embankment and walked towards Westminster. But he had not taken many steps before he stopped. He remembered that flight was impossible. Flight would be taken as proof of his guilt. He saw his name on the newspaper placards, he felt the handcuff on his wrists, he was alone in the prison-cell, he stood in the crowded law-court amid the mummery of the law and the cruel curiosity of visitors. None would pity him, unless perhaps Annie. Her name would be mixed up in this ugly business. Then Bill experienced every abject agony of terror. He trembled like a caught animal; paralysed with fear he stood, quite unable to understand the infinite complexities of the net into which a simple unpremeditated act had precipitated him. Regret for the loss of his wife had given way in the bitter stress of personal fear, and for an hour he remained on the Embankment in a sort of stupor, unable either to return or to fly from home. At last he remembered that every hour's delay would tell against him at the inquest. 'Those lawyer-chaps are very clever in making much out of little things, and if he didn't take care he'd swing for it.' He must return at once to Lincoln-lane. But he had not gone very far before he stopped – he could not overcome the horror that the half-severed neck caused him, and the fear of an accusation of murder being preferred against him grew intolerably acute. Then he prayed that she had not seen the razors, that she had not killed herself, and that if she had, she had not forgotten to leave behind some paper absolving him of share in her death. He stopped to reflect on her character. She was a good sort when not in drink; kind-hearted, but a little thoughtless – and yet he didn't know –

As he approached the lane his fears augmented, and he looked eagerly for some sign that would tell him the news. The doorsteps were as usual filled with children. Mrs Temple was coming from the mangling room with a basket of clothes. The moment she saw him she said – 'What have you done with your wife, we haven't seen her all day?' He felt the irrevocable had happened. 'Why, you're as pale as a ghost, Mr Dale.'

'I pale? Not I!' He felt that he must not give himself away, but his tongue clove to his mouth. Speech seemed impossible, the words caught in his throat. It was with difficulty that he got them out at last.

'Why, what's happened? What about my wife. Why do you ask what I have done with her?'

'Only because we haven't seen her all day. We thought she might have gone after you.'

'No, she ain't been after me to-day.'

'Well, we don't know where she is; her door's locked. We was up there about a couple of hours ago, and we hammered, fearing that something had gone wrong, but we couldn't get in.'

'That's odd. I left her this morning – the drink had made her a bit ill. I dare say you heard her; you know the way she carries on after a drink?'

'No, I didn't hear her; maybe the others did. She was very drunk last night; we was all very sorry for you. A terrible trial a wife like that is to a man.'

'As long as I don't grumble I don't see what affair it is of other folk. I'm very fond of my wife. If she do take a drop too much sometimes, who is it that don't – none in this lane.'

'If that's the way you're going to take it when we says we is sorry for you – good evening.'

'Stop, Mrs Temple; one moment. You said that you had hammered at the door and wasn't able to get in. Do ye mind coming up with me?'

'What do you want me to go up with you for?'

Dale felt that he was giving himself away, but he couldn't help it now; words came faster than his thoughts, and he begged Mrs Temple to lay her basket in the doorway and go up with him. Her round, fat, kindly face was full of compassion for her unfortunate neighbour. She liked him better for having taken his wife's part, and she put down her basket and went upstairs with him. He did not hear what Mrs Temple was saying; his heart was dead within him, and he thought only of the spectacle that would meet his eyes when they got the door open. Not many knocks or words were wasted; he put forth his shoulder and burst the door. They went in, and he saw what he had seen many times during the day – his wife huddled up in the right corner. He did not dare go near her; it seemed to him that if he were to touch her that the head would roll from the shoulders. He knew that Mrs Temple stood waiting for him to go to his wife, but he could not go. Then he saw a piece of paper on the floor, and he doubted not that these were her last words to him – her farewell. He felt that he would give the whole world to have her back again, and when he went forward to pick up the paper he felt that he had never really loved her till now, but as he examined it his face changed expression, and he said to Mrs Temple –

'It's only a pawn-ticket. She's gone and pawned the razors. I thought she was dead, and had written me a word of good-bye. I left the razors out this morning, and all the day I've been thinking that she would make away with herself. I couldn't get through my work with thinking how I should find her in that corner covered with blood, and all through my fault.'

'And she's gone and pawned the razors,' said Mrs Temple, looking at the ticket which he held to her, 'and she has got drunk on what they gave her on them. They must have been good ones. She's ten times worse than she was last night.'

'And I was thinking all day that I had as good as murdered her.'

'Well, that's about the best bit I've heard this long while! You breaking your heart, fit to throw yourself from the scaffolding! Well, that is – ' and Mrs Temple's fat body shook with laughter.

'You wouldn't laugh if she lay there with her throat cut, would you? Well, I don't see that is much better as it is. She's a nice sort of wife to help a man through life, and this is a nice sort of room to live in. A nice sort of 'ome that a man can be 'appy and comfortable in, ain't it? It looks uncommon cheerful, and it smells sweet, don't it?'

She heard him say, 'A real drunkard's 'ome,' as she went out – and that just about what it was. He was deserving of something better, but it was always the way. The good men get the bad wives, and the bad wives get the good husbands. She'd like to see Annie married to such a man. She was sorry she laughed at him, but it was that funny, say what you will. Mrs Temple leaned against the wall and held her sides, and when she related what had happened in the mangling room the house shook with laughter. The joke was clearly to the taste of the neighbourhood, and Dale knew that in a few minutes the whole street would be in roars. He felt in his pockets; he had a few coppers; what should he do, go and get drunk or throw himself into the Thames?

Several girls came out to meet him in the passage, and they besieged him with jeering inquiry. What did he feel like all day, as if he would like to chuck his little self over the scaffolding? The poor dear lying there with her throat cut, whereas she had just popped the razors and got drunk again. They could hardly speak for laughing.

Annie stood apart, and Bill saw that there were tears in her eyes. He held out his hands to her; they grasped each other's hands, their souls looked out of their eyes. Then he rushed out of the house without a word. Afterwards Annie regretted that she had not obeyed her instinct and followed him. But it was all so sudden; fate had decided too quickly.

An Episode In Bachelor Life

Mr Bryant was tall, slim, and not many years over thirty; his features were regular, but no one had ever mentioned him as a good-looking man. He lived with his mother in Bryanston Square, but he had chambers in Norman's Inn, where he wrote waltzes, received his friends, and practised wood-carving.

The service in Norman's Inn was performed by a retinue of maidservants, working under the order of the porter and his wife; but these girls were idle, dirty, and slovenly: the porter's wife was an execrable cook, and Mr Bryant was very particular about what he ate, and could not bear the slightest speck of dust on the numerous knick-knacks that filled his sitting-room. So, after many complaints, he resolved to have a servant of his own. His mother had procured him one Clara Thompson, from King Edward's School, a young girl just turned seventeen, pale-complexioned, delicate features, and blue eyes, which seemed to tell of a delicate, sentimental nature.

She stood now watching Mr Bryant eat his breakfast. He did not require her service, and wondered why she lingered.

'I'm thinking of leaving, Sir. If you don't mind, I should like to go at the end of the week.'

Mr Bryant looked up, surprised. 'Why do you want to leave, Clara?'

She told him she did not like Norman's Inn, and little by little he drew the story of her trouble from her. The porter's nephew had come to take the watchman's place until the old soldier returned from the hospital. Almost from the first he

156

had begun to plague her with his attentions. Last week Fanny had asked her to come to the Turk's Head, a music-hall at the other end of the lane. Harry had sat with his arm round Fanny the whole time, and Mr Stokes's nephew had put his hand on her knee. She could,'t get away from him, and didn't want to make a fuss. At last she had to get up, but Harry had pulled her back and told her to drink some beer. The beer was poison; she thought they must have put something in it; she had only had a mouthful, and that made her feel quite giddy.

'And the singing you heard at the Turk's Head?' asked Mr Bryant.

'It wasn't very nice, Sir; but it wasn't quite so bad as what goes on in the kitchen of an evening when all the girls are there. I do all I can, Sir, to keep out of his way, but he follows me down to the kitchen and kisses me by force. The others only laugh at me, and I'm insulted because I won't dance with him.'

'But what are these dances like?'

'Oh, Sir! I can't tell you, Sir! I try to see as little of it as I can. The other evening I said I'd stop there no longer, and walked up and down the inn until bedtime. That's how I got my cold.'

'I don't like to lose you, Clara. I can speak to Mr Stokes, and tell him that you must be let alone.'

'Oh, no, Sir! don't do that – it would only set them more than ever against me. It isn't for me to find fault, but I'm not used to such company – it was so different in the school.' Tears started to her eyes; she turned aside to hide them.

Mr Bryant was touched.

'I won't have you go down into that kitchen any more, Clara. There's no reason why you should. It is all the same to me if I pay the porter for your food or if I put you on board wages. There's a kitchen here, you'll have coal and gas free. I'll give you ten shillings a week board wages.'

'Oh, Sir, you're really too kind!'

'But you'll still have to sleep with Lizzie.'

'That doesn't matter, Sir, so long as I haven't to go much to that kitchen. I was always there, Sir, except when I was attending on you, Sir, and that was so seldom.'

'You prefer to sit in these rooms?'

'Oh, Sir!'

'You can sit in the back room and do your sewing when I'm here, and when I'm not here you can sit in this room. I'm afraid you'll find it lonely.'

'I shan't be lonely for their company. You're very good to me. I don't know how to thank you.'

When he returned from France he brought her back a shawl – a knitted silk shawl. The shawl meant that he had thought of her when he was away. She could hardly speak for happiness, and she spent hours thinking, wondering. It was such a pretty shawl . . . no other man would have chosen such a pretty shawl. There was no one like him. Her hands dropped on her knees, and she raised her eyes, now dim with dreams, and listened. He was singing, accompanying himself on the piano.

The days that he dined in the inn were red-letter days in her life, for he detained her during the meal with whatever conversation he thought would interest her, and she listened as a dog listens to its master, unmindful of the great love that consumed her or his indifference. One day there came a sharp double rap at the door which made them both start.

'That's the post,' she exclaimed.

'No; it is not the post,' she said, coming back, 'a messenger boy brought this letter, and he says there's an answer.'

Mr Bryant tore open the envelope, and Clara watched the eager expression on his face. He went to his desk and wrote a long letter. When he had fastened it she held out her hand, but he said he would speak to the boy himself.

Next morning there were several letters in the post-box: one was on perfumed paper, and she noticed that it bore the same perfume as the letter which the boy had brought yesterday.

'Any letters?'

'Yes, Sir.'

Clara pulled up the blinds and prepared his bath. As she was leaving the room she looked back. He lay on his side, reading his letter, unconscious of everything but it. After breakfast he said –

'I want you to take a letter for me.'

'Do you want me to go at once, Sir?'

'I want the letter to get there before twelve. There's plenty of time.'

'Is the letter finished, Sir?'

'No, but it will be when you have done up my room.'

Mr Bryant was sitting in an attitude habitual to him when she came for the letter – with his left hand he held his chin, his right arm was thrown forward over the edge of the desk.

'Is the letter ready, Sir?'

'Yes, here it is. Mrs Alexander, 37, Cadogan Gardens. You know how to get there?'

'No, Sir.'

'You take the train to Sloane Square, and it is within a few minutes' walk of the station.'

She had often wondered if he were in love with any woman. None ever came to his chambers. But this Mrs Alexander, who was she? He had not told her not to leave the letter if she were out . . . Then why had he told the boy last night not to leave the letter? Mrs Alexander might be a widow. The thought frightened her; Mr Bryant might marry, give up his chambers in the inn, and send her away. Perhaps this was the very woman who would bring ruin upon her. She stopped, overcome by a sudden faintness, and when she raised her eyes she saw that a lady was watching her from a drawing-room window. Was this the number? Yes, this was 37. Before she had time to ring, the door was opened, and a lady said –

'I'm Mrs Alexander – is that letter for me?'

'Yes, Ma'am.'

Mrs Alexander was a small woman, dressed in a black woollen gown, well cut to her slight figure. The pallor of her face was heightened by the blackness of her hair. She stood reading the letter avidly, the black bow of a tiny slipper advanced beyond the skirt, her hand clasping the hand of a little child of four, who stood staring at Clara.

'She opened the door herself, so that the servants might not know that she received a letter,' Clara thought, as she sat in the train studying the handwriting so that she might know it again.

'She's no widow, for if she was she'd not take the trouble to watch from the window.' Clara was shocked at Mrs Alexander's wickedness. 'Living in that fine house, a good husband, no doubt, and that dear little girl to think of. But these sort of women don't think of anything but themselves.'

One morning she found a small lace handkerchief on one of the armchairs. Had Mrs Alexander given it to him, or had she been to his rooms late and forgotten it? It had been her pleasure not to allow a speck of dust to lie on the eighteenth-century tables, china vases, and the pictures in white frames. But another woman had been there, and all her pleasure in the room was destroyed. Mrs Alexander had sat on that chair; she had played on the piano; she had stood by the bookcase; she had taken down the books and leant over Mr Bryant's shoulder.

A month later the tea table wore a beautiful white cloth, worked over with red poppies, a bottle of smelling-salts appeared on his table, and, though it was winter, there were generally flowers in the vases. Clara noticed that the stamps on Mrs Alexander's letters were different from ordinary English stamps, and when the ordinary stamp reappeared on sweet-scented envelopes she knew that Mrs Alexander had come back.

'Clara, I should like you to dust and tidy up the place as much as possible.'

'Aren't the rooms clean, then, Sir?'

'Well, I fancied they were getting rather dusty. I don't mean that it is your fault; the amount of smuts that come in from the chimney-pots opposite is something dreadful. I shall be going out in the afternoon; you'll have time for a thorough clean. You can get Lizzie to help you, and not only this room, but all the rooms. We are getting on into spring. I don't see why we should not have fresh curtains up in the bed-room, and don't forget to wash my brushes and to put a new toilet cover on the table. You might go to Covent Garden and order in some flowers – some bunches of lilac; they'll freshen up the place. I shall want some hyacinths, too, for the windows.'

Next morning the servants stopped as they went up the inn

with their trays to admire Mr Bryant's windows. He called
to Clara for the watering-pot, and sent her to the restaurant
for the bill of fare. At one o'clock the white-aproned
cook-boys came up the inn with the trays on their heads. The
oysters, the bread and butter, and the Chablis were on the
table. Everything was ready. The church clock had struck the
half-hour, and Mr Bryant was beginning to complain – to
express fear that the lady might have mistaken the day, when
a slight interrogative knock was heard at the door. In a
moment Mr Bryant was out of the sitting-room; he thrust his
servant back into the kitchen, and she heard the swishing
sound of a silk dress. A few moments after, the sitting-room
door opened, and Mr Bryant called her.

'Is the lunch all ready, Clara? Is everything in the kitchen?'

'Yes, Sir.'

'Then I'll get the things out myself. I shan't want you all
the afternoon. You can go out for a walk if you like; but be
back between five and six, in time to clear away.'

It was the sharp, peremptory tone of a master speaking to a
servant, a tone which she had never heard from him before,
and it made her feel that she was something below him,
something that he was kind to because it was his nature to
be kind.

Clara realized this with a distinctness which she was
unaccustomed to, and in a sick paralysis of mind she took the
dish of cutlets and placed it in the warmth, and was glad to
leave the chambers; and meeting Lizzie as she went up the inn
she told her she was feeling very bad, and was going to lie
down. Would she kindly answer Mr Bryant if he called, and
get him what he wanted? Lizzie promised that she would,
and Clara went upstairs.

About five o'clock Lizzie came to her with the news that
Mr Bryant was very sorry to hear she was unwell. Could he
do anything for her? Was there anything he could send her?
Would she see the doctor?

No, no, she wanted nothing, only to be alone. She caught
the pillow, rolled herself over, and Lizzie heard her crying in
the darkness, and when the coarse girl put her arms about her
Clara turned round and sobbed upon her shoulder. Bessie

161

was breathing hard, Fanny snored intermittently, and, speaking vey low, Lizzie said –

'I suppose it is that you care for him?'

'I don't know; I don't know. He don't care to talk to me as he used. I feel that miserable – I can't stop here – I can't – '

'Yer ain't going to chuck your situation for him?'

'I don't know.'

'You'll be better to-morrow – them fancies wears off. Ah, that's why you wouldn't go out with Mr Stokes's nephew. Well, he was a low lot.'

'He was quite different.'

That was all the explanation Clara could give, but it seemed enough for, as one animal understands another's inarticulate cry, so did Lizzie's common mind seem to divine the meaning of the words: it was quite different.

'A gentleman's nice soft speech and his beautiful clothes get on one somehow. I know what you means, yet Fanny says she likes Harry best when he's dirty.'

Next morning, when Clara went up with Mr Bryant's hot water, she saw that a letter from Mrs Alexander was in the post-box; he read it in bed, and he re-read it at breakfast – he did not seem even to know that she was in the room. She lingered, hoping that he would speak to her. She only wanted him to speak to her just as he used to – about herself, about himself. She did not wish to be wholly forgotten. But he was always reading letters from Mrs Alexander or writing letters to her. She hated having to take letters to Cadogan Gardens, and Mrs Alexander seemed to come more and more frequently to Norman's Inn. And every day she grew paler and thinner. She lost her strength, and at last could not accomplish her work. Mr Bryant complained of dust and untidiness. She listened to his reproofs like a sick person who has not strength to answer. One morning she said, as she was clearing the breakfast things –

'I'm thinking of leaving, Sir.'

'Of leaving, Clara!' and, raising his eyes from the letter he was writing, Mr Bryant looked at her in blank astonishment. Then a smile began to appear on his face. 'Are you going to be married?' he said.

'No, Sir.'

'Then why do you want to leave?'

'I think I'd like to go, Sir,'

'You can get more wages elsewhere?'

'No, Sir; it isn't that.'

'Then what is it? Haven't I been kind enough? Can I do anything? Do you want more money?'

'No, Sir; it's nothing to do with money.'

'Then what is it?'

'I think I'd like to leave, Sir.'

'When?'

'I should like to go at once.'

'At once! You don't think of the annoyance and trouble you're putting me to. I shall have to look out for another servant. Really, I think – of course, if you are going to get married, or if you had an offer of a better situation, I should say nothing: but to leave me in the lurch – some whim. I suppose you'd like a change?'

'I don't think that the inn agrees with me, Sir.'

'You are looking poorly. If you'd like to go for a holiday – '

'No, Sir; I think I'd like to leave.'

Mr Bryant's face grew suddenly overcast, and he muttered something about ingratitude. The word cut her to the heart; but there was no help for it – she had to go.

Her idol was taken from her – the idol that represented all that she could understand of grace, light, and beauty, and, losing it, the whole world became for her a squalid kitchen, where coarse girls romped to a tune played on a concertina by a shoe-boy sitting on the dresser.

An Episode in Married Life

On 15 May, 1885, Madame de Beausac was dining with her cousin, a well-known writer and Academician, who lived in an old street in the Faubourg St Germain. As she drove there through the clear and fine twilight of the Champs Elysées, she thought of the novel she was reading in the *Revue des Deux Mondes*. She had read the first instalment, and was interested in the story. The second instalment was just published, and she regretted she had not had time to glance through it, for she was going to meet the author, Mr James Mason, at dinner.

The roadway was full of carriages, and Madame de Beausac's throughts grew vaguer and more dream-like as she lay back on the blue cushions of her *coupé* and admired the chestnut trees, now full of white bloom. She had never felt happier in spirit or in flesh. As the *coupé* passed round the Place de la Concorde life seemed a perfect gift: the tumult of the fountains was loud in the still air and every line of roof was sharp and delicate in the elusive light. And thinking of Mr Mason and his heroine, a woman of thirty, who reminded her of herself. Madame de Beausac noticed as the *coupé* passed over the Pont Neuf that the Seine seemed a little river in comparison with the wide flowing Thames. She had spent her honeymoon in London, and she wondered if she had really loved her husband. All that was a long while ago, and young men who would declare their passion if she held out ever so little encouragement did not interest her at all. She supposed that she was different from other women. All the women she knew had lovers; she was the only virtuous woman in her set; she was the only one against whom no one could say anything. That was, at least, something.

The *coupé* entered the Rue de Varennes and stopped at a large corner house. As the coachman turned his horse into the *porte cochère* Mr James Mason slipped aside to let the carriage pass.

He was thin, tall, fair – a typical young Englishman. This was his first visit to M. Renoir; the publication of the translation of his novel in the *Revue* had procured for him the invitation. He waited on the pavement's edge, for the *coupé* was standing in the passage in front of the glass door opening on to the staircase. The door of the *coupé* opened, and, all pink, Madame de Beausac stepped out. 'There is entertainment in that waist,' thought Mason; and a love story – a vision of blue-black hair and pink dress – passed through his mind. He smiled at the idea that a passing appearance had inspired in him. But, truly, she seemed to mean more than the others; she seemed significant of something, and he regretted that he would never see her again. He heard the hollow sound of her horses' hoofs on the asphalt of the courtyard as he ran, hoping to catch a last glimpse of her on the staircase: but she had already stopped, and, looking up, he saw the entertaining waist disappearing through a door. 'I shall never see her again,' he thought. He sighed, and remembered that he had forgotten to ask on which floor M. Renoir lived, and when the *concierge* said '*Au premier*' he was genuinely taken aback. Then he would meet the lady of his sudden admiration in M. Renoir's drawing-room; they were going to dine together!

Mason had spent the larger part of his thirty-three years talking to women, thinking about women, observing women, and formulating his impressions of women. He could, therefore, divine their thoughts through their slightest actions. He had already noticed that Madame de Beausac was looking thin. But he had to speak to his hostess. When the conversation paused and he looked up, he found to his pleasure and surprise that Madame de Beausac's eyes were still fixed upon him.

'Upon my word, it would seem as if – it may be no more

than curiosity. However, I shall soon know. If she looks at me again in that way before the *entrée*, I shall know it is all right.' Mason talked to his hostess about indifferent things until the servants came in with the *entrée*. Then he looked up. Madame de Beausac's eyes were fixed upon him.

'That's all right,' he thought. And so sure did he now feel of her love that he had begun to fear the indiscretion of her eyes before the *entremet* was handed round. 'She must take me for a fool if she thinks I do not understand.' And he tried to compose a look which could be interpreted. 'We'll settle all that in the drawing-room after dinner.'

He had expected to find her waiting for him, but, very much to his surprise, she sat down at the card-table and played whist for an hour, and Mason talked to various people, looking at her from time to time, but she sat, her eyes fixed on her cards. 'Most strange,' he thought. 'I could have sworn it; I'm not often mistaken.' Soon after he heard that she was going to a ball at half-past ten. 'I shan't have an opportunity of even speaking to her,' he thought, and his eyes went to the clock. Madame de Beausac's eyes had also gone to the clock, and, seeing how late it was, she got up from the card-table, and came towards him, pulling her fingers into the long mauve kid.

They sat down together, as far from the others as possible. She told him she had often heard of him, that she had read the first part of his book, and would read the second to-morrow. She had liked the story very much indeed. If he could come and see her to-morrow, she would tell him what she thought of the second part of his novel.

'Unfortunately,' she said, raising her eyes, 'it is my "At Home" day.'

'That is unfortunate. You're going now to a ball: cannot you send some excuse?' he said, looking round to assure himself that no one was within earshot.

'Impossible,' she said; 'I have to meet my husband there,' and her black eyes seemed to look down in his very soul. 'You will come, won't you? I want to see you.'

Madame de Beausac seemed to be quite beside herself. Conversation was impossible under the circumstances.

Mason was afraid that they would be noticed. The moment was full of peril, and he was glad when she said 'I must go now, so little suffices to upset these kind of things,' and he watched her dark, thin shoulders disappear through the doorway, and wondered what developments to-morrow's visit would bring forth. Never in all his experience had he provoked so extravagant a passion, a passion so utterly uncontrollable. He wondered; he was really curious to see how it would turn out.

At the ball Madame de Beausac wore a strange, melancholy air; she danced hardly at all, and asked her husband, much to his satisfaction, to take her home before the cotillon. Not a word was exchanged in the carriage, but when they were alone in their room she said, laying her arm on his shoulder and looking at him sadly –

'I wonder, Albert, if you still like me?'

'My dear, what makes you ask such a question? I hope that no one has – '

'No, no, nothing of that. No one has told me stories about you. I was only thinking – it is four years since we were married; four years ago we were in London; I did love you then, didn't I? – and you – you were crazy about me. I wonder if you've been true to me all this while. Tell me; I shall forgive you; tell me,' she said, raising her eyes from white roses of the Aubusson carpet and looking at him earnestly.

'True to you, my dear? Of course.'

'Will you swear it?'

'Berthe, someone must – '

'No, dear, no one has. Only I want to know.'

Madame de Beausac sighed deeply, her hand fell from his shoulder, and she watched her husband take off his coat. It seemed to her that he had grown stouter since breakfast, and she took up the *Revue des Deux Mondes*, sat down, and wondered.

'Aren't you coming to bed?' he said, laying his face on the pillow.

'Not yet; I'm going to read.'

167

'I thought you had read the first part of the novel they are publishing in the *Revue*?'

'Yes; but the second part was published to-day.'

'Then, good night, dear; I'm rather tired.'

'Good night, dear.'

When her husband snored Madame de Beausac looked round and breathed a sigh of relief.

Next day, when Mason called on Madame de Beausac, the footman led him through a suite of lofty rooms filled with bronze and tapestries, and it was in the last room, a beautiful room, that he found Madame de Beausac and her company. They were seated about an open window on mauve-coloured sofas, and the green garden was full of rhododendrons. 'Just the kind of mistress that would suit me,' thought Mason. He hoped that these ladies and gentlemen would go soon, and that Madame would refrain from looking at him till they were alone. His wishes were gratified. Not once did he catch her looking at him, and he had to console himself with the thought that women always slip into exaggeration. He waited as long as he dared; more ladies arrived, and at a quarter-past four he felt he must go. He bade her good-bye; her eyes were empty of the love he expected to find there, and he walked through the rooms feeling rather crestfallen. Suddenly he became aware that Madame de Beausac had left the guests; they were alone in the ante-room.

'I've read the second part of your novel. You're the young man. Do you run away with the married woman?'

'Do you mean in reality or in fiction?'

'In reality.'

'There's no necessity in running away, is there?'

'Perhaps not,' she said. 'But we haven't a moment – someone else will ring presently. Are you going to the Prince's masked ball to-night?'

'I haven't an invitation.'

'I will send you one.'

'What time?'

'Half-past eleven,' she whispered, and flew back to her guests.

168

When Mason had gone Madame de Beausac felt that she had acted very wrongly. She could not understand what had happened to her; something must have happened, for once or twice she thought that she must be going mad. But, mad or sane, the violence of her love did not abate, and she thought vainly how she might combat it. She went to her husband, feeling that a kind word would save her. He took her in his arms, and said she was looking pale; he kissed her, and for a moment she thought she felt better. But the overmastering passion which Mason had inspired in her was not to be swept away by a little uxorial kiss. To free herself from its clutch she must appeal to her child; perhaps her baby's kisses would win her back to reason, and she took little Clare out of her cot.

'Mother is going to a ball. What would baby do if Mother never were to come back?'

Little Clare rubbed her eyes; she was not yet awake, and did not grasp her mother's meaning.

'What would baby do if Mother were never to come back?'

Clare began to cry, and hid her face on her mother's shoulder.

'What would baby do?'

'Die,' said the poor little thing, sobbing, and Madame de Beausac laid the little girl back in her cot. She walked down the passage with a firm step: her little girl had saved her; she would not go to the ball. At that moment she caught sight of the dress she had intended to wear, a pink dress, the same she had worn at her cousin's, and, without warning, all the intolerable desire came back, and for a sense of choking in the throat she could hardly answer her maid, who had come to ask her if she would dress now. She sat down, unable to decide. At last she deetermined to think no more – she would go to the ball. Going to the ball didn't mean – didn't mean – she would go the ball. She called her maid and dressed hurriedly in the strange calm of mind which follows submission to temptation.

At the same moment Mason was tying his white necktie. He stopped his cab at Baron, the costumier's, intending to hire a

Venetian mantle. But as he was trying one on a strange thought came into his mind. Never in all his experience had he provoked so uncontrollable a passion. If he were to put this frantic passion to a severe test? He smiled, and forthwith refused the Venetian mantle and paused to consider what costume he would adopt.

Madame de Beausac was dressed in the pink gown she had worn on the night she had met Mason. She carried a bouquet of orchids in her hand, and she moved forward slowly, shaking hands with her friends, searching amid the crowd for her lover. Suddenly she heard someone call her softly. She knew it was he, and she turned, her face aflame with pleasure. But the look of pleasure vanished, and a little cry of horror escaped her. A tall white Pierrot, incredibly hideous, stood beside her. The white powder seemed to have surprisingly lengthened Mason's long face – he was hideous, ridiculous.

'Don't you like my costume?' he asked.

'Oh,' she said, laughing, 'I never saw anything like it,' and she laughed again.

He asked her to dance; she excused herself, and taking a friend's arm passed up the room.

When she returned he asked her to sit out a dance with him. It was difficult to refuse, and she took his arm and they sought a quiet corner. Mason felt he had gone a little too far, but he counted on the charm of his conversation to overcome the effect of the white powder on his face. But the spell was broken – conversation was impossible. She could not tolerate the horrible white face, and got up to go. As she drove home she looked at her husband almost with the same eyes that she had looked at him with four years ago, when they were in London on their honeymoon.

When she arrived home she took little Clare out of her cot and kissed the poor little sleepy face till it was wide awake. And so did a powder-puff save a woman, when other remedies had failed, from the calamity of a great passion.

'Emma Bovary'

The Misses O'Hara arrived at Aix-les-Bains by the afternoon express from Mâcon. The month was September, the air was moveless and warm, and Ismena hoped that Letitia would be benefited by the change. Letitia had never been abroad before. Ismena had been to Paris in early youth to study art, and the drawings she had done in Julien's were tied up in a portfolio, and it lay in a cupboard in their house in Dublin. But this was more than twenty years ago, and Ismena had discovered in the course of the journey to Aix that she had forgotten a good deal of her French. As they drove to the *pension* Letitia said she was glad they were going to say where English was spoken; she had been a little bored by her sister's attempt to speak French, and when the fly stopped and the proprietress came forward she asked her in triumphant English if they could have a double-bedded room.

'I am very sorry, Mesdames, but we have not a room with two beds in it vacant, but we can give you two small rooms on the same floor.'

The sisters stood looking at each other. They had been accustomed for many years to retire at the same hour, and Ismena wondered what it would be like to awaken in the middle of the night and to feel herself alone; and Letitia thought it would be very strange to undress by herself, and to go to sleep without saying good-night to her sister.

'Your rooms will be in the same corridor,' the proprietress said.

And Ismena, thinking that she read in Letitia's eyes acquiescence in this arrangement, said –

171

'If you don't mind, Letitia.'

Ismena was tall and straight, and she was better looking than her sister. Her nose was slender and the nostrils were shapely, her eyes were clear and intelligent, her teeth were in good order, and she would not have looked her age had her hair not turned white. Letitia was stouter than her sister, her complexion was muddier, she was less distinguished looking, and her features corresponded to her character – neither was clear-cut. Her hair was an iron grey and her teeth were not so well preserved as Ismena's; the front tooth looked as if it would not last much longer, there was an ominous black speck in it.

In early youth they had lived in the west, and their habit had been to come up to Dublin in the spring and to stop for a month at a hotel. They said they came to Dublin to buy dresses, but their friends said that they came up to Dublin to look for husbands. Whatever their intentions in coming to Dublin may have been, it is certain that they received no proposals of marriage in the drawing-room of their hotel. Neither received a proposal until Ismena went to study art in Julien's and Letitia was left alone in their lodge in the west. In this interval both were on the point of being married, but, unfortunately, Ismena thought it necessary to rush back to Ireland to see her sister and to bring her suitor with her; Letitia brought her suitor from the country; and when the young men saw the sisters together neither loved his be- trothed as much as he had done before. There was no wish to change over, together neither sister seemed to please, and the young men broke off their engagements.

After this miserable adventure their visits to Dublin be- came more private, they stayed only a few days in town, returning to the country as soon as their clothes came home from the dressmaker's. Many years passed, and when they were middle-aged they had inherited a house in Stanhope Terrace, and they came to live in Dublin for good. They often said they would go abroad, but they had never dared to go until Letitia had been ordered abroad by the doctor. But now that they had got as far as Aix, there was no saying they might not go on to Rome when the season at Aix was over and if Letitia's health had been benefited by the waters. They especially looked forward to going to Geneva, and regretted Mont Blanc could not be seen from Aix. Ismena consoled Letitia. She must put Mont Blanc out of her head. She must think of nothing but her health. They went to the baths every morning after mass, and after a short walk they returned to the *pension* for lunch; in the afternoon they went for drives around the green lake and admired the mountains; in the evening there was always some music in the drawing-room, and though Letitia and Ismena neither played nor sang, they were fond of music.

True that they missed their reading a little, but about a week after their arrival they discovered there was an English library in the town.

They had begun reading Mrs Henry Wood before they left Dublin; Letitia was in the middle of the twelfth and Ismena was finishing the thirteenth volume. The librarian said he could supply them with all her works, and both women had begun to think that their journey south was a complete success. Nothing happened to mar their happiness except that they were forced to sleep in different rooms, and now the little blot on it was about to be wiped away, the people who occupied the double-bedded room were going, and the question arose if they should leave their single rooms.

Ismena, though not impatient to share her nights with her sister, was surprised to hear Letitia say it would be hardly worth while changing, now that they were returning home so soon, and she questioned her sister sharply in the baths that morning, but without obtaining any other answer from her.

Letitia had found a book in her room, and a book that had interested her more than any book she had ever read. She had had occasion to move the chest of drawers, and the book dropped down. It was a French novel of many hundred pages and very closely written, but Letitia's attention had been caught at once. She had opened the book at a page where the French was easy, and she had read of a farmer's beautiful daughter who was going to marry a country doctor. The writer mentioned that when Emma put up her silk parasol

173

the last drops splashed on the distended silk. Letitia had never ready anything like this in Sir Walter Scott or in Mrs Henry Wood. The rain-drops splashing upon the distended silk parasol excited her wonderment, the sensation was so near that she could feel and hear the cold rain on the silk, and that afternoon her sister noticed that she was a little distracted as they drove about the sailless green lake. Ismena admired the vines and thought it exciting to be in the south at the time of the vintage, but Letitia was thinking of the pages she had read before coming out to drive with her sister. They described the farmer's daughter after her marriage. One day Emma was walking in some meadows wondering if her life would always be the same, and her thoughts ran round and round in circles, like the little Italian greyhound in front of her. Letitia had been impressed by the passage, and she felt that she must read this book, not once, but many times. But they were returning to Dublin in a few days, and she could not read the book in that time, nor yet in twenty days. She felt she must read the passage about the greyhound again. The book had probably been forgotten by some former occupant of the room. She did not like to take what did not belong to her, and she could not leave it behind, for then the people in the hotel would think that she had bought the book, that it was hers, and the last three days were spent in thinking of what she should do with it. She could not put it into that trunk; Ismena would be sure to find it, and she did not want Ismena to know that she had read it; she did not want Ismena to read this book; she did not want to discuss this book with Ismena. One can discuss Scott or Dickens or Thackeray, but one cannot discuss emotions that one ought never to have felt with one's sister. Eventually she put the book into the pocket that she wore under her skirt, and it seriously inconvenienced her during the journey. It was difficult for her to get her purse when Ismena asked her for it at the ticket-offices, and the book thumped her legs when she walked, but she did not mind the inconvenience; she was troubled by the thought that she had stolen the book, but her anxiety to know what became of Emma was intense. She thought of the pleasure it would be to read this book in the garden, and almost the first thing she did was to hide her book in the tool-house. It was only in the garden she could read it; in the drawing-room she read Scott with Ismena. There was a rosewood table in the middle of the worn carpet, and the wall-paper was stained and dusty and covered with bad engravings of sentimental pictures, and there were some coloured lithographs of Pyrenean peasants and forgotten prima-donnas. It was in this drawing-room, sitting on the little green sofa or on the old armchairs, sheltered from the flare of the fire by tapestry screens, that Ismena and Letitia read the books that came every week from the circulating library. They always read the same authors, for if they read different authors they would have nothing to talk about, and they enjoyed discussing the heroes and the heroines in the evening before they took their candle and went to their bedroom. It was Ismena who decided which author they should read; her mind was more methodical than Letitia's, and she believed that to derive any considerable benefit from an author he should be read from the earliest to the latest works. Her preference for authors of historical tendencies enabled her to overrule Letitia's taste for modern sentimentalities, and she was now forcing a thorough reading of the Waverley novels upon her sister. Most of their reading was done in the afternoons and evenings. The sisters took the housekeeping and the gardening in turns. At half-past ten every morning they separated for a while. One took up the key-basket, the other looked to see if it were raining; if it were not, she put on her gardening gloves.

'You don't seem to care for *Old Mortality*?'

'I admire it, but I don't care to read it. How many more novels are there, Ismena, in this edition?'

'Thirteen or fourteen, I think, dear; we ought to get through them all before February.'

In those fourteen novels Letitia saw nothing but breastplates and ramparts, and she made up her mind to skip a number of pages when Ismena went to the kitchen.

'Before we went to Aix we began Mrs Henry Wood. You insisted on reading her and you did not finish her works.'

'I read eighteen, and then I began to get confused about the characters and to muddle up the stories. I have read now a dozen volumes of Scott, and I don't seem to have learned anything.'

'What do you mean, Letitia?'

'Well, one learns nothing of life.'

There seemed to be some truth in Letitia's remark, and Ismena thought before she answered –

'You did not like *Felix Holt*, you never finished it, and you said that a novel was intended to amuse rather than to instruct.'

'*Felix Holt*, if I remember right, is about democracy, socialism, and Methodism. I should like to read about life, about what people really feel. I cannot express myself any better, Ismena. Don't you understand that one would like to read about one's own life or about something that might have been one's life?'

'But no one could write a novel about our lives; nothing very much seems to have happened in them.'

Letitia heard her go downstairs to the kitchen, and she put the marker twenty and odd pages farther than she had read. She turned on the sofa and looked out of the window. There were clouds, but it was still fine, and Letitia decided that this was the moment to go into the garden.

Their garden was a small square facing the street in which they lived. It looked as if it should be the common property of those living in the street, but the landlord had found that if he allowed all the tenants to walk in the garden no one walked in it at all. For it to be enjoyed by someone it had to become the exclusive property of one house, and it had been given to the Misses O'Hara to keep in order. They had a pretty taste in gardening, and they kept it in beautiful order.

Along the street there were hawthorn-trees and along one wall many lilac-bushes and some apple-trees, and the lilacs grew in such abundance that their branches joined overhead, making a shady little avenue. The tool-house was at the end of this avenue, and Letitia could read there in safety; her sister could not come upon her unawares; the moment the garden gate opened Letitia could hide her novel behind the loose planks.

She could generally get about one hour a day by herself in the garden, and she read about Emma's love of Rudolph, and the scene where she sees him for the last time in the garden impressed her very much, and while talking to her sister of things that did not interest her she remembered how the ripe peach had broken from its stalk and had fallen with a thud in the quiet midnight. She had read of the passionate yearning of this wife of the country doctor, the wife always looking to something beyond her life and the husband quite contented in his life. The sensation that the book exhaled of Emma's empty days was extraordinarly intense. There was a description of how Emma looked out of the window in the morning, how she watched her husband ride away to visit his patients. Later, a clerk came to fill her empty days with desire again, and Letitia was extraordinarily impressed by a passage describing how the husband, lying by his wife's side, thinks of the child in the cradle, what she will be like when she grows up, etc., while Emmas dreams of a romantic elopement in a coach drawn through mountain passes by four horses. Letitia read that Emma hardly heard her husband's breathing, so intently did she listen to the tinkling of the postilion bells and the sound of distant water-falls.

Rudolph was a neighbour, and Emma had been able to see Rudolph in her own house or in his, but she had to go to Rouen to see the clerk, and to go to Rouen she required money, and Letitia read how Emma used to borrow from a usurer. When the usurer gave her the money all she saw in it, all it represented to her, was a number of visits to Rouen. Emma used to meet her lover in a hotel. The descriptions of their meetings frightened Letitia, and she sometimes thought she was not justified in reading any more, but her scruple died from her in an extraordinary sense of bewilderment and curiosity.

The garden gate closed with a snap, and she slipped the book behind the loose woodwork of the shed and, catching up a rake, went to meet her sister.

Ismena had come to ask her sister if she had seen the French dictionary. She had been writing to some of her friends in Aix and wanted to know how to spell a word. Letitia told her sister that she thought she would find the dictionary in the study, and she resolved to put it there when they went in to lunch.

They walked across the sward to the bare borders. The sunflowers had died and the dahlias had been put away for the winter, but the chrysanthemums were still flowering.

After lunch Ismena brought her sister out with her to pay some visits, and next day it rained. It rained all the week, and they read the Waverley novels under the great Victorian chandelier. Letitia often thought of putting on her waterproof and running down to the tool-house to fetch her book. The Waverley novels were books, and Mrs Henry Wood's novels were books, but this book was life or very nearly. Letitia knew she never would get nearer life than this book, and she waited impatiently for another dry day. Whenever there was a dry hour Ismena was with her, and it looked as if the Waverley novels would be finished before she got into the garden again. She was now trying to read *The Talisman*, but she seemed to make no progress, and she had to move her marker on several pages in order to deceive Ismena. While skipping the last half of this book she had to deceive Ismena further. She held the book as if she were reading it, and fixed her thoughts on Emma and the usurer. There could be but one end – the convent, or her husband might die and she might marry the clerk. But then she would not be punished for her sins! Then Rudolph was her first love, and to marry him not only the husband but the clerk would have to die. But these endings were the endings that Scott or Mrs Henry Wood would have chosen, and Letitia wondered.

At last a fine day came, but that morning Letitia awoke with a bad throat, and her throat grew worse all day. Next day she could hardly speak, and Ismena had to send for their doctor; but he assured her there was no cause for alarm, that her sister was not suffering from diphtheria. An hour later the parlour maid said to a visitor –

'Miss O'Hara is ill, she is in bed, but Miss Ismena would like to see you.'

Ismena explained that, although her sister could not speak, there was no cause for alarm; the doctor said so. The visitor thought she would send in a specialist, but Ismena never permitted any interference, and two days after Letitia was dead. She died the evening of the following day. About four o'clock she made signs that she wanted to write, and Ismena handed her a sheet of note-paper and a pencil, and she wrote, '*There is a brown-paper parcel in the summer-house.*' She thought that if she got better, she could read the book in bed; if she got worse, she would ask the nurse to burn it.

But it took Ismena a very long time to find the book, so securely had it been hidden, and during that time Letitia's throat had inflamed still further, and when Ismena returned Letitia was dead.

Had it not been for the garden Ismena would not have lived; it was the garden that helped her to forget her grief. She digged in the garden all the spring, and in June Ismena's flower-beds were the admiration of the neighbourhood. But one day as she crossed the sward going to the tool-house she remembered that she had gone there to fetch a brown-paper parcel for her sister. She had taken a long time to find it, and when she brought it to her sister, her sister was dead. She left the garden and searched for it; she remembered that it looked like a book. At last she found it, and it was a book. She had read it in France long ago; she remembered who had given her the book, and wondering what had become of him she stood for a long time watching the trees waving in the garden.

'But how did Letitia come upon this book? Who could have given it to her? Now I know why she sat in the garden so often. Now I know what became of the French dictionary. Oh,' she said, 'who ever would have thought this of Letitia!'

The Voice of the Mountain

Mary Cronin was an only daughter and had plenty of money, and one day coming home from Mass she told her father that she would marry Dan Coogan. Her father said:

'Well, Mary, I had hoped for a richer man, but Dan is a good boy, who will work the farm well and make you happy.'

'I'll tell him what you say,' said Mary, and she called after Dan, and from that day the neighbours looked upon them as married. There was great dancing and singing in the farmhouse on Sunday evenings, the piper did not leave the kitchen until midnight, and many a Monday morning the neighbours walked down the village street in the dawn light.

Dan lived in a hill village two miles distant, where his father worked a little farm of about ten acres. This farm was to go to his brother, and before Dan's courting of Mary Cronin the price of his passage to America had been spoken of as his fortune.

'America is the place for the man who has pluck in him and who wants to work and to make money. Here you think of nothing but spending your wages in the public-house. You are always looking for your neighbours' opinions because you've no principles of your own. That is not the way in America.'

It was thought that he might praise America without dispraising Ireland.

'You're a weak people, too lazy to make your own clothes. There is many a girl in the village who would go without a new dress if she had to make it herself.'

If another said half as much as Dan he would have been hunted out of the parish, but no one minded him. It was just as if they knew he would not be like this always, and that they must have patience with him. His words seemed unlike him, for there was a dream in his blue eyes – they seemed to say, 'I love you,' and everyone sympathized with Mary.

And now, since his marriage was settled the neighbours had begun to ask if he was going to stay with them, and the answer was that old Cronin would not let him have his daughter if he did not mean to stay at home and work the farm. Old Cronin saw the makings of a good man in Dan, and old Cronin was never far wrong. Dan was proud of his father-in-law's opinion. And he was proud of himself: in getting Mary he had 'done out' the whole country. Dan thought little of Irish courtship, 'running to the priest to ask him to make their marriages for them', he said to himself as he walked home after a dance at the Cronins', and he remembered with satisfaction how he had looked the girl straight in the eyes and put his arm about her.

He had just bidden Mary and the neighbours who had come to the dance 'good-night', and it was not many more times he'd be walking this mountain road; in a fortnight he would be living with his father-in-law, who had a farm of eighty acres, and a fine house two storeys high, and he thought of the fine bedroom he would sleep in, and the gig he would drive to Dublin. If there was one thing Dan hated more than another it was a bare mountain side, and as he walked home he gloated in the thought that his lot would be for henceforth in the snug plain beneath the hills.

He walked, swinging his stick, thinking the world very pleasant, and his own life as the principal thing in it.

His way led through a dark wood where the trees hung thickly, and a little further on there was an old churchyard, where no one had been buried seemingly for centuries, so ruinous were the graves, and a little further on there was a fragment of a church, a carved doorway, and Dan had seen many people admiring this crumbling arch. He could distinguish the carving in the moonlight, and he stood wondering how people could be so foolish as to waste time dreaming

181

over a crumbling stone. America was the country for him. But he had given up America for Mary's sake.

There was a little wind in the ash trees and the trembling foliage made him tremble. 'They seem very strange,' he thought, and Dan supposed it was the night time that made them like living things. Behind them lay the bare mountain valley. He had just been thinking that he hated this landscape, and now was surprised and disappointed to find that he hated it no longer. There was a wistfulness in the distance, and it seemed to steal into his heart and to draw him out of himself, out of the self he had known always, and into another self, an unspotted self, a second self. And in the sway of his second self he began to walk timidly, and he looked about him as one might in some sacred place; and he did not dare to swing his stick lest he should break the furze blossoms, nor did he kick the stones from the path, for he did not despise them any longer.

A little further on there was a great Druid stone, or was it a stone that some deluge had carried down the hill and left upon four upright stones? He had heard this stone had been an altar and that the Druids came there to worship the sun, but he had not listened to these stories, they had gone in one ear and out through the other as wind goes through a crack in the door. But now these stories were like music in his ears, and the earth that he had cared for only to plant potatoes in and that he had thought good for nothing else had become possessed of an extreme sweetness, and after trying to resist the impulse, for it seemed a mad impulse, he yielded to it, and flinging himself on the ground kissed the earth. Remembering how different his thoughts were a moment ago, he felt a little dazed and he thought he must be going mad.

As he rose from his knees he saw cattle grazing, and they moved so mysteriously that they seemed like exhalations, and the ash trees and the grey stones around which they grazed seemed almost as alive as they. 'We're all living together in the earth.' The words came into his mind suddenly – 'all things are part of the earth, part of its life, and we're all doing the earth's bidding.'

Through a great clearness of mind he looked back into the

time of the Druids, and after seeing them he saw the Danes, and he saw Brian in the forest, and a great king coming to meet him. For after years of war against the Danes Brian had been left with only fifteen followers, and standing in rags before the king he had told him that the stranger must be driven out. A century later a traitor had brought the English over, and the battle against the stranger had been continued through the centuries. After the siege of Limerick the 'wild geese' had fled to France and Austria to fight the stranger abroad when they could fight him at home no longer. Their desire to get rid of the stranger had never come to an end. He seemed to know things he had never learned; the earth seemed to whisper everything he needed to know; the blood that had been shed seemed his blood; the wrongs that had been done were his wrongs, and he learned all these things that night from the hill.

Half way down the hill, on a level with his eyes, there was a fir wood, and over the tops of the fir trees a long plain, and the moon shone so brightly that he could follow the lines of the field and the lines of the coast. One field fixed his attention; its lines were like the lines of a horseshoe, and about it were dim fields, and a little way out to sea Howth floated in the moonlight as shapely, as mysteriously, as an island in the legends of the Golden Age.

Dan wandered about till the moon faded, thinking of the limitless years behind him when he was part of the earth, and of the limitless years in front of him when he would be part of the earth again, and all the while he saw clouds rising up in the west, and they were blown southward. One cloud seemed to lead the others, and when the dawn began the outlines of the coast seemed to enclose his life, and the mountain seemed to whisper a message, and in their message were the names of Emmet, Wolfe Tone, Mitchell and Stephens.

'Home,' he cried; 'why should I go home? What shall I find at home?'

And he went home scared by his own folly, and lay down on his bed.

Next morning he had forgotten a great part of his ravings,

and went to his work as usual, and came to his dinner as usual. But at night a great craving came upon him, and, telling his father and mother he was going to see Mary Cronin, he walked amid the hills; every night he learned to love them and to understand them better. All this time his father and mother did not know where he went after nightfall and they wondered greatly until a goat-herd told them he had seen Dan at dawn on the brow of the hill, and then Dan had talked to him of foreign parts.

He seemed to lose interest in the ordinary things, and when they spoke of the farm, of the planting of potatoes, of the sowing of corn, of the price of pigs and cattle, he hardly seemed to hear what they were saying, and when they asked him of what he was thinking he started like one who had been awakened suddenly. When they asked him if he wished to leave them he said he did not know, and a moment afterwards he said he wished to go away; and when they asked him where, he said he saw a lonely country, and that people were marching through the hills.

'Don't ask me any more,' he said, 'my mind is wandering, and you only make it wander more when you question me.'

They thought it was to America he wanted to go, and when he said no they thought of Australia. The Coogans were afraid old Cronin would hear about Dan, and, of course, he heard of his talk of going away, and he spoke to Mary and wished her to break off the marriage. Wherever Dan might go she would go with him, she said. But her heart was very sore, and the tales she heard made her weep.

'These hills have bewitched him,' she said.

'They tell me,' said Mrs Coogan, 'that he stands for hours looking across the sea as if he were waiting for a ship to come to take him away. You'll find him under the ash trees sitting on a bit of wall.'

Mary sought him on the hillside. The landscape was reddening, the leaves hung listless, and high up in the soft autumn weather a flock of great birds with outstretched necks were flying southward.

'Winter must have begun early in the north,' said Dan; 'there must be snow and ice there or the wild geese would

184

not be flying south. They come in from all sides, it is said, to their leader.'

'It is curious,' said Mary, 'that they never miss their way.'

'Nor will that bird miss its way,' said Dan, pointing to a cuckoo perched on the wall. 'To-day or to-morrow, when the instinct is ripe in him, he will go all by himself to a place where he has never been, thousands of miles away, and there will be no mistake.'

'Why do you speak to me, Dan, about these birds? Is it because you feel like them?'

'I suppose that is it, Mary; I feel as if I must go. But the birds know where they are going.'

He got off the wall and they walked home together. But he could give her no straight answer, and he looked at her in a way that made her fear that he cared for her no longer.

'Dan, if you have ceased to care for me, tell me, but if you want me to go to America I will go. Do you not care for Ireland any longer?'

'I never loved Ireland before; it is now that I am beginning to love her.'

'And it is now,' she said, 'you want to leave Ireland.'

They entered the kitchen talking of New Zealand; but it was not to New Zealand nor to Canada that he wanted to go.

'What have I done to make you angry with me, Dan, to make you care less for me than you did?'

'You are just as young and as good and as comely as before.'

'And yet you don't want to marry me?'

'Something is calling me. Are you not afraid to marry me? You have heard them say that I was going out of my mind.'

'Oh, Dan, you want to frighten me so that I may say I don't want to marry you. But you will never get me to say that. Dan, Dan, what have I done?'

'Someone is calling me. Mary, I cannot help myself. It is as if someone was calling me from over the sea.'

When he said this they thought for certain that he was going mad and they looked round the kitchen, and only Dan was quite calm.

'I don't think,' he said, 'I am going mad, only I know that I must go away.'

Then he seemed as if he were holding something back, and they pressed him to speak, but he did not speak for a little while.

'I know no more reason of all this than you. But it is to Africa I am going.'

'Was it a fairy,' said his mother, 'that told you to go to Africa last night when you were at the top of the hill?'

'No, mother, I saw no fairy; and you may think me mad if you like and Mary may think me mad if she likes.'

He turned to go out of the door, but Mary stopped him.

'I don't think you mad. I will go to Africa with you if you think better of Africa than America.'

He looked at her tenderly, like one who appreciates a sacrifice and is not able to accept it.

At that moment a footstep was heard at the door, and the priest came in with a paper in his hand.

'There's war in Africa,' he said, 'or there soon will be. The Boers have broken out, and they say that they are going to drive the English into the sea.'

Dan stood listening, the priest seemed to be telling him of a dream he had dreamed and had almost forgotten. He stood listening open-eyed, remembering the shapes he had seen in the clouds, how one cloud had seemed like a warrior, and how clouds had come up from the west, and how the wind had borne them southward in tumult. The priest told that loyal Irishmen were flocking to the standard of another captain, an inheritor of the great tradition, and Dan knew that he was drawn by the same impulse, and he said:

'I knew of this war on the mountain. That is what the mountain was saying to me.'

'But,' said Mary, 'if you go out there, you may be killed, and what shall I do if you are killed?'

He did not seem to hear her.

'But if you are not shot by the British they may take you prisoner and they will hang you.'

'I shall not be taken a prisoner; they will take me dead if they take me at all.'

'But if you come back you will marry me.'

'I shan't forget you, dear.'

186

'But do you know if you will come back?'

'My mind is full of going, I know nothing else.'

Dan and Mary walked out of the house together, and for the first time for many weeks there was a happy look on Dan's face. He walked with his arm about her, and, standing among the furze bushes, he told her it was here he had heard the voice of the mountain.

'And you used to think that you hated this mountain and liked our snug fields far better.'

'So I did, but we do not know what is in us until the time comes. I hated that hill, for it was the barest, and it was out of that hillside that the whisper came – and it was there – it was there everything happened.'

He looked at her, wondering if she had understood him. She said that she had, and he went away very happy. But he did not leave her alone, the hills were henceforth her company. They were always responsive and always kind, and she did not look in the newspapers for news of Dan. She knew she would be the first to have news if anything were to happen to him. She knew that she would see him on the hillside.

A Flood

It seemed to him that he was in very cold muddy water full of little waves, and that by treading water and putting forth all his strength he was able to keep himself above them. But the wind blew them higher; they slapped him in the mouth, and he had much trouble in getting his breath between. All of a sudden it occurred to him that it would be much easier to abandon this painful striving and to lie back amid the waves. He took a long deep breath, the water slipped down into his lungs, and he lay quite natural and comfortable until a dinning sound began over his head. He tried to sink deeper into the stream, but the noise grew louder and he could not but think that he was rising to the surface. At last he opened his eyes.

'It's this infernal rain on the roof that makes me dream,' he said.

A bed had been made up for him in the kitchen on three chairs, and when he awoke he found himself sitting bolt upright with his arms bent as if he were treading water, his legs stiff and numbed with cold. The hearth was full of ashes with a last spark fading in the dawn light, and catching an end of his blanket he rubbed his hands against it. His perceptions lengthened out and he went to the window, but seeing water everywhere he fancied for a moment that he must be still dreaming. The pigs had broken out of their sties and were swimming amid various wreckage; the house dog was swimming alongside of his kennel; the hens rose in short flights – two were already drowned, the others were drowning – but the cock perched on his coop crowed defiantly.

A Flood

Tom looked to where the day was breaking; a thin pale light soaked slowly through the clouds, and he could just distinguish the tops of the willows above the water.

The staircase behind him creaked, and turning hurriedly he saw old Daddy Lupton awful in his night-shirt, like Death himself coming to bid him good morning.

'Well,' said Daddy, 'what do 'ee think about the jade now? She makes one feel young again. The biggest flood we've had these fifty years.'

The old man's levity inspired hope in Tom that the river would not rise any higher, and that the house was not in danger. Tom asked him if this were so, but Daddy continued to babble of a great flood of sixty years ago in which he had nearly lost his life. A big flood it was, but nothing to the great flood of nearly eighty years ago. It had carried a village quite away, and the old man followed Tom to the window, telling him how the water had come down the valley faster than a horse could gallop.

'All my brothers and sisters were drowned, father and mother too; but the cradle floated right away as far as Harebridge, where it was picked up by a party in a boat. There h'ant been no flood to speak of since then. A fine jade she once was, and when it rained like this we used to lie quaking in our beds. Now we sleep sound enough.'

'I must wake 'em,' said Tom.

He rushed upstairs, called out, and in a few minutes the pointsman and his family were standing in the kitchen: John Lupton, a tall man with a long neck and thin square shoulders, a red beard and small queer eyes and hands freckled and hairy, and Margaret Lupton, his wife, a pleasant portly woman of forty, with soft blue eyes and regular features. Her daughter, Liz, took after her father – a thin-shouldered, thin-featured girl with small ardent eyes and dark reddish crinkly hair. But Billy, Liz's brother, took after his mother. He was very like her, the same soft oval face with blue eyes and no distinctive feature; the same sweet retiring nature, more of a girl than a boy; but the boy in him expressed a certain curiosity for Tom's boat.

'Shall we go in the boat, Father?'

'What boat, sonny?'

'Tom's boat.'

'Tom's boat wouldn't hold us all.'

'We needn't all go together.'

'My boat is far enough from 'ere by this time,' said Tom, 'or most like she's at the bottom of the river. I tied her last night to the old willow.'

Tom was a fair-complexioned, broad-shouldered young fellow, an apple grower that lived on the other side of the river. He and Liz were to be married at the end of the week, and yesterday being Sunday he had rowed himself across at sundown, and they had gone for their wonted walk. When they came home supper was on the table, and the hours after had gone by pleasantly, his arm being round Liz's waist, till the time came for him to bid her good night, but on seeing the swollen river she had turned her pretty freckled face to his and dissuaded him, and they had returned to the cottage.

'I never seed the river rise so quickly afore,' said Lupton.

'I did. I did.'

It was Daddy that had answered. He was still in his nightshirt, and his last tooth shook in his white beard.

'Go and dress 'eeself, Father. And why, Mother, don't 'ee light the fire? The morning is that rare cold we'll all be the better for a cup of tea.'

'Yes, Father, I don't be long now,' and she began breaking sticks.

While the kettle was boiling Tom told them that the pigs had broken out of their sties; they lamented the loss of their winter food, and Billy burst into tears on hearing that Peter – his friend, Peter, the house dog – had gone away, swimming after his kennel.

'Come, let us sit down to breakfast,' Lupton said.

But they had hardly tasted their tea when Billy cried out: 'Father, Father, the water be coming in under the door yonder. Take me on 'ee knee, Father. 'Ee did promise to take me to Harebridge. But if I drown I shall never see the circus.'

Lupton took the little chap on his knee.

'There will be no danger of that. Grandfather will tell

190

'ee that this be nothing to the floods he knew when he was a little boy.'

The water continued to come under the door, collecting where the asphalted floor had been worn, and they watched it rising out of these slight holes and coming towards the table. It came at first very slowly, and then suddenly it rose over their knees, and while Mrs Lupton took the baby out of the cot the others searched for tea, sugar, bacon, eggs, coal, and candles.

'We shall be wanting all these things,' Lupton said, 'for the water may keep us upstairs for hours to come.'

And they were very wet when they assembled in Lupton's bedroom. Lupton emptied his big boots out of the window and called on Tom to do the same. Liz wrung out her petticoats, and standing round the table they supped their tea and ate some slices of bread and butter. The baby had been laid asleep on the bed, and Daddy sat by the baby softening his bread in his mug of tea, mumbling to himself, his fading brain full of incoherent recollections.

'The folk in them fine houses will be surprised to see the water at the bottom of their parks,' said Lupton, to break an oppressive silence.

'They be like to live so high up the water will never reach them,' Mrs Lupton answered.

'It h'ain't like them to think for to send us 'elp.'

'They 'aven't no boats up yonder,' said Tom. 'They be a good mile up from the river.'

'Tom, dear, it's a pity your boat be gone, for you might have row'd me right into Harebridge.'

'Yes, Liz, if you'd set still I might have taken 'ee through them currents, or as likely we might have gotten sucked under by an eddy, or a hole be knocked in the boat by some floating baulk.'

'I be lighter than Liz; would 'ee take me, Tom?' said Billy.

As the tops of the apple trees were still visible they judged the depth of the water to be about ten feet. Cattle passed the window, some swimming strong and well, others nearly exhausted. A dead horse whirled past, its poor neck stretched out lamentably, and they all laughed at the fox that floated so peacefully in the middle of a drowned hen-roost. The apples came by in great numbers; Billy forgot his fears in his desire to clutch some, and a little later they saw two great trees rolling towards the pointsman's box.

'There she goes!' cried Lupton. 'And how she do swim! She'd put me into the quay at Harebridge as well as a steam packet.'

There was nothing to do but to watch and wonder if the flood was rising. Liz was certain it was sinking, and pointing to a post she said there was no sign of it ten minutes before. Lupton was not so sure, and when the post disappeared, which it did a few minutes afterwards, there could be no hope at all that the flood was not still rising, and then everyone began to wonder what the cause of the flood might be, and everyone, except Daddy, waited for Lupton to speak. But he was loth to tell them that he could only understand the great rush of water if the embankments up yonder at the factories had broken, and if that were so, 'God help them!' As Lupton said these last words their faces grew paler, all except Billy, who returned innocently to his grandfather to ask if he didn't think the flood was as big now as the great flood of sixty years ago.

'It be a flood and a big one, but the biggest of all was eighty years ago, when my cradle was washed away down to Harebridge and stuck fast in the alder.' And he began to tell a story of other children whose cradles had been carried just down to the sea, frightening everyone with his loquacity.

'Tom, 'as 'ee a bit of baccy to give to Daddy to stop his jaw with?' said John Lupton.

Tom fumbled in his pockets, and when their eyes met each read his own thoughts in the other's face.

'We must be doing something, that's certain,' said Tom. 'But what shall we be doing?'

'Yes, we must be astirring,' Lupton answered. And without another word he began to look about the room. 'Now, if we 'ad but a few bits of timber we could make a raft. It's a pity that bedstead is of iron.'

Tom, who had gone back to the window, cried suddenly:

'Give a hand here, John, for 'ee was talking about a raft and blowed if I 'aven't gotten one.'

And looking over Tom's shoulder Lupton saw that he had caught a few planks tied together – a slender raft that somebody up yonder had launched as a last hope.

'Very likely so,' said Lupton, 'anyhow it is ours. It might carry one of us.'

'Yes, one of us might chance his life on it and bring back 'elp.'

'That's right enough; it's an off-chance, but one of us had better risk it. Get along, lad, get along, and come back in a boat.'

'Don't leave me, Tom,' cried Liz; 'let us be drowned together.'

'Be 'ee mazed, lass?' said Lupton; 'for Tom will manage right well on them planks, and he'll come back in a boat.'

'No, Father, no; I'd sooner die with Tom than live without him.'

' 'Ee ain't the only one; 'ee'd better let him go or yonder church will see no wedding party next Monday. Tom, get astride of them planks at once.'

'I think I'd better take this 'ere shutter with me'; and while it was lifted from its hinges Lupton lashed two broom handles together.

'Not much of a punt pole, but the best I can give, and maybe it will get 'ee out of the current.'

But Liz held Tom back.

'Yes, Liz, Tom loves 'ee and that is why he must go: Come, girl, hands off. I don't want to be rough with 'ee, but Tom must take the risk of them planks. Now, Tom.'

And away he went in a swirl, trying his best to reach bottom with his broom handles, but the raft rolled in the current, and Liz's last sight of her lover was when he attempted to seize some willow branches. The raft slid from under his feet, and he fell into the flood.

'He's gone from 'ee now, and we shall soon follow after if we don't bestir ourselves.'

'It matters naught to me now,' said Liz.

'I ne'er seen one mazed like 'ee afore.'

'But I seed many; sixty years ago all the sweethearts were parted, and by the score. The jade got them, here a girl and there a boy, all but Daddy Lupton, for a wise woman said she shouldn't get 'im, and her word came true. I ain't afeard of 'er. I've seen 'er in worse tantrums than to-day. It's the rheumatics that I'm afeard of. These 'ere walls will be that damp, will be that . . . ' The old man's voice died away in the whiteness of his beard.

At that moment three tiles fell from the roof; a large hole appeared in one of the walls, and they all felt that the house was falling about them bit by bit. But the immediate danger was from the great baulks that the current swept down. If any one of these were to strike the house, Lupton said, it must topple over into the flood, and lest their luck shouldn't last Lupton took a sheet from the bed and climbed on to the roof.

'See a boat coming, Liz?' her mother asked, for Liz sat looking towards some willows as if she saw something.

'No boat will come for me. I want no boat to come for me.'

'Come, Liz, come, Liz, I wouldn't have 'ee talk like that,' her mother answered. The baby began to cry for the breast, and while suckling Mrs Lupton raised her head to her husband sitting on the broken wall, but he waved the sheet so despairingly that she did not dare to ask him if a boat were coming.

'I can't sit up 'ere any longer,' he said at last. 'Let us do something. I don't mind what, so long as it keeps me from thinking.'

'I think we'd better say our prayers,' said Mrs Lupton.

'Prayers? No, I can say no prayers. I'm too bothered; I want something that will keep me from thinking. The babbling of that water will drive us mad if we don't do something. Let us tell stories. Liz, don't sit there looking through the room or what's left of it. You read stories in the papers, can't you tell us one of them?'

Liz shook her head. He asked for the paper; she answered that it was downstairs, and begged that she might take his place on the corner of the wall and wave the sheet on the chance that a boat might be passing within hail.

'She don't pay no attention to what we're saying,' said Lupton. 'Now that Tom's gone I think she'd just as lief make away with herself . . . and what may 'ee be smiling at so heartily, Father? 'Ee and the baby are the only two that can smile this morning.'

'What be I smiling at? I heard 'ee speak just now of stories. I can zay one, lots of 'em.'

'Then tell us a story, Father, and a good one. It'll keep our thoughts from that babbling water.'

'Well, I was just a-thinking. It be now seventy years ago . . . '

'Well, tell us about it.'

'I've said it was night seventy years ago; I was a growing lad at the time. I remember it as if it were yesterday. Me and Bill Slater was pals. At that time Bill was going to be married; I can see her now, a fine elegant lass, for all the world like our Liz. It had been raining for weeks and weeks – much the same kind of weather as we've had lately, only worse, and the river . . . '

'We don't want to hear about the river; we want to forget it. I suppose 'ee wants to tell us that Bill Slater and his lass was drowned? We don't want that sort of story, we wants a cheerful story with lots of happiness in it.'

'I only knows stories about those that the river took – plenty of 'em, plenty of 'em. The jade didn't get me, for a wise woman said that she would never get me.'

'Did she say, Daddy, that them that was with 'ee was safe too?'

Daddy was only sure of his own safety; and waking suddenly he said – 'I've 'eard John say that 'ee would banish thinking with something. Us better have some cards then. Cards will wake us up.'

'The old chap's right,' said Lupton. 'Where be the cards? Be they downstairs too? Where's Liz?' Lupton climbed to her place, and after looking round he turned to those in the room and shook his head. 'I'm afraid Liz has gone after her sweetheart.'

'Very likely,' said Daddy. 'The jade always gets them in the end. Where be the cards?'

Yes, where be the cards?' Lupton answered almost savagely. 'Be they downstairs, Mother?'

'No, John; they be in the drawer of the table.'

'Then, let's have them out. What shall we play? Half-penny nap? Come, Mother, and Billy too, and Daddy. Come, pull your chairs round. I gave 'ee sixpence yesterday, Father. Find them out; 'ee can't have spent them, and Mother have 'ee any coppers?'

'I've near a shilling in coppers. That will do for Billy and myself.'

As there were only three chairs the table was pulled up to the bed where Daddy was sitting.

'Come, let us play, let us play,' Lupton cried impatiently.

'I'm thinking of the baby,' said Mrs Lupton. 'How unsuspecting he do sleep there.'

'Never mind the baby, Mother; think of your cards.'

After playing for some time Lupton found he had lost threepence.

'I never seed such luck,' he exclaimed.

They played another round; again Lupton went nap and again he lost.

'Perhaps it will be them that loses that'll be saved,' he said, shuffling the cards.

'Father, I can't play,' said Billy.

'Why can't you play, my boy? Ain't Mother a-teaching 'ee?'

'Yes, Father, but I can't think of the cards; dead things be floating past the window. May I go and sit where I can't see them?'

'Yes, my boy, come and sit on my knee. Look over my cards; but mustn't tell them what I've gotten.'

'Grandfather seems to be winning; he has gotten all the coppers, Father.'

'Yes, my boy, Grandfather is winning.'

'And what will he do with the winnings if he be drowned, Father?'

'Grandfather don't think he will be drowned.'

A Flood

The old man chuckled, and turned over his coppers. His
winnings meant a double allowance of tobacco and a glass of
ale, and he thought of the second glass of ale he would have if
he won again.

'Whose turn is it to play?' said Daddy.

'Mine,' said Lupton, 'and I'll go nap again.'

"E'll go nap again.'

Lupton lost again, but this time instead of cursing his luck
he remained silent, and at that moment the rush of water
beneath their feet sounded more ominous than ever.

'I'll play no more,' said Lupton. 'I dunno what I be doing.
There's naught in my head but the babbling of that water.'

A tile slid down the roof, they sprang to their feet, and
then they heard a splash. The old man played with his
winnings and Billy began to cry.

'It's sure and certain enough now that no help will come
for us,' said Mrs Lupton. 'Let's put away the cards and say
our prayers, and 'ee might tell us a verse out of the Bible,
John.'

'Very well, let's have a prayer. Father, give over counting
your money.'

'Then no one be coming to save us,' cried Billy. 'I don't
want to drown, Father. I be too young to drown. Grandfather's too old and baby too young to think much about
drowning. But if we drown to-day, Father, I shall never see
the circus.'

'Kneel down, my boy; perhaps God might save us if we
pray to Him.'

'Oh, God, merciful Saviour, who has power over all
things, save us. Oh, Lord, save us.'

'Go on praying, Mother,' Lupton said, as he rose from his
knees, and taking another sheet from the bed he climbed to
the top of the broken wall; but he had hardly reached it when
some bricks gave way and he fell backward and drowned.
Mrs Lupton prayed intermittently, and every now and then a
tile splashed into the water.

'The way to manage 'er is take 'er easy. She won't stand no
bullying, and them giddy young folks will bully 'er, so she
always goes for 'em.'

197

In Minor Keys

Five or six tiles fell, the house rocked a little, and they could feel the water lifting the floor under their feet.

'Mother,' said Billy; the child was so calm, so earnest in his manner, that he seemed suddenly to have grown older. 'Mother, dear, tell me the truth – be I going to drown? We have prayed together, but God don't seem like saving us. I'm afraid, Mother; bain't you afraid? Father's gone and Liz's gone and Tom's gone, all except Grandfather and us. Grandfather and the baby don't seem afraid. Mother, let me 'ave your 'and; 'ee won't lose hold of me.'

Mrs Lupton took the baby from the bed and looked at it, and when she looked up she saw the old man playing with the coppers he had won.

'Does drowning hurt very much, Mother?'

The wall wavered about them, some bricks fell out of it; Billy was struck by one, struggled a little way, and fell through the floor. The floor broke again, and another piece of the roof came away, and Mrs Lupton closed her eyes and waited for death. But death did not seem to come, and when she opened her eyes she saw that the floor had snapped at her feet and the old man was standing behind her.

'A darned narrow escape,' he muttered. 'As near as I have had yet.'

'They're gone, they be all gone, all of them. Baby and all.'

''Ee must have let her slip when the roof came in.'

'I let the baby slip!' And looking down she saw the child floating among broken things.

'Well, that was a narrow escape,' chimed the quaking voice of the octogenarian. 'I'm sore afraid the house is in a bad way. I seed many like . . . '

By some great beams the south wall still held firm, and with it the few feet of floor on which they were standing.

'They be bound to send a boat afore long, or else the wise woman . . . Everything's gone – table, cards and a shilling in coppers.'

'They're all gone; everything is gone.'

'Yes, the jade's got 'em. She 'as brought near every one I knew at one time or the other.'

Then the wild grief of the woman seemed to wake reason

in Daddy's failing brain.

Her eyes were fixed on the bodies of her husband and child dashed to and fro and sucked under by the current, appearing and disappearing among the wreckage.

'I can't grieve like that; I ken grieve no more. I'm too old, and all excepting me baccy and the rheumatics are the same to me now.'

'Saved!' cried a voice. 'Give way, my lads, give way.'

'Saved, and the others gone!' cried Mrs Lupton, and as the boat approached from one side she flung herself into the flood from the other.

'Are you the only one left?' cried a man as the boat came alongside.

'Yes, the jade 'as got all the others. There, they be down there; and my daughter-in-law has just gone after them, jumped right in after them. But it was told by a wise woman that the jade should never get me, and her words comes true.'

'Now then, old gent, let me get hold of you. Be careful where you step. Do nothing to risk your valuable life. There you are, safe, safe from everything but the rheumatics.'

'They be very bad at times, and I must be careful of myself this winter.'

At the Turn of the Road

An Irish Girl's Love Story

The nightingales had sung to within two hours of the dawn, and when the stars receded and the moon paled in the south, the owls returned to their belfries, the kites and nightjars to their perches; already the badger was rolled in sleep in his deep burrow, the hedgehog in his nest of leaves, but even at dawn the world is never wholly silent, and a belated vixen struggled with a chortling hen in the worn cart-track leading to the village of Brandlesbury, nearly losing her hold of the fowl, so surprised was she at the sight of a girl coming from the forest at such an hour; but perceiving quickly that the intruder was deep in thought, she gripped the fowl tighter and trotted away to her cubs, already forgetful of the interruption. And in an equal forgetfulness Cicely Wyatt pursued her way down the loose, crumbling track, her shoes gathering sand at every step, till she came to Wyatt's grocery store.

She had never seen the day breaking before, and for that reason or another she stopped to admire the ascending light, and after watching some rosy clouds gathering above the sun, yet unrisen, she put her key into the lock. It was then that a blackbird began to whistle from an apple bough across the way; not long after, a thrush from a naked ash commenced to sing little snatches of song, and for nearly two hours little else was heard but these two songsters.

At six a jingle of harness jarred the sequence of sweet sounds as the carter's whip cracked on his team to their daily labour. At eight o'clock dogs were let through the doorways and ran barking down the street, and almost at the same moment the shutters of the grocery store came down with a clang, and Fred Wyatt began to consider the best display he could make of his vegetables.

His baskets of cabbages, onions, cucumbers, carrots and turnips gave him no trouble, and it was not till he came to a large sack of potatoes that he stopped to take breath.

'Now, what 'aste be thee in to open thy shop?' asked a lusty fellow, a farrier, on the way to his forge. 'A few minutes sooner than the Fitches open theirs will be all thou'lt get for thy pains.'

'I open my store when it pleases me, without a thought for when the Fitches open theirs.'

'As well thou mayst, for isn't young Sidney to wed thy daughter and make one family and one store?'

'He that has worked for forty year will work on till his breath stops altogether.' And the little fat, colourless man, whose short cropped beard was already full of grey hairs, though he was not many more years than forty, began again his struggle with the sack.

'I'd give thee a 'and, Fred Wyatt, but thou'rt wasting thy strength over them potatoes without reason, I'm thinking, for who do I see in the distance but Tom Huggett, a-coming up with big strides as if he guessed as he couldn't come fast enough to save thee from doing thyself a mischief.'

'I thank thee kindly, and will wait for Huggett to get the potatoes into line for me.'

The farrier bid the grocer good morning, and Fred Wyatt had recovered most of his breath when Tom Huggett was within speaking distance.

'Thou 'ast come none too soon, Huggett. I'm nigh gone for breath.'

'Be'ant I five minutes afore my time, Master?' Tom asked.

'I'm not a-grumbling at thee, lad. Thee canst manage big sacks better than I, though in days gone by I was 'andy enough with them. Now, Tom, the first thing I 'ave to say to thee is that a letter come last night from Mrs James saying she'd be much obliged if I'd send her order, she not 'aving been altogether herself these last few days.'

'And what may the order be, Governor?'

'A pound of bacon, a half of cheese, a half of the best fresh, and a dozen new-laid . . . We're short of biscuits, Tom; we're as low down as one tin. I'll write to Reading for three more. Cocoa – we've enough to go round till the traveller calls, but go down t'other end and see how we are off for coffee and tea and sugar. I'll say nothing about cheese and butter; I never likes to interfere with Mrs Wyatt's counter. She'll be down presently and no doubt will have her word to say on her own account. Oranges – we be out of them. All the Jaffas are gone, but the Sevilles will be coming in –

'So thou hast got thyself down at last, 'Arriet, and Tom would like to have it from thee if Mrs James wants potatoes and onions, for she 'asn't said nothing about them in her order. But what's the matter, woman?'

'Fred, I daren't tell thee. I can't say it. Go, look for thyself in the clothes closet.'

'Hast met a ghost in the closet?'

'No ghost, but thy daughter.'

'My daughter!'

'Aye, in closet, hanging by her apron strings.'

'Art still in they dreams? And last night she was out till midnight listening to the nightingales – '

'Last night is to-day . . . Here comes Sidney; and a sad tale we have to tell thee, my poor lad. Hast lost thy sweetheart and wife that was to be.'

'Something 'as 'appened to Cicely?'

'I can't speak – '

'Now, what's the matter with your wife, Mr Wyatt?'

'My wife has seen something in the closet. But sometimes people see things as others don't see, for I'm thinking as a girl don't hang herself three days before she's to be married.'

'I can't bear it. Let me in. I must see her! Wyatt, wilt come with me?' he called back from the foot of the stairs.

Wyatt stood aghast, unable to speak, and he remained speechless long after the others had gone up-stairs, Tom Huggett waiting to get a word from him. At last he said: 'Nail this on the door, Tom.'

'Six pounds of potatoes,' a customer cried from the doorway.

'The master says no business will be done in the shop to-day. You must go down to Mr Fitch.'

'No business will be done to-day at Mr Fitch's no more than here,' cried Wyatt. 'Thou 'ast no understanding of it, Tom. Somehow, I can't get it into my 'ead as Cicely is gone from us, nor can Sidney, and he is a 'ard-'eaded lad . . . Thou 'ast brought in everything – potatoes, onions, tomatoes, and the notice is on the door? Then shut it after thee . . . Ah, now they be coming down; but how slow! Is she alive, or dead, Mother?'

'Sidney says as we must touch nothing till the doctor 'as seen her and the sergeant of police. We're going along to fetch them and will be back in a few minutes.'

'If you meet any comers this day, tell them no business is being done here.'

The cat jumped from the counter, startling him, and on her reappearance with a mouse in her grip, he said: 'Something is always happening in this world,' and moved towards the stairs; but lacking courage to look upon his dead daughter, he wandered about the shop, the 'want' book in his hand. Somebody knocked.

'Can't they read?'

The customer knocked again, and to rid himself of whoever it might be, he called out: 'Go to the Fitches; no business is being done here . . . But the Fitches, too,' he reflected as he listened to retreating footsteps, 'will shut up their shop, and Sidney will be sorry for Cicely just as we are; but nobody won't grieve as I am grieving.'

Once more his mind passed from thoughts into sensations, sympathies, of old time, going back to the day he saw his daughter open her eyes for the first time. A pretty thing she was to look at in her cradle, and soon after a gay, pleasant child running about the shop, always with a little tune on her tongue. And hearing her in his thoughts singing, he was moved to go up to her, but at the foot of the stairs his courage forsook him, and he began to mutter one of her songs till tears overflowed his eyes and obliged him to desist.

'She had always a pretty ear for music, and a customer never got a wrong bill – more than the Fitches can say. Mrs Fitch – '

A footstep outside roused him; but the passer-by didn't even stop to read the notice on the door, and his thoughts ran on something like this:

'Everybody liked Cicely, but she didn't matter to them, nor they to her; not even to her mother did she matter as she does to me. A father's love for his daughter is a wonderful, mysterious thing, though I wouldn't say as her mother don't love her very deep. We shan't be able to carry on without her; the Fitches'll get all the business.'

But why, he asked, did this old jealousy intrude itself? And to excuse himself for such a thought at such a time, he muttered as he went about the shop: 'They've been striving after the custom this long while, and I don't begrudge it to them; why should I? Nothing matters now that Cicely is gone.' And again he lost sight of everything past and present till a knocking at the door roused him and he opened it to his wife and Sidney, come back with the doctor and the policeman.

'A sad story this is,' said the doctor, a fine old man of eighty, unshrunken, still six feet two and without any grey to speak of in his beard. 'A sad story, and we are all sorry for you.'

'Yes, we are sorry for you, and all the village will be grieving with you when the news gets about, Mr Wyatt.'

As Fred did not answer, the sergeant had to declare his errand.

'We've come, Mr Wyatt, to view the body and make our report.'

'The wife will take you up-stairs.' The doctor plucked the policeman by the sleeve. 'I'd liefer not see her till she is laid out.'

At that moment the cat came to show her mouse to Mrs Wyatt, and Wyatt said incontinently that the mouse was caught soon after Mrs Wyatt and Sidney had left the shop. The doctor plucked the sergeant's sleeve again, whispered, and Wyatt remained with the cat, thinking of the nestful of young mice behind the wainscot, till Mrs Wyatt called over the banisters:

'We've laid her on her bed, and thou'lt put up a prayer

with me?' He ascended the stairs, and Doctor Morgan and Sergeant Hamblin knelt with the parents and Sidney; and on rising from their knees Doctor Morgan reminded Mrs Wyatt that Sergeant Hamblin would like to ask some questions, and spoke of an adjournment to the parlour. She turned the handle, and Doctor Morgan and the sergeant found themselves in a low-ceilinged room and their eyes quickly discovered the large assortment of fancy articles with which the flowered table-cloth was bestrewed – photograph albums, cruet stands, plated ware, knives and forks, brooches, necklaces and scent bottles.

'No, no, Wife, not yet. I'll not have her presents made away with, not yet.'

'Nor is there need to remove them,' said Hamblin. 'I have my note-book with me.'

There were enough chairs in the parlour for them all to be seated.

'Doctor Morgan and I see no reason why anybody should doubt that Miss Wyatt took her own life – '

Fred cried out that he could bear it no longer, and it was some time before he was able to tell that he had never noticed any change in his daughter up to eleven o'clock last night, when she asked leave to go to the forest to hear the nightingales.

'She was the same cheerful, contented girl as always,' said Mrs Wyatt, 'and it was after finishing the shop accounts that she asked for leave to go to hear the nightingales. I was took aback, for it was, as Wyatt has told you, after eleven o'clock; but having a thought that she was to meet Sidney, I gave her the key of the front door. "You'll be back afore midnight?" I said, and she answered: "Soon after, Mother. The birds are singing their best at midnight." '

'Was she partial to the forest, Mrs Wyatt?' Sergeant Hamblin asked.

'I can't remember that she ever spoke of the forest before, though we live so near it.'

'And you, Mr Sidney, did you ever take her for walks in the forest?'

'I spoke to her once about the forest, but she said that a shady road was more cheerful.'

'And you were not with her last night?'

'No; and I can't think how she come to know that nightingales sing best after midnight. Somebody must have told her, but who? Unless it was Grigg. I met him coming away from here after tuning the piano, and he told me there were more nightingales in the forest than he had ever known before, and better singers, and it may have been from Grigg that she got the idea of going to hear them when her accounts were finished.'

'It is hard,' the doctor remarked, 'to find the crevice through which an idea enters the mind.' And Hamblin, taking the hint, said: 'You never heard your daughter speak of taking her own life, Mrs Wyatt?'

'Never a word; did we, Fred?'

'Never a word,' Fred answered, 'and we believed her to be as happy as the day is long.'

'There is always a reason, Hamblin,' said the doctor, 'but very often – and much oftener than people think – the reason is unsearchable; yet search we must, for in the eyes of the law suicide or *felo de se* is a felony, and the law forbids Christian burial to all who take their lives, unless it can be shown that they were suffering from a fit of temporary insanity at the time. A very unchristian law, I admit, for who shall look into a human mind and tell the alienation of the brain that compelled a man to take his life? You will remember, Sergeant, that she took her life three days before her marriage; and her marriage was of her own making – am I not right in saying so, Mrs Wyatt?'

'You are indeed, Doctor. Sidney was her choice, and there was no waning since the day he pushed her bicycle up the hill for her.'

'Three days ago we walked out together,' said Sidney, 'and parted looking forward to our marriage.'

'We shall meet,' said Hamblin, rising from his chair, 'at the inquest in the big room of the Hare and Hounds, and it will be for the coroner to say whether we shall hear Grigg.'

'But he'll hear Grigg, and if he don't, I say it will be no fair inquest but a hush-up.'

Sergeant Hamblin could not allow the word 'hush-up' to pass unreproved.

'We have no evidence against Grigg. You met him on his way to Lyndhurst after tuning the piano. We're all sorry for you, and understand how grieved you must be, but the story will come out clear to-morrow.'

'Come, Sidney,' said Doctor Morgan, and taking Sidney by the arm he led him from the room. Sergeant Hamblin lingered to tell Mr Wyatt that an ambulance would be sent to remove Miss Wyatt, and when he was gone a distressing silence fell. But for a long time neither could find words to break it with.

'Sergeant forgot to ask if Cicely was back afore twelve, 'Arriet.'

'She had the key, and I knew thou'd be restless if I didn't turn in with thee, and never thinking she'd stay out later, I fell asleep; and thou'ast sleeping sound enough when I waked suddenlike, asking myself if Cicely had come in. And without waking thee I lifted my legs out of bed and went in search of Cicely, and not finding her in her bed, I sat myself down upon it to harken for her key. And it must have been three or four when I 'eard it, for it was broad day at the time. I asked what had kept her out so late, and her answer was that she had gone to the forest to think.

"To think of what?" says I.

"Of my marriage, of course, Mother, for what else is there for me to think about?"

"Think about thy marriage!" says I. "But thou'rt as good as married to Sidney Fitch – in three days! Now, what did thy thinking come to?"

"To nothing good, I'm thinking."

'And then fair frightened, and feeling my wits leaving me, I said: "Thy lovely dress – the presents – the breakfast – and the dance."'

'And what did she say to all that?'

'Not a word: and not being able to get an answer out of her, I went on: "It isn't fair, Cicely, to break off a marriage within three days of the wedding without giving any reason; you are keeping something from us and Sidney. What's to become of him?"'

'And she had nothing to say about him?'

'Only as she didn't feel sure she'd be happy in married life. "But," said I, "is it only a feeling?" She didn't answer. "I've been a good, kind mother, haven't I?" says I, and she answered straight she had naught to complain of. And then suddenlike she threw herself into my arms, and when she had had her cry out I tried coaxing her, till at last she began to give way, and to hearten her I asked her if it was anything to do with Sidney.

'She said: "No, Mother, Sidney is all right. He's a good lad, but I can't marry him." More than that she wouldn't say.

'I kept on – you can call it nagging, if you like, but I was afeared, and felt I must get at the truth. That was my mistake – happen it was, happen it wasn't.

' "I don't know what Father will say when he hears it," I said; "it will break his heart." Maybe I went too far, for seeing as the words "break his heart" stirred her, I went on till she broke down again. I know I was 'ard with her, I know I was. "Thou'lt break 'is 'eart, and mine, too; both our 'earts will be broken. Thy father and I have loved thee, Cicely, all thy life. All our love 'as gone to thee. We had nobody else to love. And now it is beginning to come to thee that we're thinking only of ourselves."

' "I didn't say that, Mother," said she.

' "No, but that's what is in thy mind. I can read it in thy face."

' "If Father is that set on this marriage, and thou'rt on his side and against me, I don't know what will happen to me." Her foot was on the stairs, but I called, and she came back.

' "Thou'lt have to tell it all to Father, and he, being a man with a liking for reasons, will listen to reason."

' "To his own reasons, Mother, but not to mine."

' "I've a thought for thy meaning, Cicely, and maybe thou'd do well to tell me when the feeling began that Sidney was not the husband for thee."

' "Last week, Mother."

' "Thou'st seen nobody since walking out with Sidney."

' "Yes, I have, Mother." '

' "Nobody's been here but Grigg." And we stood looking at each other.'

'Thou hasn't told me of Grigg, 'Arriet. I can't call to mind hearing his name afore.'

'Hast forgotten the tuner, Fred, that came to put the piano right for the dance, the spare man in the brown clothes, him as trails a lock of black hair across his skull?'

'I 'eard him tuning, and being busy in the shop didn't catch sight of him before leaving. But he was here more days than one.'

'He was here twice, for the first time he couldn't get the piano right, his ear being out, so he said. He was here an hour before I came in to see how they were getting on, and for an excuse for interrupting I asked if he had tuned the piano.'

' "Of course, Mother, what art thinking of?" Cicely cried, and not being able to get an answer out of myself at the moment, I said:

' "Of course, what am I saying?" and ran my fingers over the keys for to have an excuse for complimenting him. "Why," says I, "the piano isn't in tune!"

' "I've tuned thirteen to-day and my ear is out," said Mr Grigg, "and I'll come back to-morrow and finish my tuning", which he did. And he was about going when Cicely starts talking to him about the forest, and so eager was she to hear of the Rufus Stone, the great King and Queen Oaks at Mark Ash, and the Lymington River, and he nothing loath to talk about the forest, I couldn't but ask him to stay and take a cup of tea with us.

'It was whilst we were 'aving our tea as he told us he tuned pianos all over the country – at Lyndhurst, Brockenhurst (I think he said he had some pianos to tune there), and that his round took him to Beaulieu and often to Christchurch. He had a lot to say, too, about forest glades and nightingales. Cicely and I came down-stairs to see him off, and he was barely out of sight when Cicely began to talk of the wonderful forest.

' "Cicely," said I, "I never heard thee speak of the forest afore; to hear thee one would think it had arrived no later than the day before yesterday!" '

'Maybe she went to meet Grigg.'

'Grigg was miles away. I heard him say that he was going straight to Lyndhurst.'

'Thy story, 'Arriet, seems likely enough for many another girl, but our Cicely, I'm thinking, was too natural a sort to throw over a young fellow like Sidney Fitch for the old tuner with his wisp of black hair drawn over a bald skull, no more than three days before her wedding.'

'I said nothing about a change of mind. Her words were: "Sidney's all right, Mother. Sidney's a good lad, but I can't marrry him." '

'She was willing enough to marry him at the back end of the week, so her mind must have gone over – '

'I think it was the grocery store that frightened her.'

'Frightened her! Wasn't she born into it?'

'Yes, Fred, she was; and she was contented enough in it till she took fright at the thought as her married life would be no more than her single life over again. She'd come to that time of life when a girl begins to weary of the days she has known and to long for days she don't know. Our days be like beads on a string, and a young girl wearies of the lot she has been stringing, and then it is main easy to set her off; well-nigh anything will do it.'

'I never 'eard thee speak like that afore, 'Arriet, yet we've been stringing the same beads all our lives. When I told thee that I was but a grocer's apprentice – '

'The shop was our romance, Fred, but it wasn't Cicely's. I don't say she wouldn't have gone tired of green branches and wandering after pianos to be tuned, for there are bad days in the forest same as in the store; but she'd have had her romance.'

'But why should our daughter have been that different from her mother? For when we walked the common, 'Arriet, and the gipsy tilted his horse over a gate, thou'dst no thought to jump up behind him.'

'All that is long ago, Fred, and I'm no ways willing to think myself better than my daughter. I was fond of thee, and there was no crying off, though thou wast no more than a grocer's apprentice at the time, with a good notion in thy head as Brandlesbury needed a grocery store. And for twenty year we've worked at our counters, thinking always of the five-pound note to put with the others to make a fortune for Cicely when she wedded. But she's been took from us, and Sidney.'

'Yes, 'Arriet, thou has said it. We've worked eighteen long years for her, who had no thought for us, only for herself.'

'I've told thee thy daughter's story out of my own heart, and spoilt her for thee in the telling, but thou'lt understand her presently, and after thine own heart.'

'It would have been a 'ard blow 'ad she married the tuner and gone wandering from 'ome with him, but I'd 'ave borne it.' And catching a sudden glimpse of Cicely in his wife's small, frail body, black hair, and death-pale face, he added: 'We must be careful not to speak unkind of her for what she's done, for she may still be about the house, and passing of judgement upon her may scare her ghost away for ever.'

'Cicely will not be scared away, and knowing more than before will have pity on us both.'

Fred left the parlour, and returning from the shop laid several dishes in front of his wife.

'However sick at heart we may be, we must eat. I cannot have thee ill in the house. Here – cheese, butter, biscuits, dates, apples and bananas. And after eating we might take a bit of a walk about the edges of the forest.'

'Yes, about the edges of the forest,' Harriet answered. 'I shall not be long finding a bonnet and shawl.'

The words that rose to his lips were: 'Don't hurry; we be'ant pressed for time this afternoon,' but he kept himself from speaking them, and was pacing up and down the parlour, his hands behind his back, when the front door bell began to ring. 'Now, who can this be?' and raising the window, he leaned out, but withdrew his head quickly, for the police had come with an ambulance to take Cicely away to the Hare and Hounds for the inquest . . .

'I'm thinking, 'Arriet, that the edge of the forest is no place for us to be seen walking'; and Harriet being somewhat of the same mind, each sought for some work that would distract their minds. And Fred thinking to find his in the account books, retired to his desk; but Cicely's handwriting was on

211

every page and he found only memories. And Harriet, ascending the stairs to consider what might be done with Cicely's wedding clothes, came upon a vision of Cicely going up the aisle in a muslin dress and veil, and her grief burst the restraint she had put upon it. She threw herself on Cicely's bed, and when she rose from it she said:

'This grief will last for ever. As the days go by we shall miss her more and more. But what are we to do with these clothes, the stockings, the gloves, the shoes?'

Whilst folding them into a parcel her thoughts came upon Mrs Wenman. She, too, had lost a daughter. There are moments when women want to talk to women, and in Mrs Wenman's cottage the afternoon passed away in sadness, but not in the cruel, hard, unrelenting sadness of the morning. Some of the wistfulness of the skies seemed to have come into her heart, and at the end of the day Mrs Wenman came home with her, and her companionship was so soothing that Harriet asked her in. They cooked some food together, and after eating they left Wyatt and collected what remained of Cicely's clothes; and these Mrs Wenman took away, Harriet keeping only her daughter's books and music.

'I'm glad the music was kept, for it will remind us of her playing,' Fred said, when they lay down together. 'Isn't that so, 'Arriet?'

'Aye, true enough,' Harriet answered. 'But let's not go over it all again.'

'Thou'rt thinking of the ghost that may be about the house.'

'Maybe I am, maybe I'm not, Fred' . . . And waking suddenly, she cried: 'She spoke in my ear! A voice spoke, and I heard it plain as I hear thee, Fred.'

An hour later it was Fred's turn to wake, not to hear but to see Cicely's pretty face under the lamp working at her account books. He called his wife to look, but she could see nothing, and there were many more wakings and sleepings through the long dawn that began at three and continued for hours amid the songs of blackbirds and thrushes, till the rumble of cart-wheels awoke them. Another hour passed, and then it was the jingle of harness and the crack of a carter's whip that roused them, and later the dogs that were let through the doorways and ran barking down the street.

'I'd give a good bit of money,' said Wyatt as he rose from his bed, 'if the half-day that's afore us was over.'

'Why the half-day, Fred?'

'Well, won't the inquest be over by then?' he answered, and whilst they dressed their hope was that Grigg would tell his story without straying from it; and on their way to the Hare and Hounds they were agreed that the only evidence Sidney had to give was that he and Cicely had walked out together in the middle of the week, and that she seemed to look forward to her marriage with pleasure.

Sidney, whom they met on their way thither, was calmer than yesterday and seemed to see clearly that Grigg could not be held responsible for the mischief. He was followed into the witness box by Grigg, who told his story of the thirteen pianos and created a stir of admiration – Brandlesbury did not know that it possessed so great a musician. And the end of it all was that the jury found the usual verdict, and the people dispersed, discovering many reasons for Cicely Wyatt's death in their wandering fancies.

At the end of the week Sidney came to see them, and Fred's words were:

'We be main glad to see thee, lad, for we have something on our minds, something for thee to hear. We've tried to carry on, but we can't. The missus and myself are of the same mind. We want a change – that's about it, and we'd look upon it as a kindness if thou'd look after the customers whilst our absence.'

Sidney asked if they intended to open a grocery store in another town, and they answered that they had no plans. It might be they'd start another business elsewhere, or it might be that they'd come back; they didn't know.

'And when do ye expect to leave Brandlesbury?'

Wyatt answered that they were leaving next morning, and next morning Sidney accompanied them to the turn of the road.

'Good-bye, lad.'

'You'll write to us?'

213

'Yes, we'll write.'

'If you come back you'll be welcome, and if you don't come back at the end of the year we'll buy your business from you at a valuation.'

'We'll write,' Wyatt answered.

'We'll write,' Mrs Wyatt repeated; and he watched the two old people wandering away anywhither, nowhither, feeling he'd like to wander with them, for with them he would not be as far from Cicely as he would be with his own father and mother.

The Strange Story
of the
Three Golden Fishes

A Comedy of a Man Who Always Was Lucky
– Especially in Marriage

Once on a time shipping showed aloft in the ports and
estuaries of certain Kentish and Sussex towns, but the Cinque
Ports were deserted some centuries ago by the sea, their
common benefactor, and now life moulders in Rye, Rom-
ney, and Sandwich amid recollections of better days.

A tidal river or estuary flows past Sandwich through the
marshes, reaching the sea somehow, and on the occasion of
my first visit I was grateful to two fishing–smacks and a
collier moored in its sluggish current, for these small craft by
spell of contrast reminded me of the great, square-sailed
galleons that once littered the wharves with bales of silk,
crates of rare porcelain, and barrels of wine from Lisbon and
the Canaries; and my imagination, now fully roused, perceived horses from Barbary coming ashore marvellously
accoutred, with high-pommelled saddles and a strange array
of bits and bridles. For a moment the past was again the
present; vision succeeded vision; and the gilded, painted
coaches of merchant princes rattled through the great gateway to welcome the arrival of ships long overdue.

This old town smells of story, said I to myself, and could I
but trace one to its lair . . . I had heard my friends speak of a
fifteenth-century town hall, and I inquired my way thither
from the passers by. None was in doubt as to the whereabouts of the hall. All the same, I allowed a small boy to lead
me. But the doors of the hall were locked.

A reflection that human beings rouse my imagination
when gable ends leave it sleeping carried me a hundred yards
farther into the town, and I welcomed a sudden vision of

farmers repairing to an old-time inn on market-days to drink lusty ale after disposing of the sheep that I had admired in the fields on the way to Sandwich, rough little fields adorned with thorn-bushes and watered with pleasant brooks.

On the heels of these visions, memories and reflections came a sudden sympathy with sheep and lusty ale, and determined to enjoy both, one in leg of mutton and the other in pewter tankard, I said: 'If a story awaits me in Sandwich I shall come upon it in the Royal George.' And finding the George in a triangle of small streets, almost a courtyard, I entered the parlour, saying: 'An inn of story, the veritable inn of my imagination; sanded floor, coloured prints of horses that have won the Derby, the Oaks, the Leger, and game-cocks of unrecorded exploits. Nothing lacks. The waiter is according to my aspiration; he is in perfect harmony with the town deserted by her friend and accomplice, the sea; a stocky man of sixty, over whose skull some last wisps of hair were trailed carefully this morning, and are probably trailed with the same care every morning. Trimmed away are the large Victorian whiskers he once wore; of them remain only some small bunches of curled hair looking like crisp parsley above his ears.'

It seemed to me that I had seen his long, wide mouth in many waiters before, and remarking his cumbrous, trailing gait, I said to myself: 'A man grown old in the habits of his trade, but no less a human being for that.' And satisfied that this was so, I followed him to a seat and heard him speak the words that I had already heard in my esurient imagination:

'A nice leg of mutton is ready, Sir.'

It was pleasant to watch him bundle himself out of the parlour and return a few minutes afterwards with two slices of mutton, a piece of Yorkshire pudding, a dish of potatoes and greens. I liked him to be near me while I ate; answering from time to time his questions about the mutton, and passing from mutton to sheep, I spoke to him of the flocks I had seen from the train feeding under broken hedges or collected by watercourses as in a picture. Within five minutes I learned that his name was John Selby and that he had lived all his life in Sandwich.

216

'A declining town for years,' he said, 'long before my time – declining for hundreds of years, so I have heard, ever since the sea left us. We are holding on somehow, but if something doesn't happen, Sir, a luncheon such as you are eating will be a thing of the past in the George. Pickles, Sir? Worcester sauce, Sir?'

'No thank you,' I answered. 'On second thoughts, John, I'll have both, for they remind me of the days when I ate them, days of wax fruit, antimacassars, and rep sofas.'

We spoke of the race-horses on the walls, winners of the Oaks and the Derby and the Leger and the Two Thousand Guineas, and of the game-cocks, and I heard much from John about the art of trimming cocks for battle, of the minting of spurs and the trying of them, and speaking thereof John said:

'It seems to me, Sir, that all the laws they make nowadays are to prevent people from doing something they want to do.'

'Right you are, John, right you are,' and my voice was so emphatic that it brought the conversation to a standstill.

I waited for John to resume it, but he stood embarrassed, and it was to help him that I glanced round the room, saying: 'Truly, Sandwich must have declined, for such an inn as the George to have so few customers. How many have you had this morning?'

'Only one, Sir, Mr Cather. He came in early in the day and went away in a hurry, leaving his fishing-rod and creel in the corner over yonder.'

'Forgetting them in his hurry?'

'Forgetting them?' cried John. 'He would as soon forget his head as forget his fishing-rod! He left it in my charge, and I am perhaps the only man in whose charge he would leave it, for that rod is the very one with which he caught three fish that fetched sixty thousand pounds or more.'

'Sixty thousand pounds for three fishes, John!'

'Yes, indeed, Sir.'

'But there aren't any fishes in that dirty estuary.'

'He doesn't fish in the estuary, Sir. He goes to the Bourne to fish, and he wouldn't miss an April fishing in the Bourne for any money you could offer him, not for more than sixty

217

thousand pounds. If he did, he'd feel his luck would turn. But you'd like a piece of cheese, Sir; we have some that I think you would like. And what do you say to a glass of port? We have still some left twenty years in bottle.'

'I think I can trust you about port, John.'

'You can, Sir, for I don't believe in deceiving gentlemen; the truth is best in the long run.'

'A good adage, John; truth and luck are precious possessions. A man who catches three fishes worth sixty thousand pounds certainly has luck on his side. I would hear the story.'

'So you shall, Sir; I shan't be away a minute.' And it was not long after the minute he said it would take him to fetch the port that he returned with a bottle full of promise, for the dust and the cobwebs that enveloped it were not artificially applied but the consecration of time.

'You will drink a glass with me, John? and you'll drink sitting down, for port cannot be appreciated if the bibber be not comfortably seated.'

'I don't think, Sir, that Mrs Bragg would like to catch me drinking with a customer.'

'But should she come in unexpectedly I will answer for you, John, saying that a story cannot be told standing up.'

'Well, Sir, since you will have it so and will speak to Mrs Bragg, saying you insisted.'

'I will do that and more, John; and now tell me the story of the man who caught not one golden fish but three golden fishes.'

'You are a stranger in Sandwich, Sir?'

'This is my first visit.'

'May I ask then, Sir, if you have walked about the town, and if you noticed in your walk a tall, gabled, red house?'

'Standing at the end of a short avenue,' I answered, 'with shelving lawns and comely trees.'

'The same, Sir – the house that the three Honourable Miss Pettigues lived in.'

'But what have the Honourable Miss Pettigues and their house to do with Mr Cather's luck?'

'You shall hear, Sir, all in good time.'

The words 'all in good time' caused me to raise my eyes,

and seeing that the old waiter was already enwrapped in his story, I resolved not to interrupt again, but to let him tell it in his own way.

'The Miss Pettigues had fifteen hundred a year each, Sir, four thousand five hundred between them to spend in the Red House. A great deal could be done with four thousand five hundred a year in the seventies in a country town.

'Every day the phaeton came round to the front door to take them for their drive, and they went out driving, Miss Ada and Miss Pinkie. Miss Charlotte, the eldest, was seldom seen with them, her taste being for gardening, and there was always plenty of work for her, she said, in the greenhouses at the back. I think Miss Ada and Miss Pinkie welcomed Miss Charlotte's taste for gardening – not that they didn't love their sister, or were unkind to her; far be it from me to suggest anything of that kind; but their tastes were different from Miss Charlotte's. She was the homely one, who liked her garden, and they liked painting and music.

'Fine, aristocratic women they both were, Sir, with aquiline noses, Miss Ada perhaps more commanding than Miss Pinkie, handsomer, but not so pretty. Miss Pinkie had the loveliest head of flaxen hair I ever saw in my life, flaxen with a tint of red in it; I have heard it compared to spun silk. Miss Ada sketched in water-colours. There's hardly a piece of the marsh that hasn't been painted by her, and windmills, too – she painted many, and would drive for miles around to get a good view of a watermill or an old castle.

'Why they never married was a great question in the days gone by. Some said Miss Ada looked too high, among dukes and marquises, and that she didn't think any of the gentry good enough for her. Her manner was distant, though it was part of herself, and it may have kept suitors off. But the same could not be said of Miss Pinkie. She was always ready to sing for a charity. Miss Ada, who was much interested in hospital work, accompanied her sister on the piano. A gentleman writing to the *Sandwich Gazette* said that no one could sing her own songs better than Miss Pinkie, though Miss Lind might do better in an opera.'

'You seem to have known the family very well, John, and

to have a good memory,' I said, with the intention of encouraging him to tell the story in his own way.

'Sandwich born and bred, Sir,' he answered, 'with every opportunity of knowing the Miss Pettigues, of seeing them leave the Red House in their phaeton every day of my life, and being called in when I was a mere pantry boy to help; and a great delight it was to me in those early days to leave the pantry and sit on the stairs to hear Miss Pinkie sing "Robin Adair". Mr Trout, their butler, knowing that I had an ear for a sweet tune, always let me get away – but I haven't told you about Mr Trout, who took big wages from the Miss Pettigues, as was his right, for in the trade competitions he was judged to be the third greatest butler in England, and he would have been first if he had got his due, but there's a lot of trickery in those competitions.

'However, whether he should have been first instead of third is a matter of opinion, but everybody knew him to be a fine, courtly gentleman – gentleman on his father's side, for when he had the measles his old mother came to nurse him, and she was not Mrs but Miss. It was then that we began to say: "Good blood will make a show, no matter on which side of the blanket the child may be born", and Trout must have had a long ancestry of blue blood behind him, for he ran to sixteen or seventeen stone without coarseness anywhere, neither in his face nor hands, not even in his belly, Sir, which is a coarse feature in heavy men – perhaps in thin men as well as in heavy,' John added with a snigger.

'The Derby, the Leger, and the Oaks were his favourite races, but now and again he was given to studying the weights for the big handicaps and backing his judgement, and nobody ever had finer judgement; he'd have made a great handicapper. When I saw him come down the street and go into the George I'd run after him to hear what he had to say, and everybody in the room would listen to him just as I did. It's extraordinary the commanding way he had, and without knowing it. He talked and we listened just as children listen to the parson, swallowing every word he said; and as he was in the parlour of the George, he was at the Red House.

'And to make a story that is often too long, short, one day

Trout, having taken his orders in the drawing-room after breakfast, gave the ladies notice, saying that he needed a change and was leaving at the end of the month. At which they all began to speak at once. Miss Charlotte asked if he wasn't satisfied with his room and if he would like to have a private sitting-room; Miss Ada offered him more wages; and Miss Pinkie left the piano and took her seat by her sisters on the rep sofa.

' "If Trout wishes for a change," she said, "I can recommend Scotland." '

'Trout thanked the three ladies for their different kindnesses and said he had no thought for more wages, nor did he wish for a private sitting-room, and when he had spoken of change he didn't mean change of air.

' "You have heard of a better situation, Trout?" said Miss Ada.

' "No situation would suit me after yours, Miss, but I've been in service now for a quarter of a century and, as I have said, would like a change. The lease of the George is for sale – "

' "Trout, we think you should have warned us before that you desired to leave," said Miss Ada, and Trout, who was always a little afraid of her, took his chance to dodge behind the screen and get out of the room before she could say another word. She was too proud to call him back, but every morning when he came for orders the argument began again.

' "We have tried to persuade him," said Miss Pinkie, "not once but ten times, and every day he seems more fixed in his idea than he was the day before. I am afraid there is no hope."

'On these words Miss Ada poked her knitting-needles through her worsted ball, placed it in the basket by her side, and the three sisters sat looking at each other.

' "We shall never be able to keep him unless he marries one of us," said Miss Charlotte.

' "Marries one of us!" cried Miss Ada. "We are on the eve of losing Trout, and I must remind you, Charlotte, that this is not a moment for pleasantries, and such pleasantries!"

' "You are very hard on me," said Charlotte, "very hard. But I don't see that I have said anything so very shocking.

We can't manage without Trout, and if you can suggest any other way of keeping him I should be glad to hear it. I wouldn't have proposed marriage if you had had anything else to suggest, but every morning we try to persuade Trout and every morning he tells us that he has signed the lease. And if you can't read his face, I can; he is determined to be landlord of the George, or – Well, I have told you!"

' "You think, Charlotte, that the thought has come to him – "

' "No, I don't think the thought has ever come to him; I wish it had; what I propose is that we tell him."

' "That we tell him!" said Miss Ada.

' "There is nothing else to do. You have proposed more wages, Ada; again and again you have added another and another five pounds a quarter; and you, Pinkie, have offered him a three-months' tour in Scotland. And now only three more days of our old life remain to us. In three days we start to live as best we can without Trout. You look frightened, and well you may, for though I know very little about housekeeping, you know less. You think only of your water-colour paintings and your poor people, Ada, and you, Pinkie, have your piano and your songs.

' "I have my greenhouses to look after, but coming and going from the garden to the kitchen I have picked up some little knowledge of housekeeping and dread the responsibility that is about to fall upon us. I can't sleep at night for thinking on whom we can rely to look into the coachman's bills for hay and corn. We shall never be able to cope with the cook without Trout, for being used to taking orders from Trout, she'll not take them from us. I lie awake thinking who will count the linen before it goes to the wash and count it when it comes back, and there are a hundred other things of which you know hardly anything."

' "All you say is true," said Miss Ada. "We shall meet with many difficulties, but there is Mr Maxwell."

'Miss Pinkie, who had begun to hum "Annie Laurie", stopped suddenly. "Mr Maxwell can advise us only about our investments."

' "The truth is that we know very little about our affairs," said Miss Ada. "Do you think, Charlotte – "

' "I have said all I have to say, but you will not listen to me," Miss Charlotte answered.

' "We are not angry with you, Charlotte," said Miss Ada, holding out her hand; "Pinkie is not angry with you, nor am I."

' "I am glad to hear it, for there's no use being taken aback, Ada," Miss Charlotte replied. "The thing is to find some way out. I don't think anything else will stop him, but I am sorry if I offended you. I know I am always wrong and shall say no more."

' "Charlotte!" said Miss Ada. "But what we should like to hear is what put the word marriage into your mind?"

' "Why, the dreadful difficulty we are in, of course – what else?"

' "Yes, yes, the difficulty; but how do you propose to communicate your wish? – that's what we mean, isn't it, Pinkie?"

' "Yes, Ada, Charlotte's wish."

' "Not my wish," cried Miss Charlott, "but to save you and Pinkie – "

' "And yourself, Charlotte!"

' "Yes, of course," Miss Charlotte answered.

' "But we fail to see how your wish, for lack of a better word, may be communicated to Trout. Do you propose that we should write to him?"

' "No, no, Ada, not write. What we have to propose would seem ridiculous in a letter, and if he refused all three he'd have the letter to show."

' "I have always believed Trout to be a strictly honourable man," said Miss Ada.

' "So have I," Miss Charlotte answered; "but we are creatures of circumstance, and think what our position in the town would be with our letter in the pocket of the landlord of the George."

' "Charlotte! Charlotte!" cried both sisters.

' "It's very easy to cry 'Charlotte! Charlotte!' but we are within three days of the catastrophe. You ask me what we are to do. We must just tell him to pick and choose."

' "It seems a little brutal," said Miss Ada.

' "You can put it differently, if you like; you can ask him if he ever thought of marrying one of us."

' "There is no use asking him that, for I am sure he never thought of such a thing!" cried Miss Pinkie. "And when do you propose that we should put the question to Trout?"

' "I think the simplest way, Ada, is always the best way."

' "The simplest way!" said Miss Ada.

' "But which is the simplest way?" Miss Pinkie lisped, speaking to herself.

' "Since you are willing to take him, Charlotte," said Miss Ada, "wouldn't it be better that you should put the question?"

' "But he may not choose me; he may, and very likely will choose you, Ada, or maybe you, Pinkie. You must be prepared to take him if you are chosen. I think you had better take the lead, Ada, in this matter, too."

' "You're very selfish, Charlotte!"

' "It will not be me, I am sure of it," said Miss Charlotte. "I wonder what kind of women he likes – blonde or dark?" '

'How did all this come to your ears, John – all the talk of the sisters? You prattle it all as if you had it by heart.'

'The story has been going round Sandwich for thirty years or more, Sir. I use bits of my own here and there, but I'm telling the story just as I heard it and as everybody else has heard it.'

'A legend,' said I, 'rather than a story, a legend being the work of several, a story the work of one. But continue, John.'

'Well, there they were next morning sitting on the sofa all a-row, trying to keep up their courage, Miss Charlotte being not less frightened than the others when it came to the point of popping the question to Trout.'

'Which was it, John, that spoke to him?'

'I have always heard, Sir, that it was Miss Ada, and that she said: "Trout, this is our last day together, unless you marry one of us."

' "Marry one of you!" said Trout.

' "We know you never thought of such a thing, Trout, we

know you didn't, but we had to think, and after all what is best for all of us must be the right thing to do."

' "There's a great deal of wisdom in what you say, Miss."

' "So, Trout, you are willing to forgo the George?"

' "Well, Miss, I'm so taken aback by what I've just heard that perhaps it would be better for us all to think it over. I will give you my answer the day after tomorrow." On these words Trout turned round sharply and was about to leave the room, but when he came to the door (this is how he used to tell the story himself), something seemed to speak within him. He returned to the ladies and said: "I have thought it out. I will."

' "You will take one of us?" said Miss Ada. "Then you will have to choose, Trout."

' "Oh, Miss!" Trout used to say that his heart seemed to stop beating, and that he stood like a stock before the three Miss Pettigues till at last Miss Ada said:

' "Well, which do you choose?"

'Miss Ada's words brought courage to Trout, and he said: "You do beautiful water-colours, Miss Ada, and Miss Pinkie sings like a lark or Jenny Lind; but I have no thought for such things, and you won't take it amiss if I say that I could do better with Miss Charlotte? You don't mind my frankness?"

' "Not in the least, Trout, not in the least; on the contrary, we admire it," said Miss Pinkie.

'At these words Trout was more embarrassed than before, for he didn't know how to get out of the room, nor did he know in what terms to address his future sisters-in-law; and it was whilst feeling himself the biggest fool in Sandwich, unable to go forward or to go back, that Miss Charlotte said: "Herbert!"

'It was the Herbert that woke him up. "Trout today, Miss; Herbert and Charlotte after the ceremony!"

'Miss Ada and Miss Pinkie could not keep back a smile, and the success of his quip enabled Trout to tell the ladies that the marriage would take place by special licence.

' "I must have a new dress, for I haven't had one for two years," Miss Charlotte interrupted, "and I'd like to be married in grey silk trimmed with pink ribbons. What do you say, Pinkie?"

'Trout drew himself up. No smile appeared on his face, for though a hearty, communicative man, he knew how to keep his countenance when the occasion required, and the story, as his cronies tell it, is that he spoke without faltering, though it was difficult, saying that he would advise an immediate trip to London in search of the grey silk gown and wedding presents, for – He stopped on the "for", and spoke instead of the necessity for silence. Nobody, he said, need be told of the wedding; and nobody would have known anything about it before the ceremony if the question had not arisen on the door-step whether Trout should go to church sitting inside with the ladies, or on the box with the coachman.

'Miss Charlotte was all for his sitting inside with them, but Miss Ada and Miss Pinkie thought otherwise and the bickering was only brought to an end by Trout pushing his bride inside the phaeton, jumping on the box, and telling the coachman to whip up the horses. After the wedding, of course, the phaeton was waiting at the church door to take the bridal party back to the Red House, and when Trout came out with his bride on his arm Miss Ada and Miss Pinkie whispered to him that they were going to walk home; and they walked on quickly to escape from the gapers and gazers.

'The church isn't more than a couple of hundred yards from the Red House, so Miss Ada and Miss Pinkie arrived not long after the phaeton, which had not yet left the front door. On the steps were Mr and Mrs Trout, with the footman and housemaid, and the other servants looking out of the windows, and the joke that's been going round ever since is Miss Charlotte's asking if she was to sleep in the basement with Trout or if Trout was to sleep with her in the bridal chamber.

'I don't believe myself that Miss Charlotte could have put such a question to Trout or to the head housemaid, but there's no saying what a woman without much restraint on her tongue at any time will blurt out in an emergency. If she didn't say it, it was as well invented as those remarks generally are, for it's just what she might have said.

'Hearsay, Sir, hearsay, but there's sometimes good truth in hearsay, and never has there been such hearsay about a wedding in Kent as there was about this one. Everybody's tongue was wagging for months; whoever wasn't a prophet was a prophetess. And all agreed on one thing, that Trout wouldn't be able to break with the old habit of backing his fancy for some of the big handicaps. And a number came round to the belief that Trout would waste all his wife's fortune at the George. So long as the marriage was an unhappy one, it didn't seem to matter to anybody how the unhappiness came about.

'But the marriage wasn't unhappy; Trout was loyal to his wife. He never told her to shut up – no disrespectful words of that kind were ever spoken by him. She couldn't keep her tongue quiet, which is to say that Trout didn't get his fifteen hundred a year for nothing; but he never complained, and when his wife died the gossip began again, all the prophets and prophetesses agreeing that he would marry a second time. But which of the sisters would he marry?

'Of course, they all knew that marriage with a deceased wife's sister wasn't legal; but, people said, rather than lose Trout, they'll try again! And nobody will ever know whether it was the unlawfulness of such a marriage or Miss Ada's ill health that stayed Trout from marrying again into the same family. For him to marry into another family would have been out of the question. Miss Ada and Miss Pinkie couldn't have borne it, and Trout would have been a hard-hearted man if he had brought a stranger into the Red House.

'Miss Ada was taken ill soon after her sister's death; she was an invalid for some years; and Trout continued to serve his sisters-in-law just as he had done when he was their servant, managing everything for them, his conduct never changing during Miss Pinkie's lifetime, though she outlived Miss Ada by many years. It was not until Trout had buried her that the sportsman that was always in him began to break out again.

'Trout was then worth something like five thousand a year, and a man with five thousand a year is not satisfied with backing other people's horses. Though he bet in hundreds, he was not satisfied; he must have a horse of his own. About that time Colonel McAllister's stud was up for sale, fifteen thoroughbreds, mares, yearlings, platers, and chasers, with one galloper amongst them, and it was a great day indeed for Trout, and a great day for Sandwich, when Lady Olympia won the Canterbury Steeplechase. My belief is, Sir, that when luck once gets hold of a man by the collar, whatever he does will turn up trumps. We cannot put off our luck, whether it be bad or good, no more than a hunchback can put off his hump.'

'You don't believe, then, that a man may catch another's luck?'

'To answer that question, Sir, I'd have to know whether the young man to whom Trout left all his money was lucky or unlucky before he met Trout.'

'So Trout is dead?' said I.

'Not very long after Lady Olympia's win at Canterbury, Trout's heart began to fail him. He consulted all the specialists and went abroad to take the waters, but without getting much benefit from either one or the other, and he returned home having lost three stone in weight. Every morning he began to think of his end, his will, and to whom he should leave his money. His mother was dead and he was without legitimate relations, and having given up all his life to the Miss Pettigues he found himself without intimate friends. A great number of acquaintances there were, but he came to the conclusion that it would be no pleasure whatever to leave his money to any one of these.

'The only man that he could call his friend was the solicitor Maxwell, of Maxwell and Hurt. But Maxwell, he remembered, was as old a man as himself, perhaps even his senior. All the same, he would like to talk to Maxwell about his will. So Trout told Maxwell of the fix that he found himself in.

'Maxwell was touched by his friend's kind thought of him, but he was retiring from business at the end of the year with a very comfortable competence, all of which would at his death go to his wife and to his children. "Of course," he said, "if you like to leave your money to my children . . ."

'But Trout had no care for leaving his money to acquaintances, and he promised to consider the claims of hospitals and endowment of universities, schools, and nine hundred and ninety and nine other institutions in need of money. But the more he turned the subject over in his mind the more sure he became that he would like to leave his money to somebody he liked, and he invited Maxwell to dinner.

' "Maxwell," he said, "to whom would you leave your money if you had no wife or children?"

' "It is odd," said Maxwell, "that you should ask me that question. I think I should leave my money to young Cather."

' "And who may young Cather be?" asked the dying man.

' "You know I have the fishing of the Bourne," said Maxwell, "and that for years past I have given it away – a day here, a week there, a fortnight, to different men. All sorts and conditions of men have had licence from me to fish in the Bourne, but not one of them ever left a creel of trout at my office with the exception of Mr Francis Cather, a young man for whom I have done some business, advising him about the placing of money on mortgage and such like. One of the mortgages he holds is on lands down Canterbury way and in speaking about it the Bourne was mentioned, and we got talking about angling. Well, he was the only one who ever brought me a creel of trout. I have taken a liking to the young man, and I think you would like him, too. Trout. It is my turn to ask you to dinner, and I'll ask Cather to come, too." '

'Now,' I cried, 'I see the end of the story, John! Francis Cather inherited all Trout's money, and continues to fish the Bourne in the belief that his luck is in the river. Three trout brought him sixty thousand pounds, and though the trout sometimes rise when the horses fail to get first past the post, Cather's belief is not shaken that his destiny is in the Bourne. So that is his fishing-rod, the rod that caught the three golden fishes! I thank you, John, for your story, the only one I know that follows successfully what Henry James used to call "the irregular rhythm of life." '